FOLLOWING A MAGNIFICENT VISION OF LIBERTY
AND INDEPENDENCE, BRAVE MEN AND BEAUTIFUL
WOMEN BLAZE A NEW FUTURE FOR AMERICA

GHONKABA—A warrior in the full maturity of his
manhood, inheritor of the fighting spirit of the White
Indian, he now accepts a perilous secret mission from
General Washington as the future of the entire Seneca
nation comes to rest on his mighty shoulders.

ENA—Fiery daughter of Ghonkaba, her beauty is as rare
as her skill as a scout, and her heart can only be tamed by
a brutal strength tempered by a searing love.

ANTHONY SIMPSON—Cunning and treacherous, he plans
to turn the Indian nations against the American patriots,
and his evil schemes threaten the lives of Ghonkaba and
his people.

RUSOG—Son of a Cherokee chieftain, no brave has ever
surpassed him in strength and courage, but his heart has
been conquered by a woman he can't possess.

DALNIA—A darkly lovely seductress, devious, irresistible,
and voluptuous. Her wiles will entrap a Seneca warrior
and plant the seed of corruption in the noble line of Renno.

The White Indian Series
Ask your bookseller for the books you have missed

The White Indian Series
Book X

CHEROKEE

Donald Clayton Porter

BANTAM BOOKS
TORONTO • NEW YORK • LONDON • SYDNEY • AUCKLAND

CHEROKEE

*A Bantam Book / published by arrangement with
Book Creations, Inc.*

*Produced by Book Creations, Inc.
Chairman of the Board: Lyle Kenyon Engel.*

Bantam edition / November 1984

ISBN 0-553-24492-2

Published simultaneously in the United States and Canada

*Bantam Books are published by Bantam Books, Inc. Its
trademark, consisting of the words "Bantam Books" and the
portrayal of a rooster, is Registered in U.S. Patent and Trademark Office and in other countries. Marca Registrada. Bantam Books, Inc., 666 Fifth Avenue, New York, New York 10103.*

PRINTED IN THE UNITED STATES OF AMERICA

O   0 9 8 7 6 5 4 3 2 1

CHEROKEE

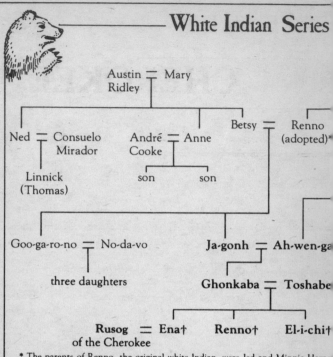

White Indian Series

Austin ── Mary
Ridley

Ned ── Consuelo   André ── Anne   Betsy ──   Renno
        Mirador   Cooke   (adopted)*

Linnick   son   son
(Thomas)

Goo-ga-ro-no ── No-da-vo   Ja-gonh ── Ah-wen-ga

three daughters   Ghonkaba ── Toshabe

        Rusog ── Ena†   Renno†   El-i-chi†
        of the Cherokee

* The parents of Renno, the original white Indian, were Jed and Minnie Harpe
they were killed by the Seneca when Renno was an infant.

† Named for an ancestor.

© BOOK CREATIONS INC. 1983

The Family Tree

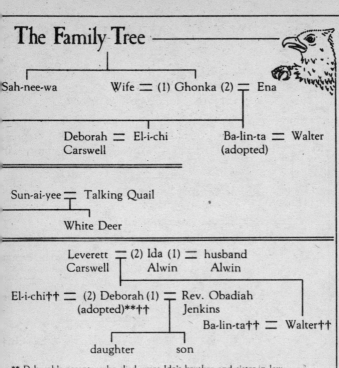

```
                        |
Sah-nee-wa        Wife = (1) Ghonka (2) = Ena


        Deborah = El-i-chi        Ba-lin-ta = Walter
        Carswell                  (adopted)


Sun-ai-yee = Talking Quail

        White Deer


        Leverett = (2) Ida (1) = husband
        Carswell     Alwin       Alwin

El-i-chi†† = (2) Deborah (1) = Rev. Obadiah
             (adopted)**††     Jenkins
                                      Ba-lin-ta†† = Walter††

        daughter         son
```

** Deborah's parents, who died, were Ida's brother and sister-in law.

†† Same as person named above.

RON TOELKE '83

Chapter I

The day was bright and clear, the sun had burned away patches of autumn frost on the earth, and the strenuous efforts of the dog now bounding in the leaves that rustled on the ground typified the spirit and energy of America.

In the middle of the previous month—October 1781—the Continental Army of General George Washington and his French allies had resoundingly defeated a British force commanded by General Lord Cornwallis. For all practical purposes, this victory guaranteed the independence of the new United States of America, although the former mother country was reluctant to admit it. British troops still occupied New York City and were active elsewhere, particularly in the South, and also to the west of the Allegheny Mountains. There they would remain until a peace treaty

1

was signed; in the meantime they were causing new troubles and forcing new battles on the former colonists who had established homes on and near the frontier.

Now, in mid-November, a small band of Seneca Indians was preparing to leave Pennsylvania for a long journey across the mountains and into the remote valleys of the Tennessee country. Unable to return to the land of the Seneca because they had cast their lot with the Americans rather than with their tribe's treaty allies, the British, they were looking forward to creating new lives for themselves in the wilderness beyond the mountains. Their departure was set for the following day.

No Seneca had ever visited the region to which they were going, though some of Ghonkaba's ancestors had passed close to it, on military expeditions, in years long gone by. It was a largely unsettled area with verdant though occasionally forbidding heights, intersected by rushing rivers. Principal among these bodies of water was one known as "River of the Cherokees," after the tribe that dwelt along its banks. Later, the river came to be known as the Tennessee, a name applied by many to the district as well. It was here that the band of Seneca hoped to find their new homeland.

Waiting restlessly for the trek to be organized, two young people strolled together in the woods near the Seneca encampment, intent on each other as much as on their surroundings.

One of them, a young woman just entering her twenties, who seemed as Indian as it was possible to be, was a direct descendant of the renowned Renno, the white Seneca who

2

had gained international fame for his exploits. With her was a blond young man who looked slightly older.

The young woman, Ena, had startling green eyes to go with her dark brown hair, chiseled features, and slender, willowy figure. She had made her mark as a scout in her own right, and with her father, Ghonkaba, had performed valuable services for the Continental Army. In so doing, she had won praise from the commander in chief, General Washington.

Her companion was Clem Dawkins, a young man who had cast his lot with the small band of Seneca that acted as scouts for the Continental Army. Tall, square-shouldered, and earnest, he knew little about warfare and even less about scouting. But he was so in love with Ena that he had joined the band of Seneca outcasts, determined to follow them to the ends of the earth.

As they wandered down the path through the woods, Ena, always serious, described in detail the duties of a scout and how to best perform them. While listening, Clem stooped to pick up a stick and threw it into the underbrush beside the trail. Ena's shepherd dog, Lyktaw, barking and yelping in delight, crashed into the brush, scattering the autumn leaves as he retrieved the stick and brought it back to Clem. Each time, he was rewarded with a pat on the head and words of praise.

Suddenly Ena stopped and shook her head, more in amusement than in annoyance. "I'm wasting my time," she exclaimed. "You're not listening to a single word I'm saying."

"I've heard every last thing you've said to me," Clem

replied. "Try me and find out for yourself. Good boy, Lyktaw!" he added as he took the stick from the dog. "Here we go, fetch again." He hurled the stick off into the woods, and the dog happily bounded after it.

"How do you find out for certain," Ena demanded, "if strangers are within a mile or two of where you positioned yourself in the wilderness?"

"That's easy—on the surface," Clem told her. "You just put your ear to the ground and listen. I've seen you do it many times. The trouble is, when I do it, nothing happens. A whole army could be marching just a few yards away and I wouldn't hear a blamed thing."

"That's just the point I'm trying to make. You don't know how to listen!" She looked at him and suddenly began to laugh.

With one accord, they moved closer together, embraced, and kissed.

Lyktaw returned, carrying the stick in his mouth, and jumped up until they took notice of him. "Good boy, Lyktaw," Clem said. "Fetch!" Again he threw the stick and then turned back to Ena. "We'll have many years ahead of us," he said, "and before you're through with me, I'll become an expert tracker. I'll never be in your class, but then, no other Seneca can equal you either. When we're married and have our home in Tennessee, it's going to be very different for both of us."

"Our future together," Ena replied, "sounds almost too good to be true."

*   *   *

CHEROKEE

Colonel Alexander Hamilton, personal aide to General Washington, threw a fresh log on the fire burning in the hearth of the study in the farmhouse that was the commander in chief's field headquarters. Then, hearing noises in the bedchamber directly above him, he hurried to the kitchen, where he notified the sergeant in charge to begin preparations for the general's breakfast. He returned to the study just as Washington, clad in a quilted bathrobe and heavy slippers, came into the room. He had slept poorly the previous night, and heavy shadows showed beneath his eyes.

"'Morning, Alex," he said. "You know, it's very strange. When the war was going full tilt, I was so busy that I slept beautifully every night, but now that we have victory in our hands, I have more time to think about the various problems that are besetting us on every side. As a result, I spend half the night stewing about them. What did you order for my breakfast today?"

"The usual, General—oatmeal, eggs, and kippers. General Knox wants an appointment with you at your first opportunity, and I gave him ten o'clock this morning pending your approval."

"I approve," Washington said promptly.

"Colonel Ghonkaba of the Seneca scouts is here to see you and insists that he has an appointment with you. I told him I'm sure that he's confused, and that you're going to be meeting with his entire unit to bid them farewell shortly before noon, but he said that you made quite a point of wanting to see him in private as well."

"Find out if he'll join me for breakfast and send him in

5

to me.'' Washington seated himself in an easy chair before the fire. A few moments later, Ghonkaba entered, his hard-muscled body trim in frontierwear consisting of buckskin shirt, trousers, and moccasins. The only indication of advancing middle age was a sprinkling of gray in his hair. Otherwise, he bore a startling resemblance to his father, Ja-gonh and to his grandfather, the great Renno, as they had looked in the prime of life.

He and Washington had known each other for twenty years, ever since Ghonkaba had acted as a scout for the young Colonel Washington during the so-called French and Indian War. They were very much at home with each other.

''You're ready to revert to an inactive status and lead your Seneca out to Tennessee, I gather?'' Washington asked.

Ghonkaba nodded as he took the chair opposite the general's on the other side of the fire. ''I am becoming a civilian again with considerable regret, sir,'' he said, ''but I can understand the point that there's little further use for my unit in the Continental Army, and that you won't have anything much for our men to do.''

The sergeant came into the room with two breakfast trays, which he handed to Washington and Ghonkaba. The general was silent until the enlisted man left the room. ''Start eating,'' he said, ''and listen to me. I am about to tell you something in greatest confidence—information that you are to regard as an official secret and will repeat to no one except Major Casno, your deputy.''

CHEROKEE

"Yes, sir," Ghonkaba said. Although he disliked oatmeal, he began to eat his porridge.

"Your subordinates," Washington said, "are being discharged with honor from the Continental Army, effective today. You and Major Casno are not being released, however, in spite of our announcement to the contrary. You are remaining on active duty, with a specific task to perform."

A feeling of great relief flooded Ghonkaba. The army was not turning him out to pasture, but had need of him. The feeling was a good one.

"Our situation west of the Allegheny Mountains," Washington said, "particularly in the Kentucky and Tennessee areas, is critical. We need that land for purposes of expansion, as new immigrants pour into our young nation, especially from the British Isles. The British ostensibly have lost the war, but they can defeat us in the long run and can reduce us once again to a state of bondage. We need the frontier country to provide us with adequate land for our immigrants, and for the growing of food for our rapidly expanding population."

Ghonkaba nodded. So far, everything the commander in chief was saying made a great deal of sense to him.

"If the territory across the mountains belongs to us," Washington continued, "the United States stands a good chance of becoming a major power. If we're confined to the Atlantic Seaboard, we'll soon atrophy and fall apart. Therefore, the British, who habitually take a long view, want to deny us those western lands at any cost. To

7

achieve their ends, they're employing an agent named Anthony Simpson. You've heard of him?''

Ghonkaba shook his head. "No, sir.''

Washington took a sheet of folded paper from his pocket and handed it to him.

Ghonkaba finished his cereal and, beginning to eat his coddled eggs, read the document carefully. Anthony Simpson had been born about forty years earlier on the American frontier, in Pennsylvania. When he was a small boy, his parents had been captured by Huron Indians, allies of the French. They had been tortured to death in his presence. He had escaped and had made his way to England, where he had been adopted by an uncle, a man of considerable wealth and stature. The boy had been reared in London, living in relatively luxurious surroundings. But he had never overcome the horror of having seen his parents' violent death. His reckless way of life ended with his being sent to Newgate Prison, and, ultimately, he had been disinherited by his uncle as profligate and lawless. Then he disappeared from sight, only to surface again a few years later. He was living among the Choctaw and had mated with one of them in a match that had produced a particularly vicious half-breed son. Meanwhile, he had become a secret agent for the British as their principal representative west of the Allegheny Mountains. To him went much of the credit for the stand taken by the various Indian nations of the region.

The Choctaw, the Creek, and the southern branch of the Tuscarora all swore allegiance to Great Britain, and the only nation of consequence still on the fence was the

CHEROKEE

Cherokee. Simpson appeared to be applying his uniquely successful brand of persuasion to the Cherokee currently. Their adherence to the British cause was anticipated at any time.

Ghonkaba read the report twice, remembering every thing that it said regarding Anthony Simpson. Then he tore up the paper and threw it into the fire. "This man appears to be very accomplished," he remarked.

Savoring his eggs, a delicacy he had been denied during the lean years of the war, Washington stopped eating for a moment. "Simpson has been called an evil genius," he said, "and that's the most accurate description that I know. He is ruthless and will do anything to win a tribe over to the British cause. Unless his activities are halted permanently, the freedom won by our thirteen colonies will prove to be only an illusion. We have won the battles, but the ultimate victory will be Great Britain's."

"It's obvious, then, that Simpson must be stopped at any cost," Ghonkaba said.

Washington tasted his kippers and found them to his liking. "That's the mission that I'm giving to you and to Casno," he said. "Find Anthony Simpson and stop him! Make it impossible for him to function any longer."

"Yes, sir," Ghonkaba said, although he had no immediate idea how to carry out the order.

"I realize you've been given an exceptionally difficult order," the general said. "It may be of some comfort to you to know that you and Casno are not alone in having been instructed to halt Simpson's activities. The same order has been transmitted to others who are in the area. I'm hopeful that, among you, he'll be found and rendered harmless.''

The twin stars on the shoulders of his field uniform that denoted General Washington's rank were faded, and the gilt that decorated the long coat was badly tarnished. But the general's voice was strong and vibrant as he addressed the Seneca Indians clad in buckskins as they stood attentively before him in the Pennsylvania woodlands.

"You, my Seneca allies, have performed brilliantly ever since the day when you joined me during the siege of Boston, so many years ago. In those years, you have not only fought valiantly and have performed invaluable service for the Continental Army and for the people of our new United States, you have suffered great hardships. You have cut yourself off for all time from your own nation, the Seneca, because of your loyalty to the United States and your refusal to accept the treaty that had bound you to our enemy, Great Britain.

"Because of your firm adherence to our cause, you have been cast out by the Seneca and by her sister nations in the Iroquois League. We know that the leaders of your tribe acted with great reluctance in this action, but they felt they had no choice.

"Nevertheless, my friends, you do not stand alone. Though I cannot confer on you that which I wish to do, let me assure you that you will enjoy the benefits of the victory that I anticipate, including those personal liberties we regard as our most precious possessions.

"Now that the war has entered a new and final phase, your services are no longer so urgently required. We are therefore pleased to authorize you to resume the lives that you have so generously given to our cause when our need was greatest. If I could, I would reward you with material wealth. Our funds, however, are severely limited. Under the circumstances, I am compelled to give you only what we consider the greatest of all boons we can present to those who have demonstrated loyalty beyond measure. Will your commanding officer come forward, please?"

Ghonkaba stepped forward smartly. He halted directly in front of the general, raising his right hand in a sharp salute. Promoted rank by rank as he led his intrepid scouts in the service of the Continental Army, Ghonkaba had achieved the rank of lieutenant colonel. He was even prouder of that than of the comparable position of war chief he had previously earned in the army of the Seneca.

An aide-de-camp handed the general a furled flag, and Washington unrolled it. Relatively small, the flag had a background of blue. On it was embroidered an eagle in red surrounded by thirteen white stars. It was the personal emblem of the commander in chief of the Continental Army.

Now the Seneca scouts would have the great distinction of owning and displaying it. Almost overcome by the honor, Ghonkaba expressed thanks for himself and his men amid the cheers of his dozen hard-bitten veterans of

11

the struggle for freedom. He then called for one of the younger members to come forward.

His younger son, El-i-chi, joined his father in front of the group.

"You and your brother will take turns marching at the head of our column," Ghonkaba instructed him. "And at all times you will display this flag." He handed El-i-chi the commander in chief's emblem.

As the ceremony came to an end, the families of the scouts crowded forward to shake hands with General Washington.

Then, at last, Ghonkaba called the Seneca to order.

"The time has come for us to take our departure, my friends," he said.

True to the Seneca tradition, the women and children as well as the adult men—about forty persons in all—were well disciplined. They promptly began to form a line of march for their great adventure. Their journey would take them into unfamiliar territory.

A small vanguard would act as advance scouts. Its leader, Ranoga, had been designated as a seasoned senior warrior after distinguishing himself frequently in battle against the British. Accompanying him in the vanguard was another senior warrior. And, surprisingly, this was a young woman—Ena.

Standing near as they made ready to depart was Lyktaw, Ena's German shepherd. Devoted to her, the dog was equally loyal to Clem, her constant companion. Ghonkaba had called Lyktaw the equal of any warrior, and anyone who had seen the dog take on an enemy knew that the description was hardly an exaggeration.

Second in command among the scouts, Casno had served as a major in the Continental Army. As the unit was reverting to civilian status, he had unexpectedly begun to fill the need for a religious leader, responding to an inner "call" for a medicine man. Now, while last-minute preparations for departure went on, he moved aside to utter a quiet, heartfelt prayer to the manitous, the eternal representatives of the gods, who watched over the destinies of all faithful Seneca.

Facing north, Casno stood erect, his arms spread. His lips moved without sound as he implored the manitous to continue to keep in mind the little band that was setting out on a new adventure.

Every Seneca regarded religion as the core of existence, to be observed and celebrated in private. Consequently, almost all of them took care to avert their eyes from Casno, even though they realized that he prayed on their behalf as well as on his own.

Only Ghonkaba, who awaited the opportunity to bid a personal farewell to General Washington, found himself drawn to Casno, whom he watched closely. Unexpectedly and suddenly, he understood why: he was being impelled by a force far stronger than himself, more powerful than any human emotion.

As he watched, a large, single bird feather, gray in color, appeared overhead and drifted toward Casno. Ghonkaba could see no bird in the vicinity, but nevertheless, the feather was there.

When it came within reach, moving in majestic, slow motion, Casno held out one hand and curled his fingers around it.

Ghonkaba felt a chill race up his spine. He recognized the feather as that of a hawk and knew that this was the manitous' response to Casno's prayer for safety and success. As the Seneca believed, and as Ghonkaba had good reason to know from personal experience, hawks were messengers of the manitous, their intermediaries in communicating with mortals. The release of a hawk feather as Casno had completed his prayers was a sign that the manitous and the gods would indeed be keeping watch over the little band's journey.

Vastly comforted, Ghonkaba turned and smiled as George Washington approached.

"The flag," he said, "was a perfect gift, sir. It will raise our spirits whenever they may be low, and in the months to come they'll be less than high on many occasions."

"Look at the bright side of the situation," Washington advised. "Colonel Dan Boone and other frontiersmen have sent word to me that the Cherokee are prepared to be friendly toward us, unlike some other Indian nations. They show no sign of wavering in their loyalty. I can imagine no reason why they won't welcome you and be extremely friendly. Surely they can find some space in the territory they control for you to make your home."

"I hope you're right, sir," Ghonkaba replied. "We're too few in number to put up a fight of any consequence.

We'll have to accept what the larger tribes of the area decree.''

"Your company," Washington told him, "has performed so many miracles in combat, I'd be astonished if you aren't entirely successful in establishing a comfortable, permanent home. In any event, please keep me informed, and I'll do everything in my power to help you to achieve a place in the America that we shall all be developing together. And I shall be grateful for your pursuit of the special mission with which I have entrusted you.''

No more needed to be said. Ghonkaba shouted an order, and the Seneca stepped out on the long march ahead. The vanguard spread out, seeking to cover each approach the column might need to take. The principal group was preceded by El-i-chi, proudly carrying the commander in chief's eagle pennant, which fluttered in the spring breeze.

The travelers were unprepossessing by any standard. Other than the well-worn garments of buckskin that they were wearing, they carried virtually no clothing. The warriors carried an assortment of weapons, including bows and arrows, tomahawks, and knives, and each man had a long rifle that had seen plenty of combat use.

Blankets, cooking utensils, and a few additional household goods were piled onto treated animal skins, which in turn were fastened to travois poles. With one end of a pair of poles over the shoulders of a woman or an older boy, the other end trailed behind, bearing the weight of the items to be transported. Travois enabled Indians on the move to go almost anywhere, easily surmounting most natural obstacles.

Toshabe, born and bred an Erie, had become more of a Seneca than virtually any other woman in the nation. Certainly none had greater natural beauty or greater dignity than did this woman with hints of gray in her hair. She was a suitable mate for Ghonkaba. Not only were her chiseled features those of a classic Indian beauty and her figure that of a woman half her age, but a rare intelligence shone in her eyes. She was endowed with the understanding and compassion necessary in the wife of a leader of people. She walked erect, a travois pole balanced lightly on one shoulder.

The other pole, on which her family's burden was laden, was carried by the elder of her sons, Renno, who bore the name of his illustrious great-grandfather. At nineteen a junior warrior who required only combat experience to qualify as a senior warrior, Renno's bearing demonstrated to all who knew him and his history that he was a worthy descendant of the famous Ghonka, of Renno the elder, of Ja-gonh, and of Ghonkaba. Under usual circumstances, he could have looked forward to becoming the Great Sachem of all the nations of the Iroquois. That had been ruled out by his father's decision to join the American forces in the war, even though that had meant banishment from the tribe and that his family could have no future associations with it.

But Renno showed no regrets, no yearning for what might have been. Like the other men of his illustrious family, he was a realist who accepted his situation at any given moment, making the best of what was available to him.

CHEROKEE

Behind them lay all the trappings of civilization offered by Philadelphia, seat of the Continental Congress and capital of a nation in embryo growing into full-fledged status. Its people, optimistic at last of victory, were planning for the unlimited future they envisioned for the United States.

Ahead, at the far end of an unmarked trail, lay the travelers' future, shrouded in the gloom of the forests that covered most of North America. No one could predict with confidence whether success or failure, joy or sorrow, awaited them.

All that was certain was their attitude. They walked without fear. Having faced the enemy for almost six years of combat, the men could hold their heads high, knowing they could confront any odds. Women who had struggled to keep their families together while living in exile rejoiced because, despite the insecurity, they were on their way, they could hope, to a new and peaceful homeland. And the young, always optimistic, always hopeful, trod the rough Pennsylvania road lightly. They alone suffered no doubts, convinced that a glorious future inevitably awaited them.

Following orders given by Ghonkaba, the party changed chores and assignments daily, giving up their work of one day and taking a fresh approach the next. In this way, they were better able to remain sharp and enthusiastic during their long, seemingly endless journey. So it happened that Renno and his brother, El-i-chi, were assigned on the same day to positions augmenting the party's regular scouts.

17

Ranoga ordered them to proceed together through the wilderness, and this they did, pushing through the foliage of early spring as they advanced. Renno was the first to find signs that the rugged hill country through which they were traveling was not uninhabited.

"Look!" he exclaimed. "We are not alone in these parts. A hunting party has been abroad here!"

Their excitement mounted when El-i-chi found some clear moccasin prints in the fresh earth. Ultimately, they could count at least twenty braves in the party.

They came to a place where a deer had been shot with a bow and arrow and the carcass butchered. Within a short time, they found the remains of a fire where meat had been cooked. Here they lingered for many minutes, examining the further evidence. The hunters had eaten not only venison. The ground was littered with corncobs and husks.

Renno felt a mounting excitement. He became increasingly convinced that the party was composed of Erie braves. "This could be an important discovery," he said, suppressing the thrill that bubbled up within him.

El-i-chi nodded eagerly. "A hunting party of more than twenty Erie braves," he replied, "can provide a target that our father and the other warriors will find too tempting to be overlooked."

At a rendezvous some time later with Ranoga and their sister, Ena, before returning to the main body, they revealed what they had found.

Ranoga was unperturbed. "We're within lands the Erie use as hunting grounds," he commented. "It is not surprising to find a substantial hunting party traveling here."

Renno shook his head impatiently. "You appear to miss the point, Ranoga!" he cried. "We have a chance to strike a great blow against a tribe that is a natural foe of the Seneca."

Ranoga said nothing but exchanged a glance with Ena, who looked at her brothers. She, too, remained silent.

"Surely you agree with us, Ena!" El-i-chi said, unable to conceal his annoyance. "We have an opportunity to take many scalps and win a great victory."

"I suggest," she replied firmly, "that you take your news to our father. He will inform you of what you are to do."

Until the day's march ended, Ghonkaba remained busy and distracted. Then he supervised setting up an overnight camp, assigning space to each family, and making certain that sentries were in place.

Meanwhile, Toshabe had prepared a rabbit stew for her family and for Clem, who had trapped several rabbits in keeping with Ena's instructions.

Ghonkaba praised the young man after he had eaten heartily.

"I'm learning," Clem replied, "that when I can see two or more ways of doing something, the simple way is almost always the Indian way. It's the Seneca genius for accomplishing what they set out to do in the most direct manner."

"That," Ghonkaba told him with a grin, "is our goal. We do try to employ direct methods. Whether we succeed in that is a question we sometimes cannot answer."

Seeing his opportunity, Renno hastened to say, "We

also seek glory when it can be found at not too great an expense." He and El-i-chi went on to describe their discovery.

Ghonkaba listened intently, his face drained of expression.

"Since the beginning of time," young Renno said enthusiastically, "the Erie have been our foes. Today the manitous are giving us the opportunity to strike a sharp blow against them at little cost to ourselves. I suggest, my father, that we set a trap for the Erie hunters. Let us overtake them, then have our warriors lie in ambush. We can take many scalps before the Erie even realize what is happening in order to defend themselves."

He and El-i-chi eagerly awaited their father's reply.

But, as Ena had expected, Ghonkaba merely looked first at his sons and then at the others sitting around the fire. "Clem," he asked, "what is your opinion of Renno's plan?"

Clem Dawkins hesitated before he replied. "According to what Renno has reported," he said, "at least twenty braves are in the Erie hunting party. In our own group, we can recruit not many more than fifteen men who can handle firearms. That's counting me and the junior warriors. That means we are outnumbered from the start. We'd have to be ready to outsmart the enemy at every turn."

"I take it for granted," Renno interjected impulsively, "that we will outsmart the Erie. We are Seneca, so we have a natural advantage!"

Ghonkaba stared hard at each of his sons. "We are Seneca," he said, "but we have no advantage. No longer can we rely on a whole nation—or a whole army—to reinforce our numbers, to supply food and ammunition, and to support our efforts. We can rely only on ourselves."

Renno looked chastened.

"What advantage would we gain if we fought the braves of the Erie hunting party and defeated them?" his father continued. "We would wear their scalps on our belts, but we already have acquired more than enough glory. The flag that General Washington gave us is far more valuable and significant than Erie scalps. We would gain their weapons, but we have all the weapons we need."

Renno began to see the point his father was making and nodded to show that he understood.

"One thing is certain," Ghonkaba said. "We would be sure to arouse the wrath of the main encampments of the Erie, and they would send war parties in search of us. Granted that we are Seneca and they are only Erie, how much chance would we have in a battle with two hundred Erie fighting men? We would be badly outnumbered—our men would be killed, our women would be taken into slavery, and at best our children would be ridiculed until they had atoned for all the mistakes of their elders. No, my sons, we shall not make the grave mistake of attacking a superior party of Erie hunters."

El-i-chi, too, grasped the significance of all that his father was saying.

"Never forget, my sons," Ghonkaba continued, "that we are members of a tiny, isolated band. We must walk softly, avoiding belligerence and taking no unnecessary risks against more powerful forces. We can depend upon no one but ourselves, now and in the future. By birth and

21

by tradition we are Seneca, but we stand alone in this world. And we must be mindful that we are to live quietly and avoid those who are stronger.''

As the exiled Seneca resumed their march toward the Southwest, the wilderness became increasingly rugged. They plunged deeper into the Appalachian Mountains, discovering that they were now in an unoccupied land. No Indian tribe called this territory its own, and none claimed it as a private preserve for hunting. Ranoga's scouts consistently reported an absence of other human beings. Consequently, the band could move more rapidly for the time being, assured that they were relatively free from danger. Game was plentiful, and the interlude gave promise of being extremely pleasant as long as it lasted.

Enjoying this atmosphere, Ena and Clem decided to travel for a day on a route some distance from that taken by the main column. They could be alone for several hours, an experience they seldom enjoyed, and they could engage in hunting, a privilege ordinarily denied them because those who were better shots took precedence whenever game was encountered.

The sun was warm, but the wind from the heights to the west was cool, and the forest cover provided ample shade. Following a course parallel to that taken by the others, they were blissfully happy, walking hand in hand among the oaks, maples, birches, elms, and beeches. In spite of her euphoria, Ena was ever conscious of the strange surroundings. Suddenly she halted and pointed to the ground some yards ahead. Then she raised a finger to her lips, calling for silence. Clem looked ahead to where Ena had pointed but could discern nothing unusual. He assumed she must have seen the track of an animal.

Quickly, Ena tested her bow, then reached over her shoulder and drew an arrow from the quiver that rested against her back.

She tested the direction in which the wind was blowing by wetting a forefinger and holding it up. Motioning to Clem to follow, she made her way in a large semicircle, approaching the area from a different angle. She advanced softly, step by step, making no sound. Clem, doing his best to be as quiet, was pleased that his own progress was virtually as silent as hers.

Ena moved slowly but steadily, appearing sure of herself.

As she halted, she raised the bow to shoulder height, pulling it taut while she held the arrow in place, ready to be discharged.

A deer, a large, handsome buck weighing at least one hundred and fifty pounds, stood proudly, facing Ena and seeming to defy her. In the next instant, when Ena's arrow found its mark, the deer crumpled to the ground.

Ena raced forward to view the fallen target, her heart swelling with pride. The first time she'd hunted without the supervision of her father or some other warrior, she had achieved startlingly successful results.

"The whole company will eat fresh meat tonight," she announced proudly. Raising her head, she made a long, low-pitched noise uncannily resembling the hoot of an owl. She repeated it again and again for three minutes before standing back to lean against a tree. She seemed to be waiting confidently.

Clem blinked, uncertain of what she was doing. After a few more minutes, an answering hoot drifted through the trees.

Ena smiled slightly and was satisfied. "Stand guard over our prize," she told Clem, "to make sure that no predator tries to take it from us."

Removing the catch from his long rifle, Clem moved closer to the carcass.

After a short wait, they could hear someone approaching. Finally, El-i-chi appeared, his eyes widening somewhat when he saw the slain deer.

"Thank you for heeding my call, my brother," Ena said. "Go quickly, if you will, and fetch our father."

Without a word, he disappeared into the screen of trees.

Clem marveled at the discipline shown by El-i-chi, like that of all the Seneca. Barely acknowledging her request, asking no questions, he had departed at the familiar Seneca trot. The pace was one that all the tribe's warriors learned from earliest childhood, and they could maintain it for as many hours as necessary.

Ena smiled at Clem, and the intimacy that bound them together was restored immediately. His questions and doubts vanished even though unanswered, for he implicitly trusted Ena to do the right thing. As he had never been in his life before meeting Ena, he felt he was at peace within himself and with the world, relaxed and feeling only warmth and goodwill.

His mood did not last long. Ghonkaba, still lean and

supple though in his middle years, appeared with dramatic suddenness. His arrival was so silent that if he had been an enemy, Clem would have lacked any opportunity to try to protect himself or his companion.

Directly behind was Ranoga, the tall, sinewy head of the company's scouts. He carried an unsheathed knife in one hand, ready for any emergency.

Thanking them for responding so quickly, Ena took unusual advantage of her femininity by giggling slightly and looking embarrassed as she confessed, "I realized only after I had shot the deer that Clem is unfamiliar with butchering, and I wanted his assistance."

Clem was uncertain whether Ghonkaba might lose his temper, but both warriors burst into laughter.

"Watch what I do, Clem, so that you may learn," Ghonkaba said. "These ways of the Seneca need no longer be strange to you." Removing from his belt a knife with a long, thin blade, he started to work on the carcass. Ranoga, too, pitched in.

Closely observing every deft move, Clem realized the accuracy of all he had heard of the Seneca treatment of slaughtered animals. They used every part of the carcass, including the skin, antlers, bones, hooves, and head. From these would be fashioned buttons and weapons, clothing, and many other items needed in daily life.

"You have watched enough," Ghonkaba said. "One learns best by doing." He handed Clem the knife.

With Ena's assistance, Clem began to carve, showing more enthusiasm than skill. They did well, nevertheless, as Ghonkaba and Ranoga stood by, correcting, advising, and teaching.

"One more lesson must be learned; and this is the most important of all," Ghonkaba said. He and Ranoga found some large, empty gourds and carried them to a stream that ran a few yards away. Dipping them repeatedly in the running waters, they poured the contents onto the ground where the carcass had lain. Some leafy plants that had been stained were uprooted and scattered where they would not attract attention. A quarter of an hour was needed, even with the help of Ena and Clem, to remove all signs of blood and to renew life to the grass that had been trampled.

"Always remember," he said, "that they who travel in the forest may leave signs of their presence. We never know when enemies are seeking our destruction. Let us not leave them signs that disclose we have been here, and also point to the direction we have taken. It's not easy to disguise the butchering of the deer, but we have to do the best we can. As it is, anyone trying to read the signs that remain is sure to be confused and upset."

Then, having done everything possible to confound any later passerby, they picked up the meat, carrying separate sections over their shoulders, and started off to rejoin their company. Ghonkaba and Ranoga let the younger couple struggle with most of the venison.

Even after they came upon the rest of the band and fell into line, at Ghonkaba's quiet instigation no one helped them carry the meat. He hoped to teach them that hunting consisted of far more than shooting an animal. It was important to butcher it, to obliterate signs from the forest that could reveal their whereabouts, before being ready to bring food to their comrades.

A short time later, when they halted for the night, Ena and Clem learned yet another lesson: their work had just begun. They gathered a large pile of wood, built a fire, and after the flames had burned down they used long, green sticks to skewer pieces of the meat and thus prepared a helping of the venison for everyone's supper.

Ravenous when he finally sat down to eat, Clem knew that he had gained new insight into Seneca practices and communal spirit.

Even now he and Ena discovered their responsibilities had not come to an end. After the meal, they faced the problem of what to do with the uncooked meat. Only a portion of the venison had been eaten; the remainder would spoil if left untreated. They gathered more wood, and then, tamping down the fire, they sliced the meat and hung it to smoke. When adequately smoked, Ena explained to Clem, venison could be preserved indefinitely. It would remain edible for months.

What impressed both of them most about the day's experience was Ghonkaba's willingness to teach by example and to guide the inexperienced into the proper practices. This, as Clem understood, was the true Seneca spirit, which this band exemplified. He knew that even though their future was in doubt, their spirit would enable them to overcome almost any obstacle.

*   *   *

Clem Dawkins struggled incessantly to carry his share of the burden. He soon learned, however, that in spite of his best efforts and Ena's loyal attempts to help him, he was not cut out for the life of a Seneca scout.

For Ena, it was second nature to read the signs in the wilderness showing that other people had passed that way recently, but Clem could fail to recognize the most obvious clue under his nose. Ena explained that this was due to his unfamiliarity with the wilderness. As a town dweller, he was almost entirely unacquainted with the ways of nature and had to strain in order to see that leaves were bent, that twigs underfoot had been disturbed, or that other signs revealed people were at hand.

His companions invariably were considerate and kind to him, and he tried to reward their trust.

His hearing had proved to be acute and his night vision was surprisingly sharp, so he was able to attain stature as a sentry, gladly taking his turn on night duty.

Rather than being given an area he was expected to cover on foot, he was assigned to one spot, well concealed, and armed with a long rifle. There he represented a formidable potential opponent as he sat awaiting the arrival of unexpected enemies who never showed up. He accepted these responsibilities without complaint and often volunteered for extra duty in place of a warrior who had spent the day ranging far ahead of the main column on scouting expeditions.

Loving him and warmly appreciating his sense of duty, Ena tried to help him without his realizing it. Regularly, she instructed the shepherd dog, Lyktaw, to join Clem on his vigil. As always, Lyktaw was faithful to the trust.

Whenever Clem was assigned to night sentry duty, usually on alternate nights, Lyktaw accompanied him and nestled down close beside him. The shepherd understood the need for silence and concealment.

Pleased by the companionship, Clem was amazed by Lyktaw's fidelity. Lyktaw never strayed from his resting place and dozed lightly for hours at a time, awakening only long enough to shift position slightly, listen intently, and be assured that all was well before dozing again.

One night began no differently from many others that had preceded it. No moon was out, but the velvetlike, blue-black sky was filled with stars intermittently visible through the heavy layer of trees. The quiet was all-pervading.

Clem lounged comfortably on the ground, his long rifle cradled in his arms. He had learned the Seneca trick of becoming sleepy, resting, and gathering his strength, yet at the same time remaining alert for any sounds that would disclose the approach of an intruder. Hours passed, and the even breathing of the grayish-brown shepherd dog told him that all was well.

Suddenly the dog stiffened and raised its head a fraction of an inch, ears pointing straight upward.

Shaking off his drowsiness, Clem immediately peered through the undergrowth but could hear nothing.

Lyktaw was endowed with an even keener sense of hearing, however, and a low, rumbling sound, menacing in its intensity, welled up from deep inside him.

Clem was taking no chances, and though he had neither

seen nor heard any sign of an enemy, he realized the dog was warning him. He removed the safety catch from the trigger of his rifle. Lyktaw continued to growl.

His hearing strained to its utmost, Clem finally discerned the sound of a small twig cracking as it broke beneath the weight of some object. No longer could there be any question: a stranger was creeping closer to the camp of the sleeping Seneca.

An immediate problem presented itself. If he sounded an alarm now, awakening the warriors, he would be inviting all of them to participate in the fight that inevitably would develop. Instead, should he seek to dispose of the intruder himself? He decided to try to handle it, because he instinctively knew that the Seneca would react the same way. If only one foe was approaching, Clem should be able to dispose of him single-handed. If the enemies should prove too numerous to handle, he then would call for help.

Again, he heard a faint crackling noise. Tensing, Clem peered down the barrel of his rifle, prepared to shoot the foe on sight.

Unexpectedly, Lyktaw began to inch forward through the underbrush, remaining close to the ground.

A dark shape emerged from the depths of the forest at the far side of a small clearing, and in the half-light Clem was astonished to see a wild boar, an ugly creature with a single horn protruding from its low forehead. Rising to full height, Lyktaw prepared to do battle against this strange enemy.

Clem called to the dog in a low, urgent voice, but it

paid no attention, obviously determined to fight to the end no matter how overmatched.

Clem was afraid Lyktaw would be easily overpowered, but he had no opportunity to shoot first because the dog had moved between him and the boar. If he fired, Clem was in danger of hitting Ena's pet.

As it peered across the open space, the boar squinted, its tiny reddish eyes gleaming balefully. Locating the dog, it pawed the ground, preparing to rush its new enemy.

Lyktaw rose to his full height and appeared to be standing indolently.

The boar moved swiftly and suddenly, lowering its head as it charged.

Lyktaw remained motionless until the last possible moment, then sidestepped nimbly. As the boar raced past, the dog reached down, his powerful jaws inflicting a nasty bite on the wild beast's back.

Infuriated by the painful injury, the boar gave a curiously high-pitched squeal as it looked around, attempting to locate its foe before charging again.

This shift in positions gave Clem the opportunity he sought. He aimed carefully, taking a bead on the beast, and pulled the trigger. His shot was accurate, and the boar dropped to the ground.

His rifle's roar awakened the Seneca camp. Ena was the first to reach the scene. She almost collapsed with relief when she saw Lyktaw proudly standing guard over the fallen boar.

When Ghonkaba arrived, closely followed by Ranoga and other senior warriors, Clem behaved with becoming modesty, attributing the victory to Lyktaw's skill both as a sentinel and as a fighter. He himself, he implied, had been little more than a bystander. Ghonkaba, however, congratulated him on his coolheaded handling of the matter.

Ena was the last to linger at the sentry outpost. When she and Clem were alone, she rewarded him with a sound kiss and then looked at him, shaking her head. "Never again," she told him, "do I want to hear you complain that you're discouraged and are too slow in learning our ways. You conducted yourself well tonight. You behaved with the skill and the wisdom of a senior warrior, and I'm proud of you. My pride will grow in the months ahead, as I've told you so frequently, and as it has been doing."

Clem tried to protest, declaring that he did not deserve such lavish praise. But Ena gave him no opportunity to interrupt. Stroking her shepherd dog's head, she said, "You and Lyktaw deserve a special reward, and you shall have it after you've been relieved of guard duty and slept for the rest of the night."

When a senior warrior appeared later at the sentry outpost, Clem immediately went off to rejoin the encampment. As he wrapped himself in his blanket, he saw Lyktaw nuzzling close to Ena, who slept nearby. Dropping off to sleep, Clem reflected that he was far more fortunate than he had ever realized. He was becoming acclimated to the ways of the wilderness in spite of his ignorance, and he was grateful for his steady improvement. He slept soundly for the remainder of the night.

In the morning, Renno and El-i-chi grinned at him while he washed in the stream before breakfast. The reason for their silent laughter soon became evident. He and Lyktaw were being rewarded in a way that neither had anticipated. Ena had fried large steaks of boar meat for them. Clem ate the meat, certain he had never tasted anything so delicious.

As the small party began to descend from the Appalachian heights, the wilderness of trees—with evergreens predominating—seemed to stretch all the way to the horizon.

Ahead of them lay the land known as Kentucky, where numbers of patriots already had settled and where talk of statehood filled the air. Kentuckians insisted that they be granted the honor of being the first to join the original thirteen states.

To the southwest stood an even more fertile and promising land, which the original settlers were calling Franklin in honor of the noted Pennsylvanian. Newcomers to the sparsely settled region later preferred to call this country Tennessee, the name given by the Cherokee and other major Indian nations of the area, principally the Choctaw and Tuscarora.

Soon the travelers would be moving away from any settled area and coming into virgin lands. Their excitement and anticipation grew by leaps and bounds, but even Clem, who had been traveling with them for so long, found it difficult to realize that the Seneca barely could curb their impatience to reach their destination, whatever it might prove to be.

Casno prayed to the manitous to lead the party directly to a land that they could call their own, but Ghonkaba knew it was too much to hope that they would reach such a place within a short time and without difficulties.

One evening after supper he was explaining to his family that the party still had a considerable distance to travel before reaching the land where they might make their new home. Suddenly Ena looked up, interrupted her father with a little cry of distress, and jumped to her feet.

Lyktaw approached slowly in obvious misery. He had encountered a porcupine and had lost the contest. His face, nose, and mouth were filled with quills.

Ena threw herself to the ground beside the miserable dog and did her best to comfort him by stroking his back.

While other members of the family stared in surprise, Clem took immediate action. Leaping to his feet, he hurried to where his belongings were stored in a travois bag and took out a pair of metal pincers. White-faced, his lips set and grim, he went to Ena and spoke to her abruptly. "Hold him steady," he ordered. "This will hurt him like the very devil, but I don't see any other way we can help him."

Ena, who understood his intentions at once, took a firm grip on the dog. Then Clem closed the pincers over a quill protruding from the forehead directly above one eye. Taking care to pull it straight rather than at an angle, he succeeded in removing it.

That was the start of a long and difficult operation. Again and again Clem's pincers closed over a quill, and he pulled it with great strength, always smoothly, never jerking, until a sizable pile had accumulated.

Lyktaw's reaction was remarkable. His spirits bolstered by Ena's constant flow of sympathy, he stood very still. Never moving, except inadvertently when he occasionally trembled from head to toe for several seconds, the animal responded to Ena's ministrations. Raising his head, the dog remained quiet, letting Clem do as he pleased. In some way that was difficult to understand, he appeared to realize what was being done for him—that Clem was not deliberately causing pain, but was actually helping, though each time a quill was removed, his face stung dreadfully. And then that pain was soon dissipated, and once it faded, it did not return.

After what seemed to Lyktaw like an eternity, the last of the quills was removed, and the operation was concluded.

Ena dipped squares of the soft inner bark of a white birch tree into the waters of a nearby lake and rinsed the blood from Lyktaw's face, the cooling water also soothing the dog.

Lyktaw no longer trembled. He showed his appreciation by licking Clem's hand; then, curling on the ground, he went to sleep, head in Ena's lap.

"I offer you my congratulations, Clem," Ghonkaba said. "Often you have been unhappy because you have felt that you show insufficient progress in becoming like the Seneca. You saved Ena's dog from a miserable existence that might have given him a serious infection and, in time, killed him. I offer you the thanks of our entire family. And I join them in their pride that you are now one of us." He turned away and went to his place beside the campfire.

Soon Clem and Ena were alone with the dog, which had fallen sound asleep, breathing deeply.

"I have loved you for a long time, for more than twelve moons," Ena said. "Now, added to my love is my great

35

admiration. When we faced a serious emergency, you not only knew exactly what needed to be done but you did it without hesitation and with great skill. You are fortunate, Clem, because you show the better traits of the white man, the better traits of the Indian.''

Her praise embarrassed him, and he flushed. "I don't deserve all that," he said. "I did what just about anybody would have done under the circumstances."

Ena shook her head. "But I won't argue the matter with you,'' she said.

They kissed and all was right in their world. No matter where the band settled, Ena and Clem felt that their own future was secure.

Chapter II

The Continental Army's most renowned unit was the regiment known as Dan Morgan's Virginia Rifles. Its four hundred hard-bitten frontiersmen from western Virginia were all expert marksmen with the long rifle of the frontier. They were led by an authentic military genius who had lacked any experience in warfare before the outbreak of the American Revolution.

Ghonkaba's veterans had served frequently with the Virginians during the long years of the war, when both units fought with high distinction. General rejoicing resulted when scouts reported one morning that they had just made contact with the outposts of Morgan's riflemen.

Soon the forces were united, and Dan Morgan appeared, riding through the little formation of Seneca, greeting all of them by name. A huge bear of a man who wore a combination of buckskins and odd parts of a Continental uniform, he was in ebullient good humor as he shouted a welcome to old friends.

When he saw Ghonkaba approaching, he leaped nimbly to the ground in spite of his great bulk.

Ghonkaba stood at attention and saluted. "General," he called out, "it's a great pleasure to see you."

"You're a sight for sore eyes, Colonel," Morgan boomed in reply and greeted his old comrade with a bear hug. "Come along to my tent for some grub and a glass of sassafras tea." Morgan threw his reins to an aide-de-camp and linked his arm through Ghonkaba's. "We have a good many things to talk over."

A short time later they were seated together outside Morgan's comfortable tent. Ghonkaba related that his unit had been demobilized and released from active service by General Washington because the need for them in the war effort had so greatly diminished.

Morgan leaned forward and lowered his voice confidentially. "You're lucky, Ghonkaba, luckier than you know. Washington sent me off with my whole fool regiment on what's beginning to look like a wild goose chase. We've spent months searching in vain in the wilderness beyond Virginia for a will-o'-the-wisp. I don't suppose you've ever heard of a British agent who calls himself Anthony Simpson?" Morgan demanded in his deep voice. "God only knows what his real name might be. He picked up the name of Simpson, as I understand it, when he was in Newgate Prison in London. Apparently he persuaded the

CHEROKEE

British that he was an expert on Indians of North America. He talked them into letting him out of prison and sending him over here. Since that time, I'm damned if he hasn't performed near-miracles.''

Ghonkaba, careful not to reveal his secret commission from Washington, gave no hint of what he already knew about Simpson. He simply waited for Morgan to explain in his own words his intense concern about the man.

''Simpson is evil, the very worst of all possible scum,'' Dan Morgan went on. ''He's personally repellent—rarely bathes, smells like an Erie brave on a hot day. He's greedy, and invariably finds ways to line his own pocket. I understand that he's become extremely wealthy on the war. If he lives to see the end of it he'll be on easy street for the rest of his days.''

Ghonkaba nodded noncommittally. ''What, in your view, has he done that makes him so important?'' he asked Morgan.

''Simpson,'' the general said, ''may be an untrustworthy, devious, two-faced cur, but he is solely responsible for keeping the Choctaw as British allies. They're the largest and most ferocious of tribes west of the mountains, as you probably know. He's also responsible for keeping the Creek in line. He has provided firearms, provisions, goods of all kinds. Our victories against the British in the East cannot guarantee who will control the West. Whoever can occupy this territory will possess it; we depend on our few Indian allies to hold the territory until we can send settlers in to claim it for the United States. Simpson stands in our way.''

"If he succeeds completely," Ghonkaba replied, "there will obviously be grave trouble. With the British pressing in from the west, the country will be unable to grow, and such a small nation will be almost impossible to defend."

Dan Morgan nodded. "You have stated almost the entire picture," he said. "Only one element is missing: the fate of the Cherokee nation. The Cherokee aren't as numerous or as belligerent as the Choctaw, nor as volatile as the Creek. But they're solid and dependable. And like your Seneca, they have a long record of winning every war they fight. They prepare thoroughly for battle, and cooperation between their units is nothing short of remarkable. It's at least as good as the best that the Continental Army has achieved after years of warfare."

Morgan's information jibed with what Ghonkaba recalled having learned about the Cherokee. Morgan continued, emphasizing his main points with jabs of his fingers.

"According to what we know from a number of frontiersmen, including Jack Sevier—you undoubtedly knew him as a colonel in the Continentals—Simpson has made repeated efforts to win over the Cherokee. He's offered firearms and vast quantities of other goods. So far, they've resisted, apparently because they seem to regard the American cause and our principles highly. We think Simpson is ready to make another effort to bring the Cherokee around. If he succeeds, the U.S. will lose all chance of getting Tennessee and the area to the south. And although we have a substantial number of settlers in Kentucky, we'd even be very hard put to retain control of that territory."

"In brief," Ghonkaba concluded, "we'd be ceding the

lands west of the mountains to the British. And guaranteeing the eventual destruction of the United States.''

"Precisely," Morgan agreed. "That's why Washington detached my regiment and sent us out here to locate Simpson and grab him. We were given four months to do it. It looks like for the first time I'm going to have to admit failure. Of all the places where Simpson has been reported, he's either long vanished or never really was there. Now the army can't spare us from field duty any longer. I'm preparing to report to Washington that our mission has failed.''

"Keep in mind, Dan," Ghonkaba suggested thoughtfully, "that we will carry on after you must leave. The mission has not failed.''

"If you see Anthony Simpson anywhere, remember that he has the potential of doing greater harm to the American cause than any other man alive. Get him before he can do any more damage, and you'll be saving the West for the United States!''

As well as Ghonkaba could estimate, his party would be crossing the border into the Western Territories somewhere in southern Kentucky. They would have to continue to travel southward in order to reach their destination, Tennessee. Although no one Indian tribe dominated the area, he felt concern that his scouts frequently found signs of large hunting parties. As many as thirty warriors at a time, all presumably heavily armed, were roaming the region looking for the plentiful game. They easily out-numbered the small band of Seneca.

But Ghonkaba's instructions to his subordinates were precise: "Avoid all contact with unknown Indians, and do not try an attack. There just aren't enough of us."

Ghonkaba knew that a half-dozen powerful tribes, some of them relatively small, others much larger, considered the hunting grounds of these forests as exclusively their own. Each tribe was at war with all the others, and their warriors fought savagely and treated prisoners with the utmost cruelty in attempts to drive out other nations. News that a company of Seneca had "invaded" the region was bound to bring reprisals.

His companions obeyed scrupulously, avoiding all con-tact with strangers. They continued their march in a south-westerly direction, minding their own business.

One night after supper, when most of the company had gone to bed, Ena and Clem Dawkins left the campsite and strolled into the forest. They were at a point roughly parallel with positions taken by the sentries. Having spent virtually no time alone for several days, they were eager to have a short visit to themselves. As they halted, Clem put his long rifle on the ground, and they embraced.

"Even though you were near," Ena murmured, "I have missed you badly these past days."

"I missed you so much," Clem replied in unromantic terms, "that my whole insides have felt like I had a toothache. How soon do you suppose we can get married?"

"My mother is sympathetic toward us," Ena said, "and I'm certain that my father will offer no obstacles, either, but both will insist, I'm sure, that we wait until we reach our destination and are settled there.''

"I don't see why we must wait," Clem objected.

"Neither do I, but I know they will say that we all face so many uncertainties that we should not add the problems that go with marriage to those of finding and making secure homes for ourselves.''

"What problems?''

"I don't know what they are," she said with a little laugh, "and I daresay we won't find out until we actually marry.''

As Ena stepped forward into Clem's arms to exchange another kiss, a seemingly disembodied, brawny arm swept downward behind her. A tomahawk barely missed her head.

Clem, astonished, managed to pull her farther aside.

Suddenly aware of danger, Ena wheeled around, at the same moment reaching for the long double-bladed steel knife she carried in her belt. She lashed out toward her unseen assailant and made quick contact. Her knife cut deeply into flesh; she withdrew it and plunged it again. Her foe staggered forward into the open from the underbrush, bleeding profusely, and sank slowly to the ground. In the dark, she could not see his war paint well enough to determine his tribe. At least a half-dozen others had been directly behind him.

Clem snatched up his rifle and braced himself for battle. The intruders' assault was centered on Ena, and he instantly went to help her. Shouting at the top of his voice to alert the Seneca, he fired his rifle at one of the braves, the first time he had ever pointed a weapon at an enemy. Unable to miss his target at such close range, he had the satisfaction of watching the warrior throw his hands high in the air above his head and collapse in a bloody heap.

Furiously angry, Clem drew his Seneca tomahawk from his belt, and although he had never before wielded it in battle, he struck another enemy so viciously that the man fell to his knees, helpless and bleeding profusely. Not satisfied, Clem continued chopping at him until that warrior, too, fell full-length on the ground and died. The attackers were all around them.

Clem barely had time to reload his long rifle before another brave jumped at him. He again fired at short range, but he missed his target. In order to avoid being shot, the warrior threw himself aside. Clem had only a respite of a few seconds.

Another of the enemy loomed in front of him now, and for the second time he resorted to his tomahawk. Wielding it with savage abandon, he found his target, slashing through his assailant's jugular vein and killing him.

Ghonkaba and several senior warriors, alerted by Clem's shout, could be heard in the distance, too far away to be of immediate help. Lyktaw, Ena's shepherd dog, raced on ahead of them.

Clem had no chance to reload. If he had been more experienced in combat, he could have grasped the rifle by the muzzle and swung it in a wide arc like a club. But he knew nothing of the tactic and instead tried to rely only on his tomahawk. More attacking braves with tomahawks closed in, forming a ring around him. Trying to come to his assistance, Ena, also surrounded, was fighting as furiously as a whirlwind. She jabbed her knife into one after another of the enemy. But there were just too many to allow her to go to Clem's aid.

Ghonkaba and the other rescuing Seneca were close enough now to use their bows, and they struck numerous targets, killing several attackers and forcing the survivors to take flight. Lyktaw leaped on an enemy just as he was about to sink a knife into Ena's chest, and he tore the Indian's throat out.

But the rescuers were not in time to save Clem. A tomahawk crashed into his forehead just above his eyebrows, and he dropped instantly. The brave who killed him was slain by a Seneca arrow only a few seconds later.

As abruptly as it had begun, the battle ended. The intruders' dead littered the ground, but the victors did not rejoice.

Lyktaw placed his front paws on Clem's chest, raised his muzzle, and wailed mournfully. The sound cut to the marrow, but Ena did not weep. True to Seneca tradition, she stood wooden-faced, staring straight ahead, a woman sorrowing over the death of her man.

For forty-eight hours, Toshabe and Ghonkaba tried their best to comfort their daughter, but Ena refused to be solaced. She did not eat or sleep and plodded wearily for hours on the daily march, speaking to no one, remaining by herself, and mourning the loss of Clem.

Seneca other than Ena's parents followed the tribe's ancient tradition of leaving her and letting her work out her sorrow in her own way. She said nothing to anyone, but after two full days on the march through the wilderness she was so exhausted that she fell into a deep sleep.

As she slept, she found herself in a pretty glade deep in the forest where the surrounding foliage was thick. In the glade, however, the sun was shining, the grass had a sweet smell, and the odor of flowers was strong. It occurred to Ena that she was dreaming, and she was powerless to prevent the dream from carrying her forward with it.

A woman materialized out of the darkness of the forest and stood at the far end of the glade. She was blond, not much older than Ena, and was dressed in a costume that once had been popular in the colonies. Oddly, she wore an Indian headband around her forehead, and fringed bands of leather were fastened at her wrists.

"You are Ena," the woman said quietly. "I have long waited to come face to face with you. Do you know me?"

Somehow the girl knew her identity and bowed her head. "You are my ancestor, Betsy," she said. "You are the wife of the great Renno."

Betsy smiled gently. "You are clever to recognize your great-grandmother. I have come to you to offer you solace in your hour of need. Try to remember the words that I say, so that they can bring you solace, although you will not remember this dream nor will you have any memory that I appeared to you and that we spoke together as woman to woman."

Ena bowed her head.

"It was the will of the manitous," Betsy said softly, "that Clem be taken from you. You consider it cruel that he lost his life at so young an age. But unfortunately he did not fit in with the hard life that you lead. And never would he have become acclimated to it. Therefore, the manitous recognized that you and he would have had an unhappy existence together. Rather than that, they preferred to spare both of you from that problem."

"I see," Ena heard herself murmur dully.

"You alone can face the will of the manitous. You alone have the strength and the courage to accept what they have decreed and to face your future. No one can do this for you."

"I will do that which I must," Ena said through clenched teeth in her dream. "I thank you, my grandmother, for your words."

"If you do as the manitous bid you, they will reward you because they are generous beyond measure. You will find happiness in your present life with another partner."

"No!" Ena cried in sudden panic. "I want no other partner. If I can't live as the wife of Clem, I don't want any other man. Please, my grandmother, convey my wishes to the manitous. Tell them they will do me no favor by giving me another romance!"

Betsy smiled enigmatically. Slowly, she began to fade from view.

Ena renewed her pleas, becoming increasingly loud, increasingly demanding. But Betsy made no reply and smiled steadily as the trees became visible through and behind her. Finally she no longer stood in the clearing. Ena was alone. Sobbing and struggling for breath, Ena tried to console herself with the realization that she was still dreaming and that no new romance was being forced on her. It was enough to know that the manitous had acted and had taken Clem from her because of his inability to adapt to the future that faced her.

Then the grove faded from view, and the dream came to an end. Ena slept soundly for the rest of the night.

When she awakened in the morning, she recalled none of the dream, but the words of her great-grandmother proved accurate. She was solaced, strangely, although she didn't know why.

She was able to eat a broiled fish, and her mother was relieved to see that the deep smudges beneath Ena's eyes were less noticeable.

As Betsy had proclaimed, Ena never knew that the appearance of her great-grandmother in a dream was responsible for helping her to overcome the greatest crisis that she had ever faced.

The exiles from the land of the Seneca descended from the higher peaks of the Appalachian Mountains into the heavily wooded hill country of Kentucky. They found the foliage thick and verdant. Though they had spent all their lives in the deep woods, they never had seen anything to equal the forests of Kentucky. Near the banks of streams, where no trees grew, a blue-green grass grew knee-high. Toshabe, who knew more about farming than did anyone else, predicted that the soil was perfect for the growing of vegetables. It was not difficult to imagine that as soon as peace was established, pioneers by the thousands would cross the Appalachians to make their homes here. Possession of such territory could make America a great nation. Settlers would be able to grow enough food to sustain the larger towns of the young nation. Kentucky and Tennessee could make a substantial contribution to its growth and well-being.

Toshabe wondered at length about the new home, toward which the party was now heading. Would she, her husband, and their children like their new land, and would they get along well with the Indians who would be their neighbors? It was impossible to guess the answers to these questions.

Toshabe found she could not dwell at length on her future in this new land because she needed to give attention to Ena, to help improve her spirits, for the young woman still was occasionally morose.

"I still am very unhappy that the manitous, whose power derives directly from the gods and are omnipotent and good, took Clem from me," Ena said one day. "Clem didn't deserve such a fate, and I don't believe that I do, either, though I have tried very hard to understand."

"It is not the place of mere mortals," Toshabe replied softly, "to question the reasons for the acts of the manitous. They have our future at heart, now and always, and they have the ability to see far into the future, a talent that is denied to us. They shape our destinies according to their own wisdom, not the puny wisdom of mere humans."

Tears had come to Ena's eyes. Toshabe took her daughter into her arms. "The only advice anyone can give you is based on common sense," she said. "A life must be lived by the living for the living. It is not for us to question the will of the gods when someone whom we love is taken from us. We must trust the gods and their representatives, the manitous, to look out for our best interests and our ultimate happiness."

"Do you honestly think we'll be happy living in a strange land, in the midst of a strange people?" Ena asked with a trace of genuine doubt in her voice.

Her mother stroked her hair. "Remember this day," she said, "and ask me that same question once again in a year's time. I cannot answer it now."

"I will remember and I will ask," Ena said.

"Until that time comes," her mother told her, "think of your heritage. Your whole life has been lived in preparation for this time of trial that you are now undergoing. You must tolerate the bad without complaint, just as you accept the good that comes to you without rejoicing unduly."

"I know, my mother," Ena said with a sudden show of spirit. "I will not forget that I am a Seneca, and I will try to live my life accordingly."

As the company pushed deeper into this strangely attractive land, Casno took his duties as medicine man more seriously than ever. Before breakfast each morning, he performed a dance to the god of the sun, and every evening, when the day's march came to an end, he prayed to the gods of the moon and stars. Together, these deities were protecting the exiles from harm and were leading them to the destination where they could settle peacefully.

Evasive action that prevented contact with superior forces continued to be the most effective strategy. Aside from the clash in which Clem had been killed, the company had been fortunate. To make certain that this would continue, Ghonkaba assigned himself the role of advance scout. The band established a semipermanent camp while he went ahead into the wilderness to scout the region. Only if he found no hostile warriors would he allow the band to continue.

He set out alone, traveling in a semicircular arc as he advanced, and he marveled at the country's vast wealth. Game, large and small, was everywhere. Ghonkaba could have shot innumerable deer or brought down smaller animals for food, but because the remains would be difficult to hide from potential enemies, he preferred to eat the dried meat he carried as emergency rations.

He was far freer in his use of plants he found. He feasted on an occasional late clump of berries, and dug up several different kinds of root that he ate after rinsing them in the clear waters of running streams.

He became conscious one afternoon of another human being nearby. It was a heavily tanned white man dressed in buckskins. As Ghonkaba watched, he started a fire and put a large slab of venison into a frying pan with some suet. Without turning, the stranger called out in an Indian tongue not wholly familiar to Ghonkaba, but one that he understood. "Don't hide in the bushes back there, warrior! Come out in the open and join me for supper. I have more than enough food here."

Ghonkaba felt certain he had hidden himself effectively in the underbrush and knew that he had made no sound and could not be seen. This man in buckskins must have

51

extraordinary eyesight or hearing to have detected his presence.

The man noted Ghonkaba's war paint. "A Seneca, eh?" he said. "You're a long way from home, warrior."

Ghonkaba was impressed that any man in these parts would recognize the colors of the paint worn by the distant Seneca. Coming into the open rather sheepishly, he moved forward slowly, holding his rifle in his right hand while he raised his left arm in the amicable sign of Indian greeting.

The woodsman, raising his own left hand in return, scrutinized him as he approached. It was evident that he had already begun to recognize and identify Ghonkaba.

Ghonkaba saw that though the man's hair was shaggy, he was clean shaven. A pair of the palest green eyes he had ever seen were examining him.

"I've heard it from more than one that you're General Washington's favorite scout," the man went on, seeming remarkably well informed.

Ghonkaba's confusion grew. "Who are you?" he demanded in English.

"My name is Boone, Dan'l Boone," the stranger replied, extending a hand.

Ghonkaba was familiar with him as a frontiersman, explorer, and hunter who had done great service for the American cause, acting as a peacemaker between warring tribes in Kentucky.

"You're no stranger to me either, Colonel Boone," he replied, and they both chuckled.

Ghonkaba helped Boone gather a number of plant roots, which they threw into a shallow pan with some water to cook and eat with the venison. Then, as their meal was being prepared, they settled down to talk.

"I heard," Boone said, "that you and your Seneca scouts would be headed this way. Therefore, I was quite prepared for the possibility that you would stumble on me."

"Yes," Ghonkaba replied. "We have our wives and children with us, and we're intending to go southwest and try to get the Cherokees' permission to settle inside their domain."

"You won't find it difficult to convince the Cherokee," Boone predicted, "provided you can assure them you are not going to bring so many Seneca that the Cherokee would have reason to feel the peaceful existence of the nation is threatened. They're honest and hardworking, and they've been steadfast in their loyalty to the United States, in spite of strong provocations. Some of them are within the region that I'm supervising for General Washington. I'm glad to say they've given me little trouble."

"Are there developments in the West that are new to me?" Ghonkaba inquired.

"That depends on what you already know. Perhaps you've heard of a British agent named Anthony Simpson?"

Ghonkaba nodded, once more noncommittal until he heard more.

"The man," Boone said with cold deliberateness, "is the lowest order of swine. He's infinitely worse than you can possibly imagine. We have hundreds of settlers in Kentucky, men who have moved here with their wives and their children, and Simpson would sacrifice the lives of every last one of them.''

Boone turned over the venison steak in the frying pan and stirred the vegetables in the little pot.

''Through the years I've worked constantly with a large number of Indian nations hereabouts,'' he said. ''I've neutralized the Miami of Ohio and I've been influential, I believe, in persuading the Cherokee to cast their lot with us. But these conditions are temporary, subject to change at any time, thanks to Simpson. He has unlimited weapons at his disposal, and he dispenses them freely. He lies to every tribe, telling the chiefs and elders only what they want to hear. He has no interest in the Indians, doesn't give a hang about what becomes of the Choctaw or the Creek in their association with the British, who will treat them as second-class citizens, taking advantage of them at every opportunity. He'll acquire grants for thousands of acres from the Choctaw and the Creek. And he'll reap profits from the trade that he encourages between the Indian nations and Great Britain.''

''What can be done to stop the man?''

Boone's eyes glistened and his face became set in hard lines. ''I know of only one thing that will stop him, and that is a bullet. One of my bullets. My orders are to dispose of the man, in addition to pacifying the frontier and making it safe for Americans here.'' He served the meat deftly and cut it in half so they could share it. Ghonkaba emptied the boiling water from the pot and distributed the vegetables. They ate in appreciative silence for some moments.

"What are you doing in these parts by yourself?" Boone asked.

Ghonkaba explained that he was traveling as a scout to make certain that no hostile Indians were on hand.

"The region is clear," Boone told him. "You can take my word for it. Not a warrior within a hundred miles of here would shoot at a Seneca. Like it or not, you've gained a reputation west of the mountains that probably rivals the name you've made for yourselves in the East, and I'm referring specifically to your company of scouts. Other than Simpson, I doubt if there's a man on this side of the mountains who hasn't heard of you and doesn't admire you."

"That's good to hear," Ghonkaba said.

"As a matter of fact, if you don't mind," Boone suggested, "I'll go back to your bivouac area with you. I'd like to meet your men. If I may, I'd be honored to speak a few words to them."

"By all means," Ghonkaba told him. "We're the ones who'll be honored."

They disdained blankets when they stretched out on the ground to sleep, and soon after dawn, after a quick swim in the nearby river, they started out together toward Ghonkaba's camp. By traveling rapidly, they reached the site around noon. Ghonkaba was astonished to find that Boone could maintain the pace of the Seneca trot for hours on end without tiring. Never had he seen a white man who could accomplish the feat.

Ghonkaba's veterans were eager to meet the celebrated Colonel Boone and were elated that he had come with their leader to speak to them. The squaws offered a noontime dinner of cold fish and herbs before the warriors gathered around Daniel Boone.

Though he had been lightheartedly joking, now that they were assembling, his manner changed and he became serious.

"I can add little to the praise of such veterans," he began. "You know better than I what you've accomplished. Your pride in your achievements speaks for itself better than any I could speak on your behalf."

The Seneca looked at one another, satisfied that the frontiersman had no intention of offering undue praise for some ulterior purpose.

"All I can do," Boone said, "is to warn you that your sacrifices and efforts are in jeopardy now. All that you have accomplished soon may be lost for all time."

His listeners stirred uneasily.

"The British realize," he said, "just as we do, that even though they continue to fight, they have lost the war. The independence of the United States is assured, and a new nation has arisen from the turmoil. But what London has failed to accomplish in one way they are scheming to achieve in another. Since the seaboard colonics were first established, their western frontier has been their lifeblood. That frontier has provided land for the immigrants who have flocked here from the Old World. America has gained her strength from the wilderness, just as the Indian nations have flourished because of that wilderness. Now the British cleverly propose to choke off this life-giving stream. They intend, in fact, to regain possession of the colonies

56

by starving us, by denying us access to our western frontier towns.''

His argument made great sense to his listeners, who nodded appreciatively.

"A British agent has provided the Creek and Choctaw with arms, ammunition, and money. If he succeeds in getting the Cherokee to change their allegiance, the West will be lost.''

"What are we to do?'' Ranoga called, interrupting him, "to prevent such a catastrophe from taking place?''

"Stop this man before he accomplishes his goal with the Cherokee. Prevent him from carrying out the will of his British masters. He is the key.''

Having concluded his remarks, Colonel Boone said that he would be on his way again. "I never stay long in any one place,'' he said to Ghonkaba. "I like to be constantly on the move. This is a way of life that I've chosen for myself and that suits me well.''

Ghonkaba walked a short distance into the wilderness with Boone. "If you run into Simpson,'' the frontiersman said jokingly, "be sure you get in touch with me, wherever I may be—I won't be satisfied until he comes within range of my gun.''

"I'll try to find a way of getting in touch with you,'' Ghonkaba replied in the same vein. "If I can't, I'll have to dispose of Simpson myself.''

Boone sobered. "I hope that won't be necessary,'' he said. "Purely selfishly, I look forward to the day when I can shoot him down. I don't think anything less will satisfy me.''

They bade each other farewell, and Ghonkaba thanked him for the advice that he had given the Seneca.

The next day, fully aware that the wilderness through which they were traveling was playing an important role in the future of the United States, the little band resumed its journey.

The Seneca crossed the invisible border separating Kentucky and Tennessee, and continued to make their way forward. The forest was the same, the growth lush and verdant, but the circumstances were far different. Instead of advancing through a land where the forest would be available to settlers who could cut down the trees and make their farms there, the party had come to a region considered a part of the domain that belonged to the Cherokee. In this portion of their hunting preserves, poachers were not welcome.

Realizing that they were treading on thin ice, Ghonkaba established some new rules. Other members of the company were not to be permitted to shoot game. Ghonkaba would bring down the animals necessary to provide meat. He hoped to eliminate random hunting that would antagonize any Cherokee who might be encountered. The new system worked well, and Ghonkaba was satisfied with it.

One morning, as the company was breaking camp, Ranoga came to Ghonkaba with word that they had exhausted their supply of fresh meat and were in need of more. Ghonkaba immediately arranged, therefore, to go ahead and, with any luck, bring down sufficient game for several days. He set out at once behind the screen of scouts, leaving Casno in charge of the rest of the travelers. Ignoring rabbits and other small game, Ghonkaba found the tracks of a deer. Following the signs closely, he increased his pace. Catching sight of his quarry, he slowed to a halt. Due south of him, a buck was grazing on some young leaves, and Ghonkaba noted with pleasure that the animal was plump and large. Stringing his bow, he notched an arrow into it, took aim, and fired.

And through great coincidence, the deer also had been sighted from another direction by Wegowa, the senior war chief of the Cherokee. At exactly the same moment, he shot an arrow at the deer.

The similarities of the two hunters were as extraordinary as the fact that they had shot at the same target simultaneously. Wegowa was the only son of the Grand Sachem of the Cherokee and was in his middle years, as was Ghonkaba. Tall, slender, and trim in spite of his advancing age, he was vastly experienced. In time he was expected to succeed his father as the leader of the Cherokee nation.

Slow to anger and deliberate in his thoughts as well as his movements, Wegowa nevertheless had a reputation among his own people for being furious in combat and refusing to give quarter to enemies who had aroused his ire.

The two hunters approached the fallen deer from opposite sides, halting abruptly when they became aware of each other's presence. They looked at each other with curiosity, without fear, and then studied the carcass carefully.

Both were astonished to discover two arrows protruding from the buck. Both had been responsible for the animal's death.

They stared at each other solemnly, then raised their left hands, palms extended, in the universal Indian sign of a peaceful greeting.

Suddenly Ghonkaba felt compelled to laugh. The situation was so absurd that it struck him as ludicrous, and although he had been trained all of his life to hide his emotions, he could not refrain from whooping aloud with laughter.

His laugh sparked Wegowa, who also broke into guffaws. Both men stood, still facing each other, rocking with unrestrained pleasure. When they regained their self-control they again looked at each other curiously after wiping their eyes.

Introductions were in order. "I am Ghonkaba, lieutenant colonel of scouts in the Continental Army of General Washington. I am the son of Ja-gonh, Great Sachem of the Iroquois League."

"I am Wegowa, senior war chief of the Cherokee nation and the son of Loramas, Grand Sachem of the Cherokee."

It was extraordinary that the Seneca and the Cherokee of the same rank and station should meet under such unusual circumstances. "This meeting was arranged in the spirit world by the manitous," Ghonkaba said solemnly.

Wegowa knew nothing of the gods and goddesses of the Seneca, but he grasped the meaning and agreed.

"It was destined by the Breath Holder that you and I should meet under these odd conditions," he replied.

"Plainly, supernatural forces are at work. The gods, yours as well as mine," Ghonkaba said diplomatically, "have arranged that you and I should meet, and they have proposed an immediate test of our friendship. Both of us have shot this deer. To which of us belongs the carcass?"

Wegowa was puzzled. "I do not know," he said. "I must appeal to the gods to decide for us."

"I propose," Ghonkaba said boldly, "that we split the carcass and that each of us take half of it. In that way, we will seal the bond of a new friendship."

Wegowa agreed readily, and they went to work with a will in butchering the carcass.

"If our paths cross again," Wegowa said, "we shall rejoice because we already know each other."

"I am certain that we are destined to meet once again," Ghonkaba told him. This was not the moment to mention that the Seneca sought the right to settle unobtrusively and peaceully in the land of the Cherokee. That would have to come after a friendship had expanded and ripened. "But I find it inconceivable that the gods should have arranged this meeting as a mere chance get-together. Our paths *will* cross again and, in one way or another, our futures will be joined."

"I'm sure you must be right," Wegowa said. "The ways of the gods are strange, but sometimes we are permitted a glimpse of the future, and I, too, am certain that we shall have a joint future someday."

They clasped each other's forearm in a sign of brotherhood, then each took his meat. They departed in separate directions. Neither suspected that their next, far more auspicious meeting would take place quite soon.

Chapter III

Winter came late this year to the land of the Seneca in upper New York State. As yet, no snow had accumulated in the fields or forest, and the hunting season was extended for several weeks.

And yet, Ja-gonh was dissatisfied. He slept poorly, often awakening hours before dawn and staying awake until daylight came and he was required to dress and perform his daily duties. He lost his appetite, too, and rarely ate more than a token amount of the foods placed in front of him.

Secretive by nature, and too proud to discuss his problems with others, Ja-gonh kept his troubles to himself for many weeks. Finally, however, he confided in his brother-in-law, No-da-vo, the sachem of the Seneca, after they had presided over a council meeting where it had been decided that the nation would formally withdraw from the war. Nominally on the side of the British since the beginning of the war, the Seneca would be neutral now, as would the other Iroquois tribes, until a peace treaty was signed. But the prospect for a benign future, undisturbed by outside forces, was very dim, and they both were realistic enough to recognize that the Seneca would be beset by problems for many years to come as a result of their choice in wartime.

Only a small fire burned in the council chamber pit, but the flames were comforting, and Ja-gonh sat close to them, staring into the fire, oblivious of anything around him.

No-da-vo lighted a pipe with a coal from the fire, and when it was burning satisfactorily he passed the bowl to Ja-gonh. "What is wrong, my brother?" he asked quietly. "I have held my tongue and kept my own counsel for many weeks, but I have seen you grieving and worried, yet you say nothing about the cause of your discontent. Perhaps the time has come to share your troubles with me."

"I think the time is at hand," Ja-gonh replied. "Know, my brother, that I have been worried about Ghonkaba and Toshabe, as well as their children. Ena, my oldest grandchild, would have married a great warrior of our nation if they had been able to remain here. Renno, who bears the name of my father, someday would have worn my feathered bonnet as Great Sachem of all the Iroquois. El-i-chi would have become a great leader, a help to his brother, and an inspiration to our whole nation. Are they alive or dead? Are they wandering aimlessly in the great forests of the West—or have they found a home for themselves? Are they in danger or do they enjoy good health and prosperity? I have answers for none of these questions, yet I'm consumed by them. It is not suitable to send a messenger in search of them, someone who can bring me word about their well-being, so I can only sit here and wait until I receive direct word from Ghonkaba.''

"It was a sad and shattering day for our family,'' No-da-vo said, "when Ghonkaba elected to take up arms on behalf of our enemies. But let us rejoice because he covered himself with glory and received many promotions from the Americans. I am sure that the manitous will lead him, his family, and those who follow him to a new home at some place in the West.''

"I hope and pray you're right,'' Ja-gonh said. "I'm afraid that even if they do find such a refuge, they will be so far removed from us that they will lose their Seneca ways. They and their children will come to worship the gods of other tribes. The proud traditions that have made them Seneca will be lost forever.''

"That is not necessarily true,'' No-da-vo argued. "Perhaps you are not aware of the ground swell in this town since Ghonkaba and his brave followers were forbidden to return.''

Ja-gonh puffed on the pipe and nodded glumly. "Yes,'' he said, "I am conscious of the feelings of people in this town, particularly members of our own Bear Clan. I've been pleased to discover that most of them would join Ghonkaba if it were possible. I can't say that I blame them, really. Life as a Seneca doesn't hold much promise. I can predict that we'll be restricted by the authorities of New York State to our own territory and to take no part in any wars or other military expeditions. We'll live strictly outside the mainstream of American life. I can't blame the authorities for their decision. Because we did join the British in the war against the Americans, we've got to pay the penalty now.''

''Aren't you being overly pessimistic?'' No-da-vo asked him.

Ja-gonh shook his head. ''I don't think so,'' he said. ''The way of life that we have known is being tragically limited. Our traditional hunting grounds are being curtailed as more and more Americans settle in the area. I can foresee the day coming when our ancient customs will be disrupted and perhaps they, too, will vanish. Since we and the other Iroquois are forbidden by the government of New York State to participate in wars, our fighting men will lose their skills and their prowess will become a thing of the past rather than an active ingredient in their lives. Furthermore, the Iroquois League itself will be disrupted and will vanish because there will be no need for it.''

''You are predicting, then, that the Seneca have outlived their usefulness as a nation, that only the individual clans will continue to exist and have cohesion?''

''I am not a prophet or a medicine man,'' Ja-gonh said, ''but I believe that is so. Our future, as a people, lies in our clans. For selfish reasons, I'm glad that we are members of the Bear Clan, which continues to thrive.''

''If I were an ordinary member of the Bear Clan,''

No-da-vo said, "I would be anxious to leave this land in which we have no hope for a real future. In fact," he went on, "you have expressed the solution to the problem without knowing it. Suppose that only members of the Bear Clan want to join Ghonkaba—which is untrue; many other Seneca are eager to cast their lot with him. Let us confine ourselves for purposes of illustration to the Bear Clan. Let us say that one-third of the members of the clan and their families want to make their homes with Ghonkaba. That means that, at the very least, an expedition of some hundreds of our people would set out for Ghonkaba's new homeland and would join him there. If you'll stop to think of it, so large a nucleus would be bound to keep alive Seneca ways and Seneca traditions, no matter where they may settle."

Ja-gonh smiled wanly and handed the lighted pipe to his brother-in-law. "As always, No-da-vo, you're incurably optimistic," he said. "Have you stopped to think that wherever Ghonkaba may make his home he'll need permission if he's going to be joined by hundreds of Seneca? No Indian nation is so large and powerful that they'll permit hundreds of strangers to immigrate into their territory, particularly hundreds of ferocious Seneca. They know us as the fiercest and most able fighting men anywhere in North America."

"You're right, at least in principle," No-da-vo agreed, "but Ghonkaba has a family knack inherited from you and Renno for being able to get his own way, so I wouldn't be surprised if he gains approval for members of the Seneca Bear Clan to join him there. Surrounded by other Seneca, your grandchildren and their children will be certain to keep alive the customs, traditions, and ancient rituals and religion of our people. Mark my words, and see if I'm not right!''

"I won't argue the matter with you,'' Ja-gonh said. "I hope you're right. All that I know now is that we're helpless, unable to do anything until we hear from Ghonkaba. Then we can consider whether to grant the wish of the Bear Clan members who want to join him.''

When Ghonkaba returned to his band's campsite with only enough meat to feed the company for two days, some of his followers were disappointed, but he remained remarkably cheerful. Withdrawing out of earshot of the others, he told Toshabe, Ranoga, and Casno about the remarkable incident in which he and Wegowa of the Cherokee had shot a deer at the same moment. "I have kept the arrow that Wegowa put into the deer, just as he has kept mine.'' He rummaged in his quiver and produced a shaft shorter and thicker than the typical Seneca arrow. "As you can see,'' he went on, "it bears only a slight resemblance to our own arrows. But, together with mine, it produced rather wonderful results.''

"I think,'' Toshabe said softly, handling the strange arrow with care, "that the manitous have produced a real miracle for our benefit.''

"No doubt of it,'' Casno said flatly, taking the arrow from her. The medicine man turned it over in his hand. "They could have chosen hundreds of ways of introducing us to the Cherokee and allowing us to become acquainted. They selected a method involving a strange sign that I can interpret only as a miracle. This is a good omen, Ghonkaba. You say that you parted with Wegowa, the war chief of the Cherokee, on the friendliest of terms. So be it. Your friendship will continue to flourish. I foresee no obstacle to a splendid, close relationship between the members of this company and the people of the nation into whose land we have come!''

Carrying his portion of the deer meat, Wegowa went directly home, about twenty-four hours distant through the forest. He went to the dwelling of the chief medicine man. It was a house that, like so many others, had a thatched roof, a fireplace and chimney for cooking, and walls of brick and wood. Unlike the Indian tribes of the North, the Cherokee had solid, permanent homes with several rooms in each. Their dwellings provided greater permanence, particularly when furnished with mats for beds, crude tables, and hassocks for sitting.

Jejeno, the chief medicine man of the Cherokee nation, sat in his living room, where he had just finished drinking a cup of herb tea. He was examining the cup's interior for the leaves, which he was reading with great interest.

Interrupting him, Wegowa presented the deer meat. ''I offer you this as special contribution to peace and harmony, O Jejeno,'' he said, bowing low.

''Do you make a guilt offering of meat because you've

once again broken the peace?'' Jejeno looked and sounded faintly amused.

The chief warrior of the Cherokee protested vehemently. "On the contrary," he said, "I have obeyed all the commands of the Corn Mother, and she and her son, Breath Holder, have honored me beyond compare."

The medicine man sat back on his haunches and regarded his visitor with a combination of surprise and displeasure. One did not idly claim the support of the goddess who ruled the universe, or of her son.

"I have chosen my words with great care, O Jejeno," Wegowa said. "I have had an experience that is unique in the annals of our people." He began to relate what had happened in the forest.

Jejeno cut him off abruptly. "Wait," he said, "let Loramas be summoned to hear, also, the words that you speak." Only the chief medicine man of all Cherokee had the right to summon the Grand Sachem of a nation into his presence. All others were required to report to the Grand Sachem at his house.

A young runner hurried to the dwelling of the Grand Sachem with the request, and a short time later, Loramas appeared, wearing his bonnet and cloak of multicolored feathers.

As the national leader of the Cherokee for more than four decades, he had left his mark on the nation. A grizzled, burly man with a barrel chest and a deep voice, he had a commanding presence. At this moment, he was thoroughly annoyed at having been summoned to his medicine man's house.

"Why have you called me here?" he demanded, and his tone suggested that his war chief and medicine man would be well advised to have a good reason.

But Jejeno was imperturbable. "Listen, O Loramas," he said, "to the strange tale that Wegowa will relate to us."

Wegowa promptly launched into his recital. At the end, he offered the arrow that Ghonkaba had fired at the deer.

"I've had such weapons described to me in times past," the Grand Sachem said at last, "but this is the first time I've ever seen a weapon of the Seneca. Did you learn the name of the warrior of the Seneca who fired the arrow?"

"He is called Ghonkaba," Wegowa said, glad that he had aroused his father's interest.

Loramas was startled. "Ghonkaba, you say? That is the grandson of Renno, the white Indian, who made the Seneca famous, and the direct descendant of the great Ghonka, perhaps the most ferocious warrior of the ages in North America! This Ghonkaba is no ordinary warrior!"

His father inspected the arrow with additional care and was satisfied. "This is an honest weapon, honestly made," he said. "It is more suited to the Seneca style of warfare than to our own." He gave it to Jejeno, who also looked at it critically and at length.

"Nothing but good can come from an association with this renowned warrior of the Seneca," Jejeno said. "He means no harm to the Cherokee, and his only feelings toward us are in harmony with our own feelings."

His use of the word *harmony* was not accidental. It was the key to the religious belief of the nation. The

Cherokee long had been convinced that the Corn Mother and the Breath Holder demanded that the people of the Cherokee live in harmony with themselves and with each other. A Cherokee's worst deed was to disturb that harmony, and the most beneficial was to create a more harmonious background for day-to-day living.

"I urge you," Jejeno said, "to encourage your friendship with this Seneca. You will benefit, Wegowa, as will the entire Cherokee nation."

"What is he doing so far from his own home?" Loramas asked.

"He did not tell me," Wegowa replied. "He said only that he and a number of his former scouts in the Continental Army are traveling in this direction. He gave no reason for their travels. I chose not to ask."

Loramas grew thoughtful. "I am curious to meet the grandson of the great Renno," he said. "See if you can't encounter him again, and then bring him to me so that I may meet him and talk with him."

When the Seneca band came to a large river that flowed toward the west, Ghonkaba decided to follow it. A short time later, the company found itself surrounded by a large band of warriors wearing the vermilion paint of the Cherokee.

Ghonkaba knew it would be imprudent to put up any show of resistance against that strong a force. To prevent any chance that an accidental show of belligerence could spark a sudden battle, he shouted, "Keep your weapons at your sides! Don't use them. And don't threaten to use them!''

More and more Cherokee appeared, but they made it evident by their attitude that they were not belligerent and had no intentions of starting a battle. Then, unexpectedly, Wegowa appeared in their midst with upraised hand.

Ghonkaba happily saluted his friend.

"We meet again," Ghonkaba said, "sooner than we expected."

"I set out deliberately with a body of warriors to find you," Wegowa told him. "I am under orders of Loramas, my father, the Grand Sachem, who wishes to greet you and welcome you in person to the land of the Cherokee."

"I know of nothing," Ghonkaba replied, "that would be a greater honor." He presented the Cherokee war chief to Toshabe and also introduced him to his children and to Ranoga and Casno.

The combined groups set out for the town of the Cherokee, but the hosts made it plain that the visitors were not captives. The Cherokee led the way, and the Seneca, following them, were not surrounded. The Cherokee braves took care not to frighten the women and children of the Seneca company, and with a quick glance Ghonkaba and Casno told each other that all was well.

Following the river, they came to vast, open fields where it was evident that a large variety of vegetables had been cultivated. The Seneca looked with great interest at these fields because their own agricultural products consisted exclusively of corn, beans, and squash. Though they had no idea what the strange produce might be that was grown here, they were nevertheless deeply impressed by land that could give rise to such abundance.

Wegowa explained to Toshabe and Ghonkaba that every family owned and farmed its own plot. The mother of the family was in charge, and everyone, including her husband and sons, was obliged to do labor in the field. The members of each family were required to work also in the common fields where produce was grown for storage for winter and for use at the communal meals. This labor was expected of each person, and no member of the community, including the highest-ranking council members, was exempt.

"I am the principal war chief of the entire Cherokee nation," Wegowa said, "yet I am required to spend as many hours at work in these fields as is spent by any ordinary brave of the tribe. None are excused, except for a woman who is about to give birth."

Eventually the town wall loomed ahead, and Ghonkaba observed with interest that the wall was built of thirty-foot poles of wood, their tops sharpened to spikes. Set close together, they formed an impenetrable barrier that would thwart any attacking force.

The entrance gate, which resembled the rest of the palisade, swung on crude but effective hinges. It was so heavy that three warriors were required to open and close it. The gate was kept closed at all times and was opened only to admit friendly persons.

The town was very impressive, reminding the visitors of the cities of the Americans because of the permanence of the Cherokee dwellings. Ghonkaba doubted that any other Indian nation had housing as comfortable and as advanced in design as these sturdy homes. The larger buildings, two stories high, were, as Wegowa explained, dormitories for single women and single braves. To the best of Ghonkaba's knowledge, no other Indian nation had buildings of more than one level.

At last, they came to a private dwelling, somewhat larger than the others, and this, it developed, was the residence of Loramas, the Grand Sachem. Here the party paused, and Wegowa led Ghonkaba and Casno inside. The rest were taken to a cavernous community hall, where they were given a meal of buffalo stew prepared with a variety of vegetables.

Ghonkaba was astonished when they walked through two rooms before coming to another chamber, larger than the others. It seemed to him that the Cherokee had a more advanced civilization, which resembled more closely that of the European nations than any of the seaboard tribes.

The massive Loramas was seated on a thronelike chair of intricately carved wood.

Jejeno stood beside his Grand Sachem, and he and Casno promptly recognized each other as kindred spirits.

As Ghonkaba raised his left arm in the customary amicable greeting, he was deeply impressed by Loramas. From the description of the great Ghonka that he remembered, the Grand Sachem of the Cherokee undoubtedly bore a resemblance to the most noted warrior in the annals of the Seneca's illustrious history.

Loramas's face remained masklike while Wegowa repeated in detail the incident when he and Ghonkaba had met. Then Ghonkaba took up the narrative of his followers' service as scouts of General Washington's Continental Army. As a result of their efforts, he explained, they were not permitted to return to the land of the Seneca because of the treaty that had bound all the nations of the Iroquois to Great Britain. His father and other leaders of the Seneca, he related, were sympathetic but left helpless to intervene on their behalf.

"What brings you to the land of the Cherokee?" Loramas inquired.

"It is our wish," Ghonkaba replied, "to settle in this land, but we do not expect to be granted the privileges that go with such a land without paying for them. Our warriors will fight your enemies together with your warriors and will place themselves under the command of your war chiefs. We will work in the fields with your people. We will do everything in our power to cooperate with the Cherokee and to bend ourselves to the will of the majority of the Cherokee."

During the long silence that followed, Wegowa and Jejeno did not dare to speak up, though both were hoping that Loramas would lose no time in granting the visitors the right to settle in the land of the Cherokee. The Seneca were reputedly the first among all Indian tribes, and Loramas was eager to incorporate into his own nation the qualities that made the Seneca great. His own mind was already made up. He would invite Ghonkaba and his followers to make their permanent home here and to make the Cherokee their own people.

At last, Loramas spoke. "This," he said, "is an important decision that I wish to convey promptly to our people.

Let us go, and I shall inform them." Without stating the judgment he had made, he rose and started toward the door, followed by Wegowa and Ghonkaba, with the two medicine men bringing up the rear.

They walked to the huge hall, where the meal was still in progress. It was plain that the Cherokee did not regard their Grand Sachem as a being on a higher plane. Many of them waved to Loramas, but they stayed in their seats at the long wooden table, eating their buffalo stew.

Loramas stood before the assemblage, and when it became evident that he intended to speak, the crowd gradually became silent.

Loramas told them that the visitors from the distinguished land of the Seneca sought a permanent sanctuary with the Cherokee and asked no favors, but were willing to take their fair share of responsibilities for daily existence in both peace and war. As Grand Sachem of the nation, he was willing to grant them the privilege, he said, provided they obeyed the ancient custom of the Cherokee. Specifically, newcomers would be accepted into the nation if Ghonkaba, their leader, could successfully meet certain conditions that symbolically would certify his people's fitness to dwell among the Cherokee and live up to their standards.

A warrior leaped to his feet and signaled for recognition. "Certain conditions?" he demanded caustically. "I feel that symbolic conditions are likely to be no condition at all. They would determine nothing and test no one."

An excited buzz of conversation greeted his words. Like all Indians, the Cherokee loved the sense of the dramatic.

"I propose," he continued, "that Ghonkaba, as the leader of the Seneca, meet a champion of the Cherokee in a genuine trial of strength."

"I accept," Ghonkaba called out instantly.

Toshabe turned pale, but her expression did not alter, and in no other way did she show that she was seriously perturbed.

Younger senior warriors of the Seneca instantly requested that they be substituted for Ghonkaba as the representative of the Seneca.

But Ghonkaba remained adamant. "I led our scouts in the war, and I led you and your families across the mountains into these lands," he said. "It is my right and my duty to represent you in this coming trial of strength, no matter what the competition may be, or what the prospective."

"Let him who will represent the Cherokee rise and stand forward," Loramas called out, apparently feeling that the outspoken warrior had forced his hand. A struggle to the finish would be inevitable.

After a pause of no more than a second, a husky young giant raised his voice. "Rusog will represent the people of the Cherokee!" he declared. Only half Ghonkaba's age, he outweighed him by easily fifty pounds.

The Seneca were dismayed by the prospect of their leader meeting this young bull in a strenuous trial of strength. Ghonkaba might easily be worn down in any prolonged contest.

Perhaps the most horrified person was Wegowa. Standing behind the Grand Sachem, he muttered, "Rusog—my son! How can my son volunteer to fight in a combat with a stranger with whom I've exchanged a vow of eternal friendship?" He knew the Breath Holder would be disturbed, and he said in a low voice, "Rusog—my son! He cannot engage in combat with one whom I've sworn as my eternal friend. He must withdraw!"

Loramas did not turn but nevertheless spoke softly. "Because Rusog is my grandson and the son of Wegowa, he must live up to his intentions and fight the Seneca. Under no circumstances may he withdraw. I forbid it. Too many warriors in the tribe will say that we are using our high rank and our official positions to protect him from possible harm. Rusog has committed himself, and he is obligated now to go through with his commitment. It is unfortunate, but it is so."

Rusog was unaware of the argument. He was strutting, preening, and carrying on for the benefit of several admiring Cherokee maidens.

No one present understood why his conduct was so boorish. Ordinarily a mild, soft-spoken, and sensible young man, he always had taken his extraordinary physical endowments for granted. Now, however, he had seen Ena in the company of the Seneca, and from the first she fascinated him. Never had any female so completely caught his total attention and admiration, and never, for that matter, had any remained so unaware of him.

For the no-holds-barred contest between Ghonkaba and Rusog, the Cherokee and the Seneca adjourned to an adjacent field used by the young Cherokee braves for a game played with a stone and curved sticks.

CHEROKEE

As Rusog strolled with several companions, he boasted of the short work he intended to make of the Seneca leader. It was not evident whether he expected only to humiliate him or to insist on slaying him.

Ena could not help but hear every word. Even granted that he had no way of knowing she was the daughter of Ghonkaba, he was behaving like such a loud boor that she looked at him with open contempt.

He saw her expression and consequently felt impelled to proclaim even more vehemently that he would annihilate his opponent.

The two principals were required to strip to loincloths and then walk into a small clearing surrounded by spectators. Toshabe, all three of her children, and the other Seneca were disturbed by the risk that Ghonkaba was taking, but he remained supremely confident of his abilities.

"Pray to the manitous, if that will improve your spirit, Casno," he said to his medicine man. "As for me, I need no prayers."

"You are overly confident, Ghonkaba, an attitude that is alien to you," Casno replied. "You must remember that your opponent has the strength of a giant bear and is capable of tearing you to pieces with his bare hands. He is many years younger, so he has far greater stamina, endurance, and strength. You will be sorely tried, even though neither of you will carry weapons."

"You are too fearful, Casno," Ghonkaba replied. "In how many battles has this Cherokee youth fought? Two or three perhaps? How often have I gone into combat? How many dozens of times have I risked my life against foes ranging from the British and the French to the most savage of Indians? There is little that I still have to learn about individual combat, and I'm willing to take my chances.'' He smiled reassuringly at Toshabe, then winked broadly at Renno and El-i-chi and saluted Ena.

When Loramas ordered the combat to begin, Ghonkaba was ready.

Seneca warriors were aware of a trick that was a great aid in individual warfare: by pressing their fingers against the wrists and ankles of their foes in a way that the enemy never learned, the Seneca were capable of paralyzing an opponent.

Rusog and Ghonkaba circled each other. Suddenly the Seneca reached out, caught his opponent's wrists, and pressed them with his forefingers and thumbs. Then he found his ankles and repeated the process.

Rusog toppled to the ground and lay still, sweating heavily as he tried in vain to regain motion in his arms and legs. Occasionally, Ghonkaba touched his wrists and ankles again in order to renew the paralytic grip on them, but otherwise, he sat on the ground with folded arms, his expression serene.

Loramas had no choice but to declare the Seneca the winner. The Cherokee Grand Sachem even showed signs of relief, though it was his grandson who had been humbled almost to the point of disgrace.

Ghonkaba was aware of the intense disappointment of the large Cherokee throng, which had anticipated a bloody battle. ''It is my right,'' he announced, ''to do away with Rusog and send him to join his ancestors, but I bear him no ill will and I deliberately refrain from this. Now, in order that the people not be deprived of their pleasure of seeing more even competition, I make the Cherokee a sporting offer.'' He turned to Loramas and deliberately challenged him. ''I suggest that each of my three children compete, evenly matched, in trials of skill against three Cherokee of their own age and level of achievement.''

To have rejected the offer would have been a sign of weakness, and the Grand Sachem did not even consider taking such a course. ''I accept,'' he said instantly.

The huge Cherokee throng roared its approval. The little band of Seneca were quietly pleased. Well acquainted with the children of Ghonkaba, the Seneca believed they had nothing to fear, and felt confident that the younger members of such a renowned family could not help but cover themselves with fresh glory. Only Toshabe continued to look concerned.

As Ghonkaba quickly dressed, Rusog discovered that powers of motion had at last returned to his arms and legs. Before he disappeared from the little clearing, he looked furtively toward Ena and then, turning away, hastily went off to fetch his own clothes. His bombast was gone, his chest was deflated, his vanity was in shreds.

''The first to compete,'' Ghonkaba announced, ''will be my son Renno and an opponent to be selected by Wegowa of the Cherokee. My son has experience as a warrior, so his opponent should be similarly qualified. They will try their skill with bow and arrow, with tomahawk, and with the rifle.''

Wegowa chose a warrior of eighteen summers to represent his people. He was given a bow and arrow, a tomahawk, which he tested briefly, and a rifle. Then he and Renno followed Ghonkaba, who walked a short distance from the front of the crowd. "In the cornfields outside the town palisade when we arrived here," Ghonkaba said, "I noticed some dummies standing guard over the crops. Scarecrows, the Americans call them. Could someone fetch two such creatures for me, please?"

A stir went through the crowd. A short time later, two senior warriors appeared, carrying life-size scarecrows. Ghonkaba set them up side by side, then beckoned the competitors and retreated sixty paces from the figures. "Listen carefully to my instructions," he told them, speaking loudly enough for the entire throng to hear. "Your first competition will be with a bow and arrow, and you will stay behind this line." He drew a long mark in the dirt underfoot with a moccasin. "You will each fire only one shot. He who is ready first will fire first."

Even as Ghonkaba spoke, Renno strung his bow and notched an arrow into it. He did not appear to mind that he was several feet behind the starting line that his father had drawn on the ground. He took careful, quick aim, as he had been taught to do in combat, and immediately let fly. The arrow sang through the air as it sped toward its target, and the spectators applauded loudly when it landed in the left eye of the scarecrow.

The young Cherokee appeared not to notice his opponent's superb shooting. Taking his time, he, too, unleashed an arrow. His shot was good, but certainly was less effective than Renno's. His arrow lodged in one shoulder of his dummy and penetrated deeply.

Without question, the Seneca had won the first round.

"Now," Ghonkaba said, "you are each allowed one shot at your target with firearms. Use the same line and make certain you stay behind it."

The Cherokee picked up an ancient, breech-loading musket, an old-fashioned weapon that had been outmoded for a half century. It was already loaded and primed, and he raised it to his shoulder. Watching him, Ghonkaba knew that he was making insufficient allowance for the weapon's savage kickback. He was eager to be the first to compete, and sighting his target down the rusty barrel of the weapon, he pulled the trigger.

The rifle gave a mighty roar: the kickback was so strong that the young warrior almost lost his balance.

Taking his inferior weapon into consideration, his aim proved excellent. A large hole had appeared in the other shoulder of the dummy. The crowd cheered its champion lustily.

Then Renno stepped to the line. His father was encouraged by the confident way that he handled his long rifle, his attitude demonstrating his familiarity with the weapon. He checked it over and squinted down the barrel. His stance alone revealed his confidence.

He squeezed the trigger, and a fountain of dried grass, small branches, and twigs shot up into the air and then fell to earth again. The Cherokee cheered when they saw that Renno had shot the head off his scarecrow. Its stuffing had risen like a plume of smoke. The headless scarecrow continued to stand, its shattered existence a testimonial to the skill of the young Seneca marksman.

Ghonkaba chuckled quietly to himself. His son had established a claim to marksmanship that could not be invalidated. It would be interesting to see how he handled the final part of the competition, using the badly disabled dummy as a target. Perhaps he should be allowed to use a new scarecrow, but Ghonkaba wanted to show him no favoritism and additionally was curious as to how Renno would handle the remaining weapon.

"Using your same targets and your same distance markers," he said, "you may fire your last weapons."

The young Cherokee stepped to the line once again, a look of supreme confidence on his face as he removed his tomahawk from his belt and weighed it experimentally in his hand. He was on safe ground now and knew it. He was handling a weapon with which he was very familiar, and he knew precisely what to do with it.

His audience fell silent as he squinted at his dummy and threw the tomahawk with a sharp downward motion of his throwing arm from shoulder height.

The weapon tore through the air and promptly decapitated the scarecrow. Another plume of twigs, dried grass, and other debris rose into the air. His expertise was unquestioned. His audience, wildly appreciative, was cheering because he finally had achieved the same results that his opponent had accomplished.

Now it was Renno's turn, and as he stepped to the line, waiting for the cheers of the onlookers to subside, Ghonkaba knew that his lack of experience with a tomahawk was making him feel far less secure.

Renno measured the distance to the target and then released the tomahawk. The form he displayed in throwing the weapon was perfect. It was the approved method and could not be faulted in any way, but his uncertainty revealed itself in his execution. The blow struck his decapitated scarecrow in the chest with sufficient force that the dummy was knocked from its feet to the ground, just as a human being would have been knocked off his feet by a similar blow. But he lacked the decisiveness of the Cherokee, who emerged the winner of that round.

Ordinarily, Ghonkaba would have judged the contest himself, but under the circumstances, he was careful to defer to Loramas. The Grand Sachem of the Cherokee had made up his own mind and, without hesitation, he awarded two of the possible three points to Renno, proclaiming him the winner in the shooting of both the bow and arrow and the firearms. Only in the throwing of the tomahawk did the young native come out ahead.

The audience determined that the judgment of their leader was correct and fair, and they applauded strongly to demonstrate their approval of his decision.

The next contest pitted El-i-chi against a junior warrior of the Cherokee who was also seventeen summers in age. The requirements for this match, determined by the Cherokee, involved ability to mount a moving horse. To the best of Ghonkaba's knowledge, his younger son was considerably lacking in experience in such an endeavor and would come out a very poor second.

What he had almost forgotten, however, was that during one winter that his family had spent with the Continental Army, El-i-chi had received instructions in horsemanship. His lessons were in the hands of members of Lighthorse Harry Lee's Virginians, a scouting unit of cavalry that had been responsible for capturing large quantities of British food that winter.

A senior warrior of the Cherokee held one end of a long tether. The other end was looped around the neck of a small but exceptionally lively horse. Running rapidly around the field, he encouraged the animal to move at a graceful trot, and the contestants were expected to run up alongside the horse and then mount while it was in motion.

The young Cherokee, familiar with the contest, went first. He made up in vigor what he lacked in expertise. He ran beside the horse until their speed matched. Then, suddenly, he hurled himself at the animal's back and landed, grasping almost desperately at the beast in order not to lose his grasp. He succeeded in staying on, and managed to right himself sufficiently to earn the applause of the onlookers. His effort had been far from graceful, but at least he had succeeded in accomplishing his goal.

Ghonkaba's concern for his younger son increased. He was not only afraid that El-i-chi would show up badly as a contestant, but he might be hurt severely as he tried to mount the moving gelding. It was impossible for him to intervene, and Ghonkaba could only hope for the best. The experience with a rider appearing out of nowhere had made the horse somewhat skittish, thus heightening the danger to his potential rider. El-i-chi showed no concern, and Ghonkaba had to admire his poise. Regardless of how badly he came out in the test, he showed no fear and no sense of hesitation.

The youth began to run as the senior warrior who was handling the horse urged it to greater speed. The gelding was moving at a rapid trot now.

El-i-chi did not run parallel with the horse but came at it from an angle. When he still appeared to be some distance from it, he suddenly sprang into the air. To the pleased surprise of his father and the delight of the crowd, he landed in a sitting position and quickly adjusted to the jarring motion of the rapidly trotting horse. Using his knees as a way of signaling the animal, he slowed it somewhat, then increased his pace to a slow gallop. It was evident that the boy knew precisely what he was doing and was achieving his ends with a minimum of effort.

El-i-chi circled the field twice, then gradually slowed the horse, and before the animal came to a complete halt, he leaped gracefully to the ground. He landed on his feet with no apparent effort, as though accustomed to accomplishing such a trick regularly.

Loramas proclaimed him the winner, and the crowd, doing its best to be fair, thundered its appreciation of the victor's efforts.

Chapter IV

Loramas and Wegowa were deeply impressed by the skills displayed by the younger generation of Seneca. Certainly they, of all the Cherokee present, realized that it was not accidental that young Seneca were so clever.

"The final contest," Ghonkaba said, "will be an exercise in scouting."

Before the third contest could be determined and its rules decided, Rusog jumped to his feet. The young Cherokee warrior was still suffering from the humiliation of the defeat he had suffered and was more anxious than ever to redeem himself. Thumping his chest, he proclaimed loudly that he was a scout second to none: among the braves of any nation on the North American continent, no tracker was his equal, he declared, and he challenged the Seneca to name a champion who could beat him.

Ena was so disdainful that she averted her face so that neither Rusog nor any of his compatriots could see her expression.

But Ghonkaba proved equal to the occasion. "You claim," he said quietly, "that you have no equal as a tracker among all the nations of the wilderness. I say you are wrong, and I am prepared to prove it."

Rusog laughed scornfully. "I am prepared to wager any sum you wish to name that no tracker is my equal."

Loramas cut him off sharply. "You'll make no wager, my grandson," he said. "Far more important matters are at stake."

Rusog reluctantly bowed his head and accepted the Grand Sachem's dictum.

"I will gladly prove before the brothers of the clan and the braves of your nation that you are in error," Ghonkaba said. "Let my daughter step forward."

When Ena joined him, many of the younger Cherokee warriors seemed resentful. Ghonkaba was quick to interpret their anger. They thought that he was insulting them by calling on a woman to engage in combat with Rusog.

"To those of you who think I am mocking you and that I am making light of your manhood," he said, "let it be known that General George Washington himself has commended my daughter for her contributions as a tracker to the cause of the Continental Army."

Some of his audience accepted his words, but others,

Rusog in particular, did not. The young giant looked Ena up and down slowly, then laughed loudly.

She clenched her fists and forced herself to bare her teeth in a semblance of a smile. While this wordless duel was taking place, a hawk appeared high in the sky overhead and gradually circled lower and lower. The entire assemblage watched in fascination as the bird came down almost to a treetop level. Rusog picked up a bow, took an arrow from the quiver at his back, and, stringing it, prepared to shoot.

But Ena, acting quickly and decisively, stepped forward and wrenched the bow from him. She had no time to explain, nor did she think it was any of his concern that the hawk was a sacred bird to the Seneca. A symbolic messenger of the manitous, the hawk undoubtedly had been sent to notify Ghonkaba and his family that they were still under the protection of the mightiest forces of the spirit world. What they were doing was right and proper, and their efforts would not fail.

While Rusog glared at her, she paid no attention to him and looked with profound satisfaction toward her father.

Then facing Loramas, she said clearly, "I will accept, O Sachem, any terms of a tracking competition with Rusog that you may care to name."

Rusog's hearty, contemptuous laugh was the first reaction to her offer.

Loramas remained unmoving and finally he spoke, proposing an exceptionally difficult test. Two foxes, recently captured, were being kept in captivity for the coming trials of youths about to go through the manhood rituals that tested their courage and their strength. He proposed that they be turned loose simultaneously, but sent off into the forest in opposite directions. Ena was assigned to track one and Rusog would track the other. Each would be followed by a few Cherokee and Seneca senior warriors in order to make certain that each abided by the basic rules of tracking.

No more difficult a test of skill could have been devised, Ena knew, but she looked at the Grand Sachem and said courageously, "I accept the terms, and I will gladly compete in the name of the Seneca."

Rusog was busily studying Ena in a way that revealed his keen interest in her as a woman, even while he was, on the surface, looking at her with contemptuous superiority. Ena wanted nothing to do with the man she regarded as a boor and a lout. She was so disgusted that she refused to hide her low opinion of him and turned her back rather than engage in conversation until their ordeal could begin.

Lyktaw, sensing the growing tension, became excited, roaming restlessly from one member of the family to another, then jumping up on each in order to draw attention to himself. Because no fox could be released in the presence of a dog that would be certain to follow and kill it, Toshabe leashed the shepherd dog. Straining and tugging, he proved too strong for her to handle, so she gave the leash to Renno, who had enough strength to keep Lyktaw under control.

The two foxes were carried to the scene in containers that resembled wicker baskets. The one Rusog was to follow was taken to the north side of the clearing and cover was removed from the basket. A reddish-brown streak was visible as the fox made a wild dash for safety and freedom in the forest.

Rusog could not begin his hunt immediately, but was obliged to wait for a specific signal from Loramas. The animal had to be given time to vanish and to cover its tracks.

The beast Ena was to track was taken to the clearing's south side. It was released to the accompaniment of loud barking from Lyktaw. The dog almost snapped the leash in an effort to break away, but Renno hung on.

Ena remained tranquil and paid no attention to the sounds made by the rapidly vanishing fox in the deep woods. She would have ample opportunity soon to study its trail.

She chatted quietly with her mother and father while ignoring the steady stares of Rusog, who seemed to have nothing better to do than to ogle.

After about five minutes, the Seneca and Cherokee each selected four of their senior warriors as judges' assistants. Loramas assigned four warriors to Rusog and the others to Ena, then instructed the contestants to begin.

In spite of the constant interest that Rusog had displayed in Ena, he appeared to forget her completely now. He headed into the woods, quickly picking up the trail of the fox.

The difficulties of following it were evident, but Rusog's boasting had not been without basis. He quickly proved himself indeed an expert tracker. Once he found the trail, he managed to follow it, his task made much easier because the fox, having been held in captivity, was so eager to flee that it paid no attention to its telltale trail.

Rusog pushed ever deeper into the forest. Ranoga, one of the Seneca assigned to observe him, admitted that he was able to make following the trail seem a simple matter.

After pushing through underbrush for a half hour, Rusog came at last to a deep gully. There, the trail stopped. Halting, he examined the ground with great care. Finally, he found a faint clue, which led toward the bottom of the gully and became stronger again on the opposite side. By the time he reached level ground, he had established the course the fox had taken. All four judges were forced to concede that he had done superbly. Ranoga, who prided himself on his own abilities as a scout, had never seen a better tracker.

From the outset, Ena took her time, advancing slowly through the forest. The fox she was to follow was smaller and somewhat more volatile than Rusog's, so she had a more difficult task. When running across a grassy opening, the fox caused less evident indentations in the grass and displaced fewer stones and twigs. On the other hand, Ena was aided by her knowledge of the fox's habits, having studied it during her training period.

The four warriors with her were ready to certify that she was an expert tracker, as good as they could have expected. But that was not satisfying to Ena. "I've been assigned to find the fox," she said, "and find him I shall. Come with me or not, as you choose!"

She kept going, and the senior warriors followed. After another half hour, they grew restless. But Ena remained fresh, still determined to succeed.

She reasoned that the fox, having spent several weeks in

captivity, would grow weaker rather soon. Therefore, she told herself, she would be able, with any luck, to do far more than follow its trail. If she persisted, she might actually be able to encounter it.

Yet another half hour passed and the judges murmured in irritation. Regardless of whether they accompanied her, she intended to carry on to the end, she told them.

By this time, Rusog and his judges had returned. The judges made their report to Loramas. Rusog, however, overcome with curiosity about his opponent, followed her party through the forest and, ultimately, caught up with it.

Ena, who was fully concentrating on her task, ignored him. Snubbed, he stayed on nonetheless.

Suddenly Ena changed her tactics. She slowed her pace to a crawl and made no sound as she crept forward through the heavy undergrowth. The warriors had no idea what she was attempting to do now, but they realized that she must have valid reasons. Rusog, bringing up the rear, knew that if he made any noise he could spoil her chances. He was tempted but refrained. Much preferring to win by honorable means, he remained absolutely quiet.

At last, Ena came to the rotting, crumbling portion of a hollow log. Part of it had fallen away, and its interior was dried and pulpy. She took a long stick and poked it gently into the opening. The warriors were astonished to see a reddish-brown paw striking at the stick.

"There, my judges," Ena said conclusively, "is the fox that we have followed." The four warriors could scarcely believe what they were seeing and hearing. Even more stunned, Rusog found it impossible to believe that Ena had actually tracked the fox to its hiding place.

"There is no need," she said, "for us to kill him. He earned his freedom, and I shall give it to him." She turned and started to retrace her steps, walking rapidly.

Rusog said nothing and continued to bring up the rear of the column. Though he had done well, she had outdone him. Through some accident of nature or some other freak happening, she had stumbled across the fox's lair. He could see no other way to explain her success.

At last, the group arrived back at the field near the town, where Loramas and Wegowa waited for the report of Ena's judges. The Grand Sachem's face remained impassive as the warriors told him their remarkable story. Then he decided to question them. "You say that she tracked the fox for a great distance from this place? And you actually saw it with your own eyes at the end of the hunt?" When they nodded in affirmation, he turned to Rusog. "You, too, saw the fox?"

The young warrior was impelled to reply truthfully. "I saw the fox with my own eyes," he said. "I would have liked to believe that it was another fox, but I'm sure it was not. It was the same animal that was released here. She followed it until it lodged itself in the hollow log. Never," he added with unexpected generosity, "have I seen such expert tracking."

Loramas promptly declared Ena the winner. Having expected exactly that outcome, she was not surprised, nor was her father.

Rusog realized that he no longer could call himself the

foremost tracker in America, and this took the wind out of his sails. He was annoyed with Ena for having beaten him but was furious with himself for having candidly acknowledged her superiority. Having been shamed by Ena, he felt he could no longer hold up his head in the company of his comrades. He looked at her with what seemed to be dislike in his eyes. But Ghonkaba, who intercepted the expression, could see a great deal more in it.

Later, he described his analysis to Toshabe. "I've told none of this to Ena. She feels only contempt for him, and she would object if she knew that he seems to have fallen in love with her."

His wife smiled. "You were right to say nothing to her," she said. "You are growing wiser in the ways of women."

"I do not sit in judgment on Rusog," Ghonkaba said. "While I cannot deny that he is annoying in his boasting, I think that basically he is trying to impress Ena. Unfortunately, he creates the opposite effect."

"You're quite right," Toshabe agreed.

"I am strongly tempted to have a few words with Rusog," Ghonkaba said. "Perhaps I can urge him to mend his ways. In so doing, he will improve his chances with our daughter."

"Don't interfere!" Toshabe said sharply. "You and I found each other with no help. I think we should let them do the same."

"I agree with you to an extent," Ghonkaba said, "but I can see other elements that cause me to wonder. We are far from our homeland, and I don't hold a position of rank and distinction with the Seneca. As paupers, we must rely on strangers for any stature we may be able to achieve. Rusog is the grandson of the Grand Sachem of the Cherokee and the son of the principal war chief. The parents of many maidens in this land would gladly welcome him as a son-in-law. Certainly, he has a standing worthy of Ena's heritage. Although she lacks rank and position, her ancestry is distinguished; Rusog does live up to it.''

''Say nothing to Rusog,'' Toshabe told him. ''And also nothing to Ena, although I grant you that he is of a stature that would commend itself to us as a son-in-law. We cannot allow ourselves to interfere in something that is none of our business. If he continues to brag and preen, he will lose her. If he learns a lesson and mends his ways, she might soften. But all you and I can do is observe, not comment!''

Evening was approaching and the Seneca had no idea where they would be allowed to spend the night. But they were encouraged when Loramas asked them to come to his house.

Jejeno took it upon himself to advise Ghonkaba. ''All the Seneca who intend to dwell in our land should be here,'' he said. ''The women have a far greater importance in the land of the Cherokee than in other Indian nations. Your women are to be present in the house of the Grand Sachem.''

The women and children were summoned, and the entire group crowded in to hear the decision made by the leader of the nation.

"In your contests with warriors of the Cherokee," he said, "the Seneca have earned the right to dwell among us. I have had words with the senior warriors and the medicine men who represent our people. They are unanimous in their opinion, which I share. Therefore, I invite the Seneca to make their home among us and to share the future and the fortunes of the Cherokee."

Ghonkaba thanked the Grand Sachem and made a solemn promise on behalf of the Seneca to obey Cherokee laws and customs and to work for the safety and the good of the nation.

That ended the formalities. On behalf of his father, Wegowa led the newcomers to a row of unoccupied houses and told them to make themselves at home. They would be expected to repay the Cherokee by doing their share of work in building more houses that would go up soon. Ghonkaba's family, which was the largest, was given the most spacious dwelling. It had three chambers for sleeping: one for Ghonkaba and Toshabe, another for their daughter, and the third for their sons.

In an arrangement unique to the Seneca, a wife became the owner of each dwelling. The house was the property of Toshabe rather than of Ghonkaba, and she had the right to determine its use in various respects.

The wives of Wegowa and Jejeno came by to conduct Toshabe and Ena to the cultivated lands outside the town walls. Here they were presented with their own plot of land. Ena was also told that if she married, she would acquire land of her own, but it was made clear that their men—Ghonkaba and his sons—would be required to do their share of work, not only on this land, but also on the common land owned by the tribe.

Demonstrating boundless hospitality, the Cherokee women provided Toshabe and the other women of the Seneca with raw materials for the evening's supper and for the morning meal. Toshabe was impressed by the variety of vegetables. Green peas were new to her, as were sweet potatoes and cauliflower. The bulk of the meat that she received was buffalo rather than deer. She found, as she had been told, it required a longer time to cook.

Renno, El-i-chi, and Ena were interested in these new foods. They were excited by the prospect of hunting for buffalo.

"All of us have much to learn, my sons," Ghonkaba said to them. "We must learn the tricks to the hunting of buffalo, just as we know it does little good to hunt deer without knowing how the deer will behave. I shall find out when the next party to hunt buffalo will go out, and I'll try to arrange for us to be included."

In the days that followed, the Seneca learned much that was new to them. They liked the different foods and were particularly pleased by the taste of buffalo meat and of the fish from the nearby rivers. These were unlike the firm-fleshed fish of northern New York.

After about ten days, Ghonkaba and the other Seneca males were invited by Wegowa to take part in a buffalo hunt. To their surprise, fifty Cherokee warriors joined the party, many times the number that would go at one time on a deer hunt.

Renno, El-i-chi, and the other Seneca youths old enough to participate carried only their bows and arrows, as did their fathers. None knew quite what to expect.

The difference between the Seneca and the Cherokee showed markedly in the wilderness. Like the braves of so many Indian nations, the Cherokee had mastered the art of traveling silently through the forest. They were sufficiently experienced to make no sound, but the Seneca traveled at their own trotting pace and were still fresh, able to continue at the same speed when the Cherokee were forced to halt and rest. Consequently, no more than three hours after the journey began, the Seneca, who had been in midcolumn at the beginning, now were ahead with the vanguard.

At last they came to a huge expanse of treeless, rolling plain, where the grass was knee-high. In the distance, Ghonkaba, who was endowed with the gifted eyesight of the original Renno, could see bulky figures that he thought might be buffalo. Wegowa confirmed his guess. "I believe," he said, "that we are seeing the sentinels of a large herd grazing in the meadow."

Ghonkaba was surprised. "Sentinels?" he asked.

"The organization of the buffalo is very complex. They have sentinels and guards, and others who keep strays in line. They have special units on their flanks and others that bring up the rear, as you shall soon see."

At his direction, his braves built a small fire, the smoke curling upward and moving away from the buffalo.

"We're fortunate," Wegowa said, "that the wind is not

blowing toward the buffalo. Then nothing would cause them to come near us. We would need a completely different strategy.''

Ghonkaba realized that the buffalo would be wary of human smells, but he did not understand the reason for the fire and asked about it.

''The buffalo are very large and strong,'' Wegowa replied. ''But they are handicapped by very poor eyesight. In fact, when the wind is right it is possible for us to approach very close on a flank without being noticed. I ordered a fire lighted so that the flickering of flames and the rising of smoke into the air would attract their attention. Their sentinels are now approaching closer, followed by the main body of the herd.''

The bulls whom he called sentinels were slowly grazing closer and closer to the fire. Large numbers of other buffalo, including many cows and calves, were moving in the same direction.

''Time to move into formation!'' Wegowa decreed, quickly assigning the Seneca to places in both the front and rear rank. Ghonkaba and his sons were in the front rank toward the left, and Wegowa took his own position beside them. ''Position yourselves no more than an arm's length apart,'' he told them, ''and be prepared for an order to wave your arms at your sides violently. That will prevent the buffalo from running you down when they advance.''

Ghonkaba did not understand what he meant.

''Use your bows and arrows freely,'' Wegowa went on, ''and fire as often as you will. Aim for their vital parts, so that you may bring down even the largest bull quickly and effectively. But I beg you, in the name of the Corn Mother, do not unloosen an arrow prematurely. Hold your fire until I give you the signal. If you shoot too soon, the herd will take fright and vanish before we can kill a single buffalo.''

The buffalo "sentinels," bulls in the prime of life, edged closer still to the double line of Indians. They were closely followed by the great, massive herd, with a line of cows in the lead.

Wegowa's quiet chuckle showed that he was pleased because his strategy was turning out to be so effective. He called, "Give your arm signals, now!"

The Cherokee extended their arms, touching each other on the shoulder, and then began to raise and lower them methodically. The Seneca did the same.

The buffalo, their attention riveted on the spectacle, began to run toward it. They invariably spread out, rather than heading toward the center of the Indians' ranks.

Ghonkaba felt a great sense of relief. If one of the shaggy, ungainly creatures came thundering directly at him or one of his sons, instant death would have been the result.

Joining the younger bulls in the front rank now were a number of older bulls. Their hair was matted, their coats dusty and spotted. As they approached, they picked up speed, and the earth underfoot trembled as hundreds of them sped toward the Indians.

Wegowa was shouting but could not make himself heard distinctly above the thunder of hooves. Ghonkaba grasped the Cherokee war chief's probable meaning: he was urging everyone not to panic. Anyone who gave in to a sense of panic and tried to flee would be pursued and run down by scores—or even hundreds—of buffalo.

It seemed the buffalo were simply following their leaders as they ran faster and faster. But Ghonkaba had been trained as an observer, and even though his heart was pounding, his brain continued to register the amazing scene coolly and calmly. The leaders had decided to gallop, and a full-fledged stampede was in progress.

At the left end of the front rank, Ghonkaba could see the leaders of the avalanche approach, kicking up a huge dust cloud. In self-defense, the Indians waved their arms in order to divert the thrust.

Wegowa called out another order and reached over his shoulder for an arrow in order to notch it into his bow.

That was good enough for Ghonkaba, who did the same. Taking careful aim, he put an arrow beneath the eyes of a charging young bull.

The animal faltered but continued to thunder forward. Ghonkaba quickly inserted another arrow into his bow and fired it. This time he placed it an inch beneath one of the creature's tiny red eyes. The bull stumbled and fell.

Other buffalo continued to rush forward. Suddenly they were upon the Indians, who were quickly surrounded. The stench of the animals was overpowering as they continued to press on in their senseless dash, but the Indians—certainly the more experienced Cherokee, whose efforts were soon copied by the Seneca—needed no instructions now. Dozens of arrows were fired, and while a few missed their mark, the majority struck home. The bigger bulls weighed as much as a ton each; even the calves carried hundreds of pounds.

Some buffalo were downed with very few shots, while others required as many as a dozen arrows in order to dispatch them. Still the main body of the beasts continued to press forward. Undeterred by the killing, they seemed crazed as they panicked with one aim: racing toward an unseeable destination. Ghonkaba, who had never seen a buffalo stampede, found it awe-inspiring, and he was glad that the waving of arms was enough to send the buffalo in another direction.

At last the charge came to an end. The bulls in the vanguard slowed when they saw the forest behind the Indians looming up. Gradually the entire column grew calmer. Before disappearing in the woods, the buffalo became docile, and the sound of their retreat gradually grew dimmer. At least a dozen of their number lay dead behind them.

The warriors began to butcher the carcasses immediately, taking care to save the hides, which would be used to make clothing, capes, and blankets. The horns of the bulls would make knives and other instruments. Virtually every portion of each beast was used in some way; nothing was wasted. Large quantities of meat were cut and packed, ready to be carried.

Ghonkaba estimated, accurately, that the meat provided by a single cow buffalo would provide for two evening meals of the entire town. The rest of the meat, preserved by smoking, went into a warehouse for common use. The wife in any family could obtain enough there for her daily needs, and she could draw on the rations as long as they lasted. The Indians trusted their neighbors not to exceed their needs. Their honor system was effective, observed by every family.

Ena, regarded as a full-grown woman by the Cherokee, was given responsibilities accordingly. She was assigned to prepare one meal each week for the unmarried men and women of the Seneca. Required to attend the meetings of the group, she could cast her vote on issues that came before it.

To Ghonkaba's surprise and pleasure, he and Casno, as his medicine man, were permitted to sit with the Grand Council of the Cherokee. They attended council sessions with Loramas and the nation's other leaders to determine questions of war and peace.

Attending his first meeting of the council and listening to addresses by Loramas and others, Ghonkaba was confirmed in what he already had guessed: as the only major Indian nation west of the mountains to have cast their lot with the new United States, the Cherokee were in an awkward position, even though their alliance was not formal. Every other major tribe had become allies of the British thanks to the tireless activities of Anthony Simpson.

Ghonkaba felt compelled to make a brief statement, so he delivered a pungent address, stressing that the British colonies that now called themselves the United States could be expected to win their full independence.

This prospect seemed, however, to make very little difference to the Cherokee, in this land where settlements by American pioneers were sparse. British-controlled Indian nations carried out raids of terror on these settlements. Even the Cherokee wondered whether they should join with the Creek and Choctaw in taking their own share of the spoils.

Ghonkaba argued ably against such a course of action. "America will soon be free and independent," he said, "and the Continental Army, having vanquished the British, can be expected to cross the mountains and punish any Indian tribe that has wantonly killed its women and children, that has raided farms indiscriminately."

Ghonkaba knew from the reactions to his address that his arguments would stave off any attacks on settlements. At the same time, he was unprepared for the remarks made by one of the leading firebrands among the Cherokee.

"We have heard the words of our new brother," he said, "and I agree we should do nothing for the present. But my reasons are not the same as his. Anthony Simpson, a man who describes himself as the close friend and representative of the British king, is due to visit us soon. We should listen with care to what he says to us. The Choctaw and the Creek have grown wealthy, thanks to the generosity of Simpson and of the British. I look forward to the day when the Cherokee, too, will share in this outpouring of wealth. Let us weigh his words and then we will be far better able to determine what course the Cherokee will follow."

His argument apparently made a deep impression, for the council agreed that the nation would await the coming of Simpson to determine whether, belatedly, to make common cause with Great Britain.

* * *

Ena fashioned a hoe out of a thin-edged slab of stone, and although the Cherokee used virtually no tools in their own gardening, she found it very useful in preparing the plot that was to be her mother's garden. Allowing no one else to take a hand, she sent her brothers fishing and then put some of their catch into the soil with the hoe. She was feeling a sense of real accomplishment when she recognized a deep voice directly behind her. "Your relatives in the Bear Clan," Rusog said, "congratulate you on a job well done. One day you will have the finest vegetable garden in the entire land of the Cherokee."

She froze, glaring at Rusog.

"I'm not making a joke at your expense," the young giant protested. "I am a member of the Bear Clan of the Cherokee, as I understand you are among the Seneca."

"That," Ena said icily, "is unfortunate. But it's an accident that cannot be helped."

Rusog studied her at length. "Why do you dislike me so intensely?" he demanded.

"I neither dislike you nor like you," she said haughtily. "I'm totally indifferent to you and to what you do."

He chose not to believe her, because he found it inconceivable that any woman would not somehow respond to him.

"One does not react with pleasure to everyone whom one meets," he said, "so it may be that, for reasons I cannot understand, you have a hatred toward me. But I cannot believe that you are truly indifferent."

108

CHEROKEE

Aware that she had found a chink in his insufferable armor, Ena exploited it. "Suppose it is true," she said, "that we are both members of a Bear Clan. That is nothing but a coincidence, and it does not mean that we are related. Should you be honored as a great warrior? I think not. In how many battles have you fought? In my family, we have warriors whose names strike terror into the hearts of braves from every other nation. Ghonkaba, my father; Ja-gonh, my grandfather; and Renno, my great-grandfather, are known wherever Indians live. Do you compare with them? I think not. Are you renowned for your wisdom? Surely you do not compare yourself with your own grandfather! Loramas, a man of wisdom, has earned his place as Grand Sachem, but you do not compare with him. And surely you don't regard yourself in such a light, so why should I honor you? Because your gods made you large and gave you physical strength? Physical strength without cunning is nothing. Prove that you are worthy of being honored and then I will so regard you. Until then, leave me alone. And don't bother me with your childish posturing!"

Despite the reproach in her tone, much could be said for the validity of Ena's criticism, and Rusog took her words to heart. Instead of responding with bluster, he fell silent. For a long time he made no reply. "I know in my heart that I will become a great warrior and a great leader of the Cherokee," he said at last. "But that is all in the future. I cannot expect you to share my vision. First, I must achieve. And only when you see my accomplishments will you honor me as I believe I will deserve. Until then, I cannot blame you for feeling that I am like the wind that blows loudly but does nothing.''

He actually sounded sobered and chastised, Ena reflected. In spite of herself, she looked at him closely. She could see no bragging, no bravado in him now. He seemed to be speaking honestly and contritely. This was the Rusog behind the pose, and she realized that she could not help but be impressed. Only a man of great inner strength would admit that he had been boasting prematurely and that another day would have to come before others would share his vision of himself.

Ena wanted to apologize for her own behavior and to suggest that perhaps they should make a fresh start. Could they, she wondered, simply try to achieve a friendship rather than the romance Rusog seemed to have in mind?

He gave her no opportunity, however, to suggest that they clear the air. Her steady scrutiny unnerved him, and he backed away several steps, nodded abruptly in farewell, and, turning on his heels, stalked back toward town, never once looking back at her.

To Ena, it seemed that she had won this exchange and that Rusog was in full retreat. But, for reasons she could not discern, she found herself unable to savor her victory and enjoy it.

A messenger came to Ghonkaba to tell him that he was needed in a meeting to be held soon at the house of Wegowa. He postponed a lesson in military tactics that he was giving his sons and departed at once.

CHEROKEE

A white man sat cross-legged on the ground conversing with Wegowa, and Ghonkaba realized instantly that this was Anthony Simpson.

At first glance, the notorious agent appeared wiry and thin. But on closer examination he was positively gaunt. His long hair was unkempt and hung in thin strands around a stubble of beard on his cheeks. He seemed incapable of meeting anyone's gaze directly, an impression created, at least in part, by the cast in one eye. His face, Ghonkaba decided, was that of a ferret, an impression heightened by his gimlet eyes, which showed sly cunning and wariness.

When Ghonkaba forced himself to politely raise his left arm, he noted, even at a distance, Simpson's fetid breath with its stale odor of rum.

Simpson clearly tried hard to establish friendly terms with Ghonkaba, though he had no way of knowing whom he was meeting. He exerted an oily charm and did his utmost to win approval.

Ghonkaba, however, said very little and deliberately refrained from revealing his ability to speak and understand English.

Wegowa had invited several of the nation's leaders to this informal session, and the purpose was soon made clear. Speaking in the language of the Cherokee, Simpson regaled them with the benefits that the Creek, the Choctaw, the southern branch of the Tuscarora, and other tribes were enjoying as a result of treaties with Great Britain. He also suggested that the leaders of those nations had benefited personally. They were the owners of the latest rifles, pistols, and swords. They owned not only blankets, but bolts of fine cloth for clothing. They now had many iron cooking utensils and other gifts.

Simpson's words were highly effective. The Cherokee listened intently, their eyes glistening as he enumerated the gifts.

Ghonkaba listened in silence, saying nothing to contradict Simpson. The time was not yet ripe for a direct confrontation. It would be better, Ghonkaba thought, to hold his fire until the council meeting, and then to employ whatever ammunition was at hand.

Eventually they all adjourned to the council building, where other leaders of the Cherokee were gathering. Ghonkaba found Casno awaiting him. They entered together, taking seats at the rear.

The members of the council lighted pipes and, making themselves comfortable, sat cross-legged on the floor. This was a solemn occasion devoid of joking or idle conversation.

Loramas introduced Simpson as "one who calls himself the friend of the Cherokee." The agent arose, brushed off his stained buckskins, and began to speak.

"Let me tell you of a true happening," he said, "that will explain to you far better than anything I might say of the situation that faces the Cherokee today. All who are gathered here have heard of the nations of the Iroquois League."

Ghonkaba was astonished, but he made no move. His face became a mask. He had no idea what would follow but prepared himself for any eventuality.

"The nations of the Iroquois first cast their lot with the Americans at the beginning of the war that has been waged for years. They were misled and misguided by the tales of the colonists that they would be fighting for their own liberty and would win a glorious freedom for themselves." Simpson paused dramatically. "But the Americans repeatedly broke their promises, cheating the Iroquois, murdering warriors and their families, and otherwise leading them to destruction while continuing to smile at them and profess great friendship for them. In time," Simpson went on, "the Iroquois learned a great lesson. Led by the ferocious warriors of the Seneca and by the wise Mohawk, they broke their ties with the Americans and cast their lot with the British. They have fought on the British side from that day to this, and they have not regretted their move. The Cherokee, too, can benefit, and in return for a formal agreement, obtain much property and money."

Ghonkaba and Casno were equally startled and outraged. Simpson's story had been made up out of whole cloth, and Ghonkaba had no intention of tolerating such a deception. Jumping to his feet, he called out, first in the language of the Cherokee and then in English, "Simpson, you lie! There is no word of truth in what you have said!

"You have made a serious error by choosing the Iroquois as the subject for your lies. I am Ghonkaba, a war chief of the Seneca, the son of Ja-gonh, the Great Sachem of the Iroquois, and the nephew of No-da-vo, the sachem of the Seneca. I am the grandson of the great Renno, who, together with his father, Ghonka, whose name I bear, inspired the Iroquois League. I repeat, not one word of truth is in what you have said."

Simpson realized he had indeed chosen the wrong subject for his deceit and tried to rectify his mistake.

But Ghonkaba gave him no chance to speak. "Long ago," he declared, "before anyone now in this chamber had been born, Ghonka, my ancestor, made a treaty of alliance with Great Britain. That alliance was kept up by Renno, my grandfather, who formed intimate ties with the American colonists. He married my grandmother, a native of Virginia who was the daughter of a colonel of Virginia militia. When my father's turn came to be Great Sachem of the Iroquois, he, too, kept up that treaty. Then the war came. Because the Seneca—and all the other Iroquois— regard treaties as sacred instruments, the nations of the Iroquois League abided by that treaty. They became the allies of the British at the very beginning of the war. My fellow Seneca and I, who have come now to the land of the Cherokee, could not tolerate such an arrangement. Therefore, we fought with the Americans against the British. We would be fighting still, but victory and liberty, freedom for all, is now assured. For that reason, we were relieved from active duty. There, my new neighbors and friends, you have the true story of the Iroquois in this war of American versus Englishman. Let anyone who doubts my word question any member of my party. Talk to the women, talk to the youngest children, talk to anyone you wish, and you will be told the same truth, word for word, as you've heard it from me."

Anthony Simpson had worked himself into a tight corner. The only way he could extricate himself was by casting doubt on the truthfulness of the Seneca who had called his bluff. He did not hesitate to compound his story. "When I told you the sad account of what befell the Iroquois, I did not realize a spy in the pay of America is in our midst. But I know it now, and so do you. His imagination is as fertile as that of a cunning snake. He speaks no word of truth because the truth is alien to his nature."

Continuing his diatribe, Simpson arose to a triumphant climax. "I do not know the true identity of this person, but I guarantee you he is no Seneca, much less is he the offspring of the famous leaders of the Iroquois, whom he claims as his ancestors!"

Ghonkaba had heard enough. The warnings of Washington, Morgan, and Boone about Simpson came back to him in full force. He realized it was a useless waste of time to exchange words with the villainous English agent.

The easiest way to dispose of Simpson would be by throwing a well-aimed tomahawk at him and decapitating him, but such a plan was far too simple to be accomplished realistically.

Ghonkaba could not allow himself to lose sight of the all-important fact that he himself was a guest of the Cherokee, and they would regard it as a flagrant abuse of their hospitality if he harmed or murdered a fellow guest in their council chamber. Such an act would be contrary to the moral values of every Indian nation on the continent.

All the same, he had to get rid of Simpson before the agent succeeded in persuading the Cherokee to become the allies of Great Britain. Therefore, he determined upon a bold, immediate course of action that was predicated on the fact that comparatively little was known locally about his prowess. Neither the Cherokee nor Simpson himself realized that like his direct ancestors before him, Ghonkaba was uncannily accurate in his aim with a tomahawk, as he was with any other weapon. His one real aim now was to frighten Simpson so badly that the man would flee from the scene before reaching his goal.

Raising his voice in a bloodcurdling Seneca war cry, Ghonkaba drew his tomahawk from his belt and hurled it with all his might at Simpson.

Instead of striking the British agent in the head, Ghonkaba's blow only removed Simpson's hat and pinned it to the wall behind him.

His aim was far too accurate for Simpson's comfort. Not waiting to give the outraged Seneca another opportunity to kill him, he turned and, proving his cowardice by not staying and challenging his assailant, he cravenly fled from the building. As he vanished, Simpson proved his lies about Ghonkaba not being a Seneca, by shouting, "You haven't seen the last of me, Seneca!"

By the time that several Cherokee decided to follow and question him, they discovered that he had disappeared into the wilderness. At least for the moment, he had abandoned his attempt to persuade the Cherokee to join forces with the British.

Ghonkaba apologized to Loramas for having acted out of turn. Not until he grew calmer did Casno point out to him that his tactics, although violent and crude, certainly were effective in exposing Simpson as a liar. He had forced him to give up his efforts to win the Cherokee as new allies. And the Cherokee remained the informal allies of the Americans.

But Simpson still lived, and Ghonkaba knew he would carry on his masterful conniving at the expense of the new country and its Indian allies.

Chapter V

Loramas bore a striking resemblance to the picture of the typical Indian leader that was forming in the consciousness of the American people. Tall and still fairly slender in spite of his advancing years, he carried himself with the natural dignity of one long accustomed to command. His sense of humor was limited, and the wrinkles in his aquiline face caused him to appear to be perpetually scowling. The feathers that denoted his high rank were set inches apart in the scalp lock that trailed down his back, and he wore the scar of a long-ago battle on one cheek with great pride. He invariably wore full war paint whenever he appeared in the presence of subordinates, and when a matter of state required determination, he invariably went into seclusion while pondering it.

This he did immediately following the council meeting from which Ghonkaba had driven Anthony Simpson.

He decided the issue of Cherokee alliances without actual consideration of the American and British positions. As he told his council, for many generations the Cherokee had been the enemies of the Creek and the Choctaw. At least once in every decade, they fought the Creek. Although they had not recently engaged in active hostilities with the Choctaw, that nation remained the greatest threat to their peace. Therefore, Loramas concluded, the Creek and Choctaw alliance with the British made it logically impossible for the Cherokee to take up Britain's cause. The nation therefore would stand by its loose agreement with the Americans.

The decision satisfied Ghonkaba. A long-term threat potentially remained, but meanwhile his Seneca would have time to accustom themselves to the ways of the Cherokee and to make themselves secure in their new homes. It appeared unlikely that the Cherokee would be taking part in any battle of the American Revolution.

All that changed one day in the late fall when young Renno came to his father with surprising news. "An old friend of yours has just arrived, my father," Renno said. "Colonel John Sevier of the Tennessee Frontier Regiment is visiting Wegowa."

Sevier, who looked, thought, and fought like an Indian, had been in overall command of the Continental Army scouts in a number of battles in which Ghonkaba had participated. Ghonkaba's eyes shone with pleasure as he jumped to his feet. "Is he at the house of Wegowa at this moment?"

"He is," Renno told him.

Waiting to hear no more, the Seneca ran to the chief warrior's dwelling.

As he approached the house, a great roar of recognition sounded from inside. Seated near the window, Sevier could see Ghonkaba nearby. And a moment later, he raced into the open, embraced Ghonkaba, and pounded him enthusiastically on the back. "Ghonkaba, you miserable old horse thief, how in tarnation are you? What are you doing here? And what's new with you? This is where you and your lads have finally landed?"

Laughing heartily, Ghonkaba had no opportunity to answer his questions.

"Come inside and join us," Sevier continued. "Your presence here may be the very break that I need." Throwing an arm impulsively around Ghonkaba's broad shoulders, he dragged him into Wegowa's home.

"Colonel Ghonkaba and I were comrades during the war," Sevier explained to Wegowa.

Sevier, swarthy and heavily tanned, had a mercurial temperament; he seemed to live on nervous energy, sitting still for hardly a moment and moving restlessly about.

"My scouts and I are making our home here with the Cherokee now, as you gathered," Ghonkaba told him at last. "We recently rid the immediate countryside of Anthony Simpson, so it seems we're doing some good."

"You have a chance to do a great deal more," Sevier replied. He began to speak the language of the Cherokee

121

for the benefit of Wegowa. "It is an omen of the gods that I have found my old comrade-in-arms here at a time when I need him the most. I have come here to seek the assistance of the Cherokee nation in a campaign that I will be leading."

"The war has moved to the West at last," Ghonkaba observed shrewdly.

"It sure has," Sevier replied. "East of the mountains, the redcoats have lost their shirts, you might say. They're barely hanging on. They're eventually going to be forced to leave New York, the only town of any consequence they still hold. They'll gather their forces for one final battle. It won't be fought this year and maybe even won't be ripe next year. But sooner or later they must put up a final show of force in the East. In the meantime, their strategy has moved to these lands west of the mountains. They think that if they can use their Indian allies to seal off the West and take possession of it, they can freeze the United States east of the mountains and ultimately weaken the Americans enough that they—the British—will be able to conquer the country that refuses to be subdued. We've developed a counterstrategy. General Washington can't spare his Continentals for duty this side of the mountains because he's got to keep them ready to meet the last British thrust in the East. I've been given command of a small force that is expected to foil the British strategy. So far, I have only a single regiment of about eight hundred men, all volunteers, pioneers with experience in fighting Indians. Most of them are landowners here in Tennessee, chiefly from the eastern part of the region, but quite a few come from Kentucky. I'm here to propose that the Cherokee supply a force, too; a force as large as it's possible to muster. Then we'll take on the Creek and fight them to a fare-thee-well. And we'll take on any other Indians who don't like our new American flag.''

Ghonkaba whistled softly under his breath. "Aren't you taking a bite that may be too big to chew, Johnny?''

Colonel Sevier nodded solemnly. "That's possible,'' he said, "maybe even probable. Even if the Cherokee are right generous and give me as many as five hundred warriors—and I can't reasonably ask for more than that— we'll sure as shootin' be outnumbered every time we go into battle. But the way I figure it, though the Choctaw and the Creek may be armed with the best English muskets, they don't know how to shoot the durn things. And I figure we have a natural advantage over 'em, so we'll more than hold our own, and that's no fooling. You'll join me, won't you, Ghonkaba?''

"I'd like nothing more,'' Ghonkaba replied, "and I'm sure that all my men will feel as I do. But I'll need the permission of the Grand Sachem before I can go off to battle with you. Don't worry, Johnny, I'll do my utmost to get his approval at whatever point may seem to be suitable.''

"What about you, Wegowa?'' Sevier demanded bluntly. "Do I have your support?''

"Our warriors,'' Wegowa replied slowly, "would be taking great risks. Never have we faced both our major enemies at the same time. We are no more expert than are they in the handling of firearms. Even if we had the most modern rifles, I am uncertain that we'd handle them well

123

enough to assure victory. This is a question that cannot be determined lightly or quickly.''

His caution was echoed by Loramas when Colonel Sevier finally met with the Grand Sachem. Although sympathetic to the American cause, Loramas made it clear that he would have to summon the leaders of the Cherokee nation to a grand conclave. There the issue would be discussed at length and settled.

Late that same day runners were sent to the other towns and villages of the nation. The leaders, including the medicine men and the war chiefs, were summoned to a vitally important meeting.

After three days, all had assembled. Ghonkaba and Casno were present, but they promised each other that they would remain silent. New to the Cherokee, they thought it wise not to intrude their views.

The council building was crowded for the session, and the air was thick with the smoke of pipes. Jejeno opened the session with a fervent prayer to the Corn Mother and the Spirit Holder to guide the Cherokee.

Loramas presented Sevier's proposal that the Cherokee launch a major campaign together with Sevier's regiment against the Choctaw and Creek. No British troops were west of the Appalachians. It did not appear, therefore, that direct action against Great Britain would be involved.

In Ghonkaba's opinion, the Grand Sachem was very fair in his presentation of Sevier's views; he did not hesitate to point out the possible dangers involved.

The first to respond was Loramas's son, Wegowa. Ghonkaba and Casno were surprised and, judging from the reactions of the nation's leaders, so were the Cherokee. Briefly, Wegowa advocated caution, a position for which none of his colleagues were at all prepared.

He was willing to admit that Sevier's regiment would be a powerful ally. He again warned, however, that their foes comprised an overwhelming force. The Cherokee risked losing and being humiliated for all time.

"Perhaps," he suggested, "an all-out war could be avoided." Perhaps the Cherokee could better achieve their ends by maintaining a precarious neutrality. They had won the approval of the Americans without raising their hands in battle, and they might best be able to survive by keeping out of the war. He insisted on reiterating these points.

His arguments were specious, Ghonkaba was convinced, angered by Wegowa's astonishing timidity. Not only was his speech unexpected, but in Ghonkaba's opinion, the conclusions were, without exception, false. The only saving aspect of it was the promise that he added, assuring the council of his readiness to accept its decision, whatever that might be.

Suddenly Ghonkaba was on his feet requesting permission from Loramas. In spite of his self-imposed promise to stay out of the discussion, he felt compelled to make his views known.

"In the war between America and England," he cried passionately, "no neutrality is possible! The Cherokee have done well by themselves in making an alliance with the Americans and have guaranteed themselves a safe and reliable future. If they go back on their word now, they will cause themselves great harm.

125

"Immigration from the British Isles and from the continent of Europe remains heavy on the far side of the mountains. There, most of the many new arrivals settle. They number well over two million persons now, and their number grows very rapidly—already more than in all the Indian nations on the continent. These people are motivated by a passionate love of liberty. That is what has enabled them to make many sacrifices in beginning new lives. They continue to make these sacrifices now that the war is being waged. They fight because they do not want to be ruled by the British, and they fight even while they cope with innumerable hardships. And this is going to bring them victory in the war. No longer is there a question about their success. They are certain to win their freedom from Great Britain."

His listeners nodded, and it appeared that they were greatly impressed.

"It may be that the war here in the West must be postponed until the Americans have troops to spare that they can send across the mountains. But they are certain to win these lands later, if not sooner. Then they will remember their friends, just as they will not forget their enemies!

"I urge you, my new brothers: do not lose the goodwill of the people of America. Stand by your alliance. It will serve the interests of the Cherokee to cooperate with Colonel Sevier and to make war on the treacherous tribes, your own enemies, that ally themselves with the British!"

Having said more than he had intended, Ghonkaba sat down abruptly.

His words were not cheered, but nevertheless they made

CHEROKEE

a deep impression. Speaker after speaker rose to his feet to
concur with his views and to express similar sentiments.

It soon became clear that he had swayed the assemblage
sufficiently to put it squarely in favor of sending an expedition with Sevier. Ghonkaba realized that he should be
pleased that his views had prevailed and that he had won
over the conniving Simpson. He was disturbed, however,
because of the attitude of his first friend among the
Cherokee. Perhaps he had misjudged Wegowa, but he was
seldom badly mistaken in his judgment of character.

That night, Ghonkaba and Toshabe sat up late talking
while drinking gourds of birch beer that she had brewed. A
popular drink with the Seneca, it was finding favor with
her new friends and neighbors.

"Must you go off to war again?" Toshabe asked, melan-
choly but resigned.

"Our unit was fortunate to have the opportunity to make
new homes," Ghonkaba replied. "Most of the Continental
Army has remained on regular duty all this time. Until a
peace treaty is signed, they will be ready to fight. The
least that we Seneca can do is to help out whenever and
wherever we're needed."

"I do not mean to complain," Toshabe said, "but I
have spoken with some of the women, and all feel that the
Cherokee are taking too heavy a burden by going to war
now. Even with the leadership of Colonel Sevier's regiment,
no easy task awaits you."

"I don't know of anything in war that is easy," Ghonkaba

answered. "The manitous have been good to us and now we can repay our debt."

She took a small sip of birch beer. "Which of the children would you take with you?"

"Only Renno. He qualifies to earn his laurels as a senior warrior. El-i-chi should remain here with you."

"He'll be most unhappy," Toshabe said with a faint smile, "but I'll do what I can to help him accept it."

"He must learn patience," his father said. "That's the first attribute of a warrior."

"I'll remember that." Toshabe hesitated. "You have no intention of taking Ena?"

"I do not!" he said emphatically. "I'll grant you that she won distinction for herself in two campaigns and won a commendation from Washington. But I never approved of her going on scouting expeditions. Ena may be superior to most men, but nevertheless, I don't consider an active campaign is any place for her."

"I'll talk to her," Toshabe said, "and I hope I can dissuade her from trying to go."

"Perhaps I'd better have words with her," Ghonkaba said, "and forbid her to come with us."

"Please don't, my dear. You know Ena. I'm sure you realize that you could simply be goading her and forcing her to prove again that she's the equal of any man."

"As I think about it," he said, "I'm sure you're right." He sighed, then added, "Why we should have been burdened with such a contradictory daughter, I don't know. She's unique among all the young females I have ever known of."

"She's *your* daughter," Toshabe answered with a smile. "Remember when your parents shook their heads over you as you now deplore Ena's headstrong ways!"

"At least I was a male, so there was some excuse for me. I feel sorry for the poor warrior who marries her. He'll be stepping into a nest of hornets!"

Ghonkaba was eating breakfast with his family in front of the fireplace when a loud rapping noise sounded at the door, and Loramas entered.

Surprised that the Grand Sachem had come to see him rather than summon him, Ghonkaba was on his feet at once offering hospitality. Toshabe, too, tried to make Loramas welcome.

But the Grand Sachem declined, explaining he had already eaten. "Would you care for a stroll?" he asked Ghonkaba.

Sensing that Loramas wanted to confer with him in private, Ghonkaba quickly agreed. They went out, leaving behind the town and the fields beyond its palisade, and wandered into the forest. Here, Loramas spoke in a soft but distinct voice. "The Seneca have proved beyond any doubt," he said, "that they have no equal as trackers and scouts. They are unique in that realm. The daughter of Ghonkaba demonstrated that she is better than the best of the Cherokee."

Ghonkaba bowed his head to acknowledge the accuracy of Loramas's observation, but he couldn't understand why the Grand Sachem was bringing up such a matter.

"Am I right to assume," Loramas asked, "that you and the other Seneca intend to volunteer your services in the coming campaign?"

"All of us will volunteer," Ghonkaba told him, "and our ranks will be augmented by two newcomers, youths who have come of age. One of them," he added proudly, "is my own son."

"Your company," Loramas said, "achieved renown when you served as scouts for the Continental Army. Would you honor our much smaller corps by performing the same function for us?"

"Nothing would give us greater pleasure," Ghonkaba said. Then as quickly, he added, "Provided, of course, that the commander of the expedition approves."

"I discussed it earlier with Wegowa, and he's eager that the Seneca accept. He asked that I speak to you because he thought that I would have a greater influence and that you'd be more likely to go along with such a request."

"We want to serve where we can do the most good," Ghonkaba said, "and help our forces achieve victory as soon as possible."

The Seneca were pleased to learn they were being given responsibilities of a kind that they performed well. They were confident of their success. Best of all, they had relied on one another for so long that they were thoroughly familiar with everything they would be required to do.

Renno was elated that he had been elevated to the status of an adult and would be given responsibilities expected of a man. Ena, as her parents had anticipated, was thoroughly unhappy and sulked because she had to stay behind.

"I was good enough to work as a scout for the Continentals," she said. "I was good enough so that General Washington asked for me and gave me work to do. I don't see why I'm not good enough to take part in this campaign."

Her father did his best to control his temper. "Washington had a specific need for your talents, and that's why he asked you to serve and exercise those talents."

Before Ena had a chance to reply with still more arguments, they heard a knock at the door. Sent to answer the summons, El-i-chi returned, grinning at his sister as he spoke to his father. "Rusog has come and asked for an audience with you."

"With me?" Ghonkaba was mildly surprised. "Very well."

In the front room, he found that Rusog was tense and anxious to come to the point of his visit. "I have volunteered to take part in the campaign against my nation's ancient enemies."

"Good," Ghonkaba replied. "Then we shall see much of each other in the wilderness."

The young giant held himself erect and his eyes were solemn. "I have come here to seek your permission to visit Ena in the days that remain before we go off into the wilderness. Do I have your approval to court her?"

"Sit down," Ghonkaba ordered, deciding to deal candidly and honestly with the young man. Not particularly surprised by the request, he wanted to clear the air.

"I would have no objection to you as a son-in-law, Rusog," he said. "In fact, I admire the honorable way in which you've conducted yourself. Your behavior has been splendid, in spite of provocation to the contrary. For some time, I have been aware of your interest in Ena. In fact, I would be blind if I had not seen it. But it occurs to me that you may not be aware of the direction in which you're moving. I think you're unprepared for Ena's temperament.''

Rusog was startled and blinked in surprise.

"She is determined to have her way," Ghonkaba continued. "The very concept of compromise is almost unknown to her. It would be impossible to live under the same roof with her if she did not realize that as her father I will tolerate no nonsense. Only that knowledge and the caution she displays in her dealings with me make it possible for me to keep her here. I warn you that Ena can make life hell for a husband who fails to master her completely.''

Rusog listened quietly but then he could not resist boasting. Striking his broad chest, he declared, "If any man is capable of handling Ena, I am that man!''

Her father and suitor were astonished when Ena suddenly appeared in the doorway. She had been engaging in eavesdropping.

She was accompanied by Lyktaw, who spoiled her entrance by going to Ghonkaba to be petted, and then wandering over to Rusog.

"You are right, my father," she declared, "when you say that I respect you. I honor you as I pay honor to all my ancestors. But what you fail to understand is that I am now an adult and have outgrown your direct control. At the risk of my life, I served in the Continental Army, where I was treated as an adult. I insist on being similarly treated by you.''

Before her father had a chance to reply, she turned to Rusog, her hands on her hips, her eyes blazing.

"As for you, sir," she declared with lofty contempt, "you make a laughingstock of yourself when you say that you can handle me. Are you nimble enough to catch the moon in both your hands late in the night as it drops below the surface of the earth? Have you the strength to harness the sun and force it to do your bidding when it rises and changes night into day? Are you man enough, using only a smile and a word, to persuade a maiden to submit to your lovemaking and to climb into your bed with you? The answers are no—and again, no—and again, no!''

Her diatribe would have withered most men, but Rusog courageously tried to stand up to her. Ena gave him no chance.

"I have heard your name mentioned often by the unmarried women of the Bear Clan in this, your land," she went on. "And I'm amused because their opinion of you is the same as mine. You remind them—and me—of a pot of water that boils and emits clouds of steam but serves no useful purpose until all the water has vanished. You are like the scarecrows that stand guard in the fields. You present a massive appearance, but in reality you are empty, a man of sawdust and twigs and dried leaves, who would blow away in a stiff wind." She laughed condescendingly, then turned to leave. Unfortunately, Lyktaw spoiled her exit, just as he had ruined her entrance, by bounding playfully around the room.

She had to call the dog several times before she could sweep out of the room.

Once the hurricane had passed with Ena's departure, Ghonkaba turned to Rusog, intending to apologize for his daughter's conduct.

But Rusog was the first to recover his voice. Clearing his throat, he sounded hoarse and strangely feeble as he said, "I sometimes wonder how much she means when she loses her temper."

Ghonkaba's shrug was eloquent. He had never experienced conduct quite like his daughter's, which had become much more untamed since Clem's death.

"It would be wrong," Rusog said, "for a mere suitor to express himself properly with her and bring her under control. That is a task that must be performed by her husband."

"True," Ghonkaba said, "but the question is, when she is so mean-tempered, how can you—or any other man—achieve the status of husband to her?"

They looked at each other blankly, tacitly admitting that the question was beyond their ability to solve, at least for the moment.

Ghonkaba decided that it was past time for Ena to mend her manners and to be more civil toward Rusog. He and Toshabe detained her for a talk after supper that evening. Ghonkaba's patience was frayed, and consequently he was in no mood for a long, gentle talk. He behaved accordingly, speaking curtly to his daughter. "I find no justification for your harsh treatment of Rusog," he said. "He may have faults, as we all have, but most of them are easy enough to correct, and I see no reason for such cruel treatment of him."

Ena merely sniffed and made no reply.

"In any event," her father continued, "he asked for my permission to pay court to you, and I granted him the right freely. I assume you know that, since you indulged in the unseemly practice of eavesdropping."

"You're wasting your time, mine, and Rusog's," Ena answered, biting off each word. "I wouldn't marry him if he were the last man on earth!"

"Why not?" Ghonkaba demanded. "He's an honorable warrior, his family background is suitable, and he can exhibit great charm. I think you're fortunate to have attracted his interest."

Ena laughed. "He exerts what you call his charm a little too freely for my taste," she replied. "In my opinion, he's a boor, and nothing will change my mind. I cannot stop you, my father, from granting him permission to pay court to me. That is strictly your own affair. But that doesn't mean that I must be receptive to him. This I refuse to do."

She was being so headstrong that Ghonkaba wanted to shake her.

Toshabe felt it necessary to intervene. "I cannot agree with the old Seneca way of doing things," she told her husband. "In the time of your grandfather, his parents would tell him whom he could marry, and he obeyed them. The youths of today have more liberty to make up their own minds. Therefore, it is right that Ena should have a voice in the selection of her husband.''

Ena looked pleased, but Ghonkaba glared at his wife.

Toshabe paid no attention to the reactions of either. ''At the same time, a young woman who recognizes the wisdom of her father and acknowledges that he is a leader of his people should have the sense to listen and to heed his judgments. He may see qualities in a suitor to which she is blind.''

Ghonkaba felt very much relieved. He told himself he should have known that Toshabe would side with him.

Ena bridled. ''You have accepted the word of my father as final in so many matters, my mother, that you have lost your capacity for independent thinking and action. I will tell both of you only this: no power on earth can force me to marry Rusog. No power can compel me to accept him as a suitor. I prefer to stay single for the rest of my days, rather than become his wife!'' Having expressed her views with great vehemence, she stalked out of the room.

Toshabe made certain that her daughter had left the house before she reacted. Then she began to laugh and could not control her mirth.

Ghonkaba was astonished when she said at last, ''I can't tell you how pleased I am by the strong interest in Rusog that Ena is showing.''

Her incredible remark about their daughter's attitude was so bewildering that Ghonkaba deliberately dismissed it from his mind. It was sufficient, he thought, that he knew warfare intimately and was something of an expert on tribal government. In no way, however, could he claim to understand women or the way they thought.

Even though the Cherokee had an illustrious military tradition of their own, they took no particular note of the departure of their warriors for combat. In the land of the Seneca all other activities came to a halt in a town when warriors were ready to march off to war. Old men gathered, young girls made a point of waving at the stalwarts, and the little children and their dogs enjoyed a special holiday.

Five hundred senior warriors were taking part in the expedition, and they left quietly, without fanfare, and without a celebratory atmosphere.

Ghonkaba and Renno said good-bye to Toshabe, Ena, and El-i-chi in the privacy of their home. Toshabe, long accustomed to such farewells, was stoic in the Seneca tradition. Ena was cheerful, almost too cheerful, as Ghonkaba later had cause to recall. Only El-i-chi was sad because he could not go, and his father promised him that his turn would come sooner than he might think.

In a last-minute development, Ghonkaba consented to take Lyktaw, which delighted Renno, who assumed charge of the dog's care. Ena said a long farewell to her pet, and when father and son finally departed, the dog trotted happily at Renno's heels.

The thirteen men of the original Seneca company, augmented by Renno and another young warrior, took their accustomed place at the head of the column. Behind them, the Cherokee, resplendent in their vermilion war paint, gathered under the command of Wegowa.

The force would rendezvous in two days' time with Colonel Sevier's regiment, whom they would meet at a designated place in the forest.

As always, the Seneca carried emergency rations of parched corn and dried strips of venison. The Cherokee preparations were more elaborate; they carried rations of smoked buffalo meat, beans, and other supplies that they could prepare with little effort.

A few of the Cherokee were armed with old-fashioned muskets that fired so inaccurately the Seneca regarded them as virtually useless. The Seneca were armed with the long rifles of the Continental Army. These fired with far greater accuracy than any other firearms yet available. All the warriors of both nations also carried tomahawks and bows and arrows. Some were armed with knives as well.

The Seneca immediately spread out in the forest. Each member was thoroughly aware of his own duties and responsibilities. They traveled at their usual pace, the Seneca trot, which they could maintain for days if necessary. They rapidly outdistanced the Cherokee. Ghonkaba was greatly relieved to be making his way through unknown wilderness again, and he knew that his companions shared his feelings. They were doing what they knew best and were demonstrably superior to any other men in North America in the performance of their duties. They could put behind them all the petty problems of daily living in a strange community and instead devote themselves to military concerns.

Two days after they left their home base, the Cherokee met John Sevier's regiment. The Seneca were the first to make contact. Ghonkaba liked what he could see of the militiamen. Seven hundred and seventy strong, all were woodsmen experienced in wilderness warfare, and none was likely to panic. They knew how to get along in the deep woods and to take care of themselves. Without exception, they were expert riflemen and were familiar, too, with Indian weapons.

By unspoken consent, Sevier took command of the combined units, with Wegowa deferring to the colonel. Sevier followed a practice of keeping his senior unit commanders informed of his plans. He called his own battalion heads and the war chiefs of the Cherokee together as soon as the united expedition got under way. It was strange, Ghonkaba realized, but he had missed such staff meetings since returning to civilian life. Like all veterans of long standing, he found that military existence had become second nature to him.

"I aim to penetrate as far as we can get into the land of the Creek," Sevier announced. "That means we'll be operating in the southern part of this territory, and we'll dip into the new Alabama territory as well. I understand that a large column of Creek and Choctaw is forming somewhere in the region. They're to be joined by token forces of Tuscarora and Seminole as well. They're organizing for the express purpose of attacking the villages of our pioneer settlers. They can have no idea, I'm confident, that we're ready to meet them and to halt them before they even begin their operation."

"How many men is the enemy putting into the field?" one battalion commander asked.

"I'll have to hazard a guess on that and say that they're going to operate with a minimum of fifteen hundred to two thousand effectives, Colonel Bryan," Sevier replied. "After we find them and establish solid contact, Colonel Ghonkaba will be better able to answer your question accurately."

The officers were silent, realizing again how much they would be outnumbered. Their own expedition numbered approximately thirteen hundred men. But Sevier was unworried, Ghonkaba seemed unconcerned, and therefore the more dubious Cherokee took heart.

"Our biggest enemy," Sevier said, "isn't the force of British-supported Indians we're going to meet. It's the time element! Unless they're particularly careless in covering their tracks—which we must doubt—we'll come upon them quite suddenly. When we do meet them, I'm counting on the element of surprise. In other words, we'll launch an attack as rapidly as we can be ready. That means we should be prepared at all times to fight on very short notice. Our entire expedition will pounce in right at the very start, and every man will do his utmost to win a quick victory. If we're compelled to fight a long campaign, we'll be beaten. Our best hope of success lies in winning as decisively and as fast as possible. The Creek have solid reputations as fighting men, but they can be beaten. I see Colonel Ghonkaba agrees with me. Would you care to tell why you feel as you apparently do?"

"The Iroquois," Ghonkaba said readily, "have engaged in combat with many of the most ferocious tribes in all the continent. But we have found that the reputations of those nations often are badly exaggerated—they lack staying power in battle.''

Several of the frontier regiment's officers failed to grasp his meaning, and one asked him to clarify.

''They are fierce,'' he explained, ''and are full of courage and determination when they first attack. But when they are repulsed they lose heart quickly. They seem unable to fight until a balance is restored and they have a chance to renew their assault. When they fail in their first effort, they are ready to flee from the field of combat, to give up the struggle completely, and give the victory to their foes.''

''That's as accurate a description as I've ever heard,'' John Sevier announced, ''and it tells perfectly what's required of us in battle. We've got to hold on and let the enemy wear himself out in his initial assault. If we hold firm, we can turn the tables quickly and with relative ease. And if we persevere, we can drive them from the field.''

''The Seneca,'' Ghonkaba added, ''have the reputation for being invincible in battle, and so they are. They have never lost a single conflict in my lifetime, in the lifetimes of my father, my grandfather, and even my great-grandfather. We have always employed the strategy that Colonel Sevier has just outlined to you.''

''And it's exactly the strategy that we're now called upon to employ,'' Sevier said. ''We must be ready to use it without fail.''

Chapter VI

As they advanced through the strange wilderness, the Seneca enjoyed themselves thoroughly, always keeping slightly ahead of the slower-moving frontier militiamen and the main body of Cherokee. Averaging twelve to fifteen miles a day, about half of the territory they were accustomed to covering, they saw no sign of Creek, Choctaw, or any other tribe.

The forest was thick with game, and the Seneca became the hunters for the entire expedition, bringing down enough deer with their bows to feed both the regiment and the Cherokee. Ghonkaba forbade the use of rifles in order to avoid calling attention to their presence.

Members of the little company invariably saved some of the choicest cuts of venison for themselves. Each night

143

they feasted on the steaks and on the wild roots and berries that they had collected during the day.

Ghonkaba shared the bounty, usually eating supper with Casno and Ranoga, his deputies. A few days passed before he discovered something out of the ordinary in the behavior of his band. When he visited their campfires, they seemed inclined to be secretive and withdrawn. They were not purposely avoiding him but instead acted distinctly uncomfortable in his presence. He thought of mentioning the matter to Renno until he realized that Renno, too, was acting exactly as were the others. For a time, he wondered if his own imagination was playing tricks on him. Finally deciding that his complaint was legitimate, he mentioned it one night to Casno and Ranoga.

Casno showed genuine bewilderment. But Ranoga surprised Ghonkaba by reacting as the other Seneca were behaving. He became withdrawn and appeared thoroughly uncomfortable.

Ghonkaba's face remained bland, his eyes veiled, and he said nothing. He seemed to be waiting patiently for Ranoga to speak.

It became so quiet that the crackle of their little cooking fire sounded like a roar.

Ranoga could not tolerate the silence. "The fault is not mine, Ghonkaba," he said, "although I acknowledge that as her first teacher in the art of scouting, I certainly must share the blame."

"I don't know what you're talking about," Ghonkaba replied stiffly.

"He speaks of Ena, your daughter," Casno said.

144

A terrible suspicion rose within Ghonkaba and threatened to choke him. "Where is she?" he demanded.

"I don't know for certain," Ranoga replied. "I assume, however, that she's somewhere in the forest beyond your vision, and that she's eating supper there."

Ghonkaba used great willpower to quiet himself so he could speak with a semblance of calm. "Fetch her," he commanded. "I wish to see her at once!"

Ranoga rose to his feet, and his manner attracted the attention of the other members of the company, who sat nearby at their own campfires. They seemed to understand immediately that the secret was out, and they showed varying degrees of apprehension and guilt.

Casno laughed unhappily. "Look yonder," he said. "You and I appear to be the only ones who weren't sharing the secret."

Ghonkaba raised his head and looked past two campfires, where his gaze happened to meet that of his son. Renno was staring at his father surreptitiously, his manner extremely uncomfortable. When he realized that Ghonkaba was looking at him, he ducked his gaze and seemed to freeze.

Ena appeared at the end of the little clearing and walked toward her father. She carried herself with her chin high in the air, her shoulders held back as she looked defiantly at him, her green eyes blazing. She wore her hair in two thick braids that fell forward over her shoulders. She was wearing a buckskin shirt, trousers, and moccasins, as were the men, and she was armed like them. In one hand, she carried a rifle; a quiver of arrows and a bow were slung over one shoulder; a tomahawk was in her belt. Lyktaw bounded beside her, happily unaware of the trouble in which his mistress now was involved.

Casno withdrew discreetly, leaving Ghonkaba alone to face his daughter.

Young Renno started to rise, apparently intending to support his sister if he could, but he changed his mind and wisely kept his distance.

Showing no fear, although it was evident that some of her self-confidence was deserting her, Ena headed straight for her father. Ghonkaba had to admire her unflinching courage as he regarded her stonily.

"I offer no excuse for my conduct," she said. "I knew I would be denied permission to take part in this campaign, so I planned from the beginning to join the company in secret. I take full responsibility for the silence that your warriors have shown. All have kept their pledge to me."

Ghonkaba spoke for the first time. "I wish," he said icily, "that they would demonstrate the same loyalty to me that you command from them."

"I know my capabilities, and I have amply demonstrated them in the past. They require no further words from me. I was eager to contribute to this expedition and to the victory that I feel certain we shall win."

"You are a female, not a warrior," Ghonkaba told her coldly. "Your place is at home. And I feel it necessary to say to you that your conduct has been no less immature or boorish than that of Rusog, whom you scorn and deride."

"It was my urgent desire," she said, "to do what no one else is capable of doing in this campaign. I have not

146

forgotten that, although I am only a female, General Washington said that I am the equal of any warrior.''

Ghonkaba decided that a change of tactics might help to overcome his daughter's superficiality. ''You have been critical of Rusog,'' he said. ''The cause of your contempt is that he behaves impetuously, like a junior warrior who has not learned the meaning of responsibility.''

His changed approach almost succeeded. He saw doubt creep into Ena's eyes, and she hesitated for a time, moved by his words. Then her stubborn nature reasserted itself and her icy glare returned.

''I see no comparison,'' she said, ''between my conduct and that of Rusog. He behaves like a fool, but I am sensible.''

''The rebellion that is part of your makeup is natural to you,'' Ghonkaba said in one more effort to counter her. ''When I was your age, I, too, was a rebel. I caused great concern for my parents before I decided to change my ways. I have an understanding of the way you must feel.''

Ena was in no mood to compromise, to meet her father halfway. ''My feelings are irrelevant,'' she said coolly. ''The one thing that matters is my duty, as I see it, and my duty is clear.''

Ghonkaba rose to his feet. He should have known better than to enter into an argument with her, because she always managed to get the last word. ''Wait here,'' he said. ''You are confined to the company's bivouac area until I return.''

For the first time, she showed apprehension. ''Where are you going?''

"To decide your fate," her father told her, and left the area to make his way to the tent of Colonel Sevier in the nearby regimental encampment.

Ghonkaba saw that Sevier was still at supper and that with him was Wegowa. It was just as well, Ghonkaba thought. He would have to explain his dilemma only once. He went straight to their campfire and apologized for his intrusion.

"Not at all," Sevier said cordially. "Sit down and have a plate with us."

"I've already finished my supper, thank you," Ghonkaba said. "I've come to relate a discovery that I find extremely upsetting and distasteful."

The frontiersman and the Cherokee war chief both stared in surprise.

He went on to relate that his daughter had joined the expedition without his knowledge, acting as a scout since the beginning of the campaign with the protective silence of all members of the scouting company.

Colonel Sevier chuckled and slapped his leg. "Durned if that doesn't sound like some of the stories I been told about her in the Continental Army," he exclaimed. "Seems like she's one female in a million!"

"Never have I known a woman like her," Wegowa said.

"I hesitate to let her travel alone through the wilderness for many days," Ghonkaba said, "but I can hope that, since the land we've crossed was empty of enemies, it will stay that way so Ena will be unmolested as she makes her way back."

Sevier looked at him in consternation. "You're sending her home?" he demanded.

"I have no choice, Johnny," Ghonkaba replied. "She's a fine scout, but she is a female and we're at war!"

Sevier spoke more softly and his tone became cajoling. "We need every advantage in this campaign that we can possibly scrape together," he said. "Who knows how much good she can do us? Washington told me she was the equal of a whole regiment of scouts. Maybe she can be influential in tipping the balance in our favor for this campaign. The good Lord knows we need all the help we can get. I can't order you to let your daughter stay, of course, but I appeal to you to give serious consideration to my request."

"I agree with Colonel Sevier," Wegowa said. "I am not trying to interfere with your authority as a father, but I saw the miraculous tracking she is capable of doing. Since she has come all this distance with us I urge you to let her remain."

Ghonkaba was stunned by their attitude, feeling that the ground had been cut from beneath his feet.

Promising only that he would do what he regarded as best for Ena and for the expedition, he took his leave and went slowly back to his own bivouac area, his mind whirling. What worried him more than anything else was the prospect of sending Ena alone through the wilderness. He could not afford to spare an escort to accompany her, and he realized he would be taking a terrible risk by sending her alone.

The prospect of finding an alternative strongly appealed

to him. She could prove useful to the expedition inasmuch as she had joined it, and it was equally true that she was far safer here than she would be alone in the wilds.

By the time he arrived at his bivouac, he had made up his mind. Ena was still standing where he had left her, and he noted at once that his warriors were still subdued. Only Lyktaw showed any evidence of pleasure; he raced to Ghonkaba, jumping up and putting forepaws on him as he wagged his tail. Ghonkaba responded by scratching the dog behind the ears. Of all the members of the scouting company, Lyktaw would be happiest when Ghonkaba's decision became known.

Taking care to avoid looking in the direction of either his son or his daughter because his expression might give away his decision prematurely, Ghonkaba said curtly to Casno, "Assemble the company."

All the Seneca heard him, and all automatically obeyed without the need for Casno to repeat the order. Glancing around the gathering, Ghonkaba noted that Ena was standing next to Renno, who almost concealed her.

"Ranoga," he said, "add the name of Ena to the roster and put her name on the list for rations. It no longer will be necessary for members of the company to sacrifice some portion of their food for her. She can eat her own."

Although the Seneca were noted for being wooden-faced in moments of emotional drama and stress, the men now grinned broadly, and the tense spell was broken.

"Casno," Ghonkaba went on, "be good enough to include Ena in your schedule of scouts hereafter. She'll be added to the daytime list, but she will not participate in any operations after dark.''

''Yes, sir,'' Casno replied crisply.

''The company is dismissed,'' Ghonkaba said. ''Ena, I want a word with you.''

The men scattered, and Ena came forward slowly, expecting to be severely chastised. Her brother accompanied her.

Ghonkaba looked at Renno. ''I was unaware that you were invited to attend a private conference,'' he said.

The young warrior stifled a sigh, and looking at his sister, he withdrew, his expression showing that he had tried to stand by.

''Sit down,'' Ghonkaba said. Ena sat.

''I am well aware,'' Ghonkaba went on, ''of your desire to make a contribution to our cause to the best of your abilities in a military campaign. I sympathize with that feeling, and I applaud it. At the same time, I must deplore your lack of military discipline. The first rule of any warrior is to obey the orders of a superior without question. You were told to remain at home with your mother. You deliberately disobeyed. You placed me in an untenable position. I'm not able to send you back because that would involve your traveling alone through long stretches of wilderness. I have no idea if the enemy has sent braves to follow our force, and I cannot risk your life in finding out. Consequently, it is necessary to keep you with us. As long as you're going to accompany us, you will do your utmost as a scout, with no favors being shown.''

Ena knew that she deserved the harsh rebuke. ''I

understand, sir," she said. "I'm truly sorry I disobeyed you, Colonel, and I'll try to make it up to you by my conduct in the field."

Ghonkaba was reminded of his own behavior at his daughter's age. As he had tried to point out to her, he, too, had been a rebel who had caused great hardship and heartache to his father. It had taken him many years to live down his past and win his promotion to war chief.

"All that I ask of you," he said, "is that you make my burden lighter, if you can, rather than compound it."

"I shall do my best," she replied, reflecting that she had never felt more abashed. She had won her own way in a battle of wills with Ghonkaba, but she could not help but feel ashamed. She had regarded her contest with him as a game, and in the past had always felt delighted when she had "won," but today all that was changed. She saw clearly that she had added to his responsibilities and his worries, and she wished she could do something to relieve him; at the moment, she knew of nothing. She had willed herself into a combat situation, and she had no choice now but to follow it through and do her best to serve her father and the Cherokee.

She preferred now to avoid Renno's company and went off to a nearby place in the forest where she could be alone. Her brother might think of her as a heroine, but she didn't feel like one.

Brushing a pile of leaves from a boulder, Ena sat on the stone, glad to be alone, relieved to have the opportunity to straighten out her thinking. She soon was lost in thought.

After some time, she heard heavy footsteps approaching

and automatically reached for her rifle. Then, as she realized that the sound came from behind her from the direction of the Seneca and Cherokee camp, she relaxed and let her rifle stay on the stone. In due time, Rusog came into view, his face a study in concentrated concern.

Ena neither called out to him nor raised a hand in greeting. She knew she was being unnecessarily rude to him, but her father's criticism, comparing her conduct with Rusog's, still smarted, and as she looked at the Cherokee her hostility almost overwhelmed her.

"I wanted to make certain that you are all right," he said simply, and with evident sincerity.

Ena wanted to reply mockingly but refrained. She owed it to Ghonkaba to make his task easier rather than more difficult, so she kept her temper in check and addressed Rusog with polite civility.

"Yes," she replied. "I joined the column soon after its departure. I've been in advance of the warriors ever since. You're marching with the main body of foot soldiers?" she asked.

He nodded. "I am. In fact," he went on with no bragging in his voice, "I'm an acting war chief while the head of our division recovers from a tooth that had to be removed from his head." Ordinarily, he would have boasted loudly to her, but today he spoke softly and claimed no credit for his temporary promotion.

In spite of herself, Ena was impressed. She knew that as a leader Wegowa was much like Ghonkaba and that he would go out of his way to make Rusog earn any advancement. Therefore, she concluded, Rusog must be a talented fighting man. To be awarded even a temporary post as a war chief before he reached the age of thirty summers was an accomplishment that not many Indians achieved. He had every right to be proud.

She was surprised to hear herself say, "I congratulate you on your advancement."

"It's a temporary promotion at best," he announced quite modestly. "I'll be moved back to my usual rank when the gods relent and relieve the pain that my war chief is suffering. Besides, I wouldn't be able to keep the position in any event. Another task, far more important, awaits me."

"What is that?" Ena asked.

Rusog shifted his weight again and again from one foot to the other. "I intend to go to our principal war chief this very night and petition him to release me from my duties. There's a special task that I am eager to perform." He swallowed hard, then his face burned as he added, "I'm going to ask Colonel Ghonkaba to appoint me as a special guard to stand watch over you."

Ena, appalled, ordinarily would have let him know, in no uncertain terms, how she felt, but she was mindful of her pledge to herself to make her father's burden easier. Because of this, and for another reason that she did not quite understand, she decided to deal leniently with the Cherokee giant.

"I greatly appreciate your regard for me, but I can't accept the assistance that you offer. If I'm to perform ably as a scout, I must be free to go where I please, when I please, and I can't have a bodyguard trailing me through the wilderness. I'm indebted to you for your concern, though, and I thank you for it.''

"It's wrong for you to run such grave risks with your safety!" he said in alarm.

Ena smiled and shook her head. "The Cherokee should know better than anyone else that women are as strong and as resilient as men. In your nation, women are as important as braves, and they take risks every day. If you take a chance on losing your life in combat for the sake of your nation, I have the right to run that risk for the same reason. I don't lack courage, and I'm convinced that our gods are watching over me, just as you depend on your gods for your safety.''

Rusog was as bewildered by her attitude as he was confused by her arguments. Never had he encountered such a contrary woman who was the equal of any man in what was exclusively a warrior's activity.

"If you change your mind," he said, "and decide that you want my help, all you need to do is ask, and I'll be there. I would very much prefer to guard you in the wilderness than to march with my own unit.''

Ena knew he was sincere. She could not help but feel sorry for him and impulsively reached out and touched his arm. "Thank you, Rusog," she said softly. "I appreciate your offer more than I can tell you.''

He reacted almost as though he had been struck by lightning. Rubbing his arm where she had touched him, he looked at her, so overcome that he was robbed of the power of speech.

Ena could see how much he was in love with her, and

she was glad that she was treating him with kindness rather than with the usual scorn. She had no desire to be cruel, and she hoped that he would recover from his infatuation.

In the meantime, she was free to continue openly with her scouting, and she was pleased that she would have no interference. As to the possibility that her relationship with Rusog could become more complicated, such an idea did not enter her mind.

At the end of each day, the scouts—except for those on night duty—gathered to prepare their evening meal. Ghonkaba's habit was to meet individually and jointly with his men at this time to learn whatever they might have to report. Even a total lack of information about the enemy could be significant.

Immediately thereafter, while his supper was cooking, he went to the rear and reported the various findings and conclusions to Colonel Sevier and to Wegowa. He sometimes found them together, but more likely each in his own headquarters.

One night, when he reported to Wegowa, the war chief acted strangely, as had been the case on frequent recent occasions.

He heard Ghonkaba's report in silence, nodding occasionally, but withholding comment.

Ghonkaba sensed a distinct hostility in the Cherokee war chief's attitude. He seemed withdrawn and indifferent to what he was hearing. When Ghonkaba finished his report,

Wegowa turned away and began to speak in an undertone to one of his own warriors.

Feeling rebuffed, Ghonkaba returned to his bivouac area, trying to figure out what had changed Wegowa's feelings toward him.

He found Casno roasting a venison steak over a small fire and cooking a pot of vegetables. Sitting cross-legged near the fire, Ghonkaba waited for his comrade to finish preparing the meal. Searching his mind with care, he tried in vain to think of any way he might have insulted Wegowa.

When the meal was ready, Casno offered a prayer to the manitous, asking for their continued guidance and protection. Then he and Ghonkaba ate in silence for some minutes, and as they finished, Casno could no longer control his curiosity.

"Something is troubling my friend," he said.

"You are right," Ghonkaba replied. "I am indeed sorely vexed."

"What is it that upsets you?"

Ghonkaba hesitated and then decided to tell the whole story.

"Ever since we have come to the land of the Cherokee," he said, "it has been my conviction that Wegowa is my friend and my brother. But his conduct toward me has become very strange of late. Every evening when I report on the scouts' activities, he seems to lack all interest in my words. He is indifferent and in fact treats me with great rudeness. Only because he is the commander of this army am I willing to tolerate his behavior."

Casno was not surprised. "I have been wondering how

long it would be," he said, "before you awakened to this. You will recall our surprise when he advocated extreme caution in the Cherokee council."

"Then you, too, are aware that something is amiss!" Ghonkaba exclaimed.

"Yes," Casno told him. "I have known of his estrangement ever since we left."

"Then perhaps you know the reasons?"

"I do," Casno said. "They are as plain as his conduct itself."

"They're not so plain to me!"

"Wegowa," Casno explained, "is the second-ranking member of the Cherokee hierarchy. His father is Grand Sachem, and as the principal warrior he stands next in line. Presumably, he will succeed his father when the time comes."

"What has that to do with me?"

"Have patience and listen! In a meeting so strange that it won the approval of the gods of both nations," Casno declared, "Wegowa met the grandson of the most famous warrior of all Indian nations in the past one hundred years. There, in the flesh, was the inheritor of the mantle of the great Renno. Not only that, but Ghonkaba had won fame in his own right. He had served with great distinction as a scout for General Washington and had won the rank of lieutenant colonel in the Continental Army. Keep in mind, if you will, that the Cherokee have been at peace with other Indian nations, with the United States, and with Great Britain for many years. They maintain a precarious relationship with the Creek and Choctaw, engaging in only limited warfare with those tribes. They have sided with the Americans, but they are not so involved that they have had to fight the British or their allies. Wegowa is the commander of this expedition, yet he never has been tried in combat. From the oldest Cherokee warrior to the newest junior warriors tasting battle for the first time—all are familiar with the exploits of Ghonkaba. They look up to him. At the same time, they know their own war chief is as new to combat as they themselves are. They have no cause to pay him respect.''

"But I am not Wegowa's rival,'' Ghonkaba protested. "I have no desire to supplant him as the head of this army. Nor do I hope to become the principal warrior of the Cherokee. What I cannot see,'' he added passionately, "is how I can be seen as a rival of Wegowa when I would refuse his positions if they were offered to me!''

"You know this to be a fact,'' Casno told him, "but Wegowa does not know it. Whether he would accept the truth from you, I cannot say.''

"Then I must reach him,'' Ghonkaba said. "I must go to him and explain my position, and in that way I shall clear up this unfortunate misunderstanding that has risen between us.''

For seventy-two hours, Ghonkaba tried in vain to see Wegowa alone. The Cherokee war chief seemed to have sensed that the Seneca desired confidential discussion, and then to have made up his mind that no such talk should take place. Not knowing what Ghonkaba had in mind, he was stubbornly avoiding the possibility of real communication between them. At least two of Wegowa's lieutenants were with him at all times. He took pains to keep them on hand.

Finally, after doing his best to arrange a meeting for three days and nights, Ghonkaba grew tired and stopped trying.

"I'm sorry," he told Casno, "but Wegowa is determined not to meet me alone. My dignity makes it impossible for me to beg him, and I must therefore abandon my efforts."

"Put your faith in the manitous," Casno advised, "and trust them to guide you in the right direction. If it is their wish that you meet with Wegowa, they will arrange for it in spite of his attempts to evade you. But if they have reasons for deeming it best that you do not confer, then you can be sure that it will not come about. Do as they say, follow in their footsteps, and all will go well with you!"

Accompanied by Lyktaw, her shepherd dog, Ena began her scouting duties at sunup every day. She worked steadily until sunset, scouring the wilderness in advance of the main army and leaving no territory uncovered. Like the other Seneca scouts, she had found no evidence of enemies, but that only encouraged her to do a thorough job, making sure she did not overlook key evidence.

Early one afternoon, when she was least expecting it, Ena stumbled across signs of the presence of a large enemy force. On the far side of a little river she saw many footprints leading away from the water in the soft clay earth of the riverbank. The telltale prints extended for more than twenty yards along the river. Whoever had been there had removed their moccasins but had made no attempt to obliterate the footprints.

Ranging up and down the river quietly while Lyktaw walked in the water behind her, Ena efficiently gathered information about the size and identity of the enemy force. Some facts were clear to her, others required intuitive deductions, and a few were impossible to understand. Nevertheless, she returned to the bivouac area for the night with much more information than anyone else had uncovered.

Reporting to Ghonkaba and Casno, she described the evidence in a dry, unemotional voice.

"This afternoon," she said, "I found solid evidence of a war party of at least fifty Creek between two and a half and three miles from our main force." She explained that she had found the footprints leading away from the river and running parallel to the direction taken by Colonel Sevier and Wegowa.

Ghonkaba was immediately alert. "Were they scouts?" he asked.

She shook her head. "The best that I can determine is that they were warriors belonging to the main body of the Creek force," she said. "Scouts would have avoided leaving their footprints in the riverbank. Only a body of warriors so confident that they became careless would make a mistake of that sort. When I say fifty warriors, I estimate that as a minimum. I counted forty to fifty different sets of footprints in the mud. There could have been many more, but they were obliterated by those in the rear. The reason I believe them to have been made by the Creek is because no other nearby nation has had their success in combat in recent years. Their victories have made them careless. Therefore, they did not remove the prints after they crossed the river. The Choctaw, the Seminole, and certainly the Tuscarora would have exercised greater caution.''

"Your reasoning is sound,'' Ghonkaba told her. "Come along and tell the high command what you've found. Supper can wait.''

He took her to the headquarters of Colonel Sevier, who summoned his own principal officers as well as the leaders of the Cherokee force. Then, at his request, Ena repeated her story and the reasoning behind her deductions.

Her listeners were impressed by the conciseness of her report, and Colonel Sevier asked, "Would you say that this force of Creek is sufficiently large to try us in combat in the immediate future?''

"You're asking me to deduce the intentions of the enemy based on my limited findings. I'm afraid, sir, that I can't do that. I can't go beyond the actual evidence that I unearthed.''

Although Sevier appreciated her candor, he was distressed by her unwillingness to guess what might be the intentions of the Creek. To him, the war plans of the enemy were of paramount interest. "Ghonkaba,'' he asked, "do you have an opinion?''

Ghonkaba knew precisely what Sevier wanted to learn. "In my opinion, Colonel,'' he said, "we should be prepared to take action with our entire force at any time. The Creek are not known for large-scale maneuvers unless they're prepared to do battle at once. I suspect they're ready for hostilities without warning. We'd do well to be prepared to respond if we encounter the warriors whose presence Ena uncovered.''

The militia's battalion commanders and the leaders of the Cherokee agreed heartily with his estimate of the outlook. They decided to put the entire expedition on combat alert.

As father and daughter returned to their own area, Ghonkaba said, ''It may be that you'd be wise to remain at headquarters tomorrow rather than take your regular turn on a scouting mission.''

''Why is that?''

''For the same reason that I gave to the command. It could be that the Creek are preparing to attack. If they do, our scouts will be the first to feel their sting.''

''That is all the more reason, then, that I should take my regular duty,'' Ena declared quietly.

Her father sighed and made no further attempt to persuade her. He realized she had made up her mind and that nothing would stop her from taking her regular place with the scouts.

Ena ate a breakfast of strips of smoked venison and corn bread that had been cooked at suppertime the previous evening, then she and the other members of the daytime watch spread out in the thick forest ahead of the army. As usual, Ena took the extreme position on the left flank.

Accompanied by Lyktaw, she made good time through the underbrush and was faintly annoyed when the dog halted several times and turned to growl at something behind them.

"Behave yourself, Lyktaw!" she whispered urgently. "No one is behind us except our own army. We're searching for signs of enemies up ahead."

In spite of her warning, Lyktaw continued to growl at intervals throughout the morning, but she paid little attention to him. Then, as noon approached, a crisis arose suddenly and swiftly.

Ena caught a glimpse of a Creek warrior, his black war paint heavy on his face and torso, lying in wait for her directly ahead. To make the situation even more ominous, she realized that a second warrior was in the underbrush to her left and a third could be distinguished in the thick foliage on the other side. She was virtually surrounded and badly outnumbered.

Like all Seneca on scouting duty, she was armed only with her tomahawk and a long double-edged knife. A bow would impede a scout's ability to make swift progress.

She knew that she had to act swiftly and decisively. Drawing her tomahawk, she measured the distance to the Creek warrior ahead and let fly. Her aim was perfect and the brave crumpled to the ground, her tomahawk in his forehead.

She had only one knife to deal with both of her remaining opponents. Lyktaw looked ready to spring at the brave in the underbrush to the left. Knowing that he would never survive the attack, being an easy target for the Creek's bow, she murmured, "Don't move, Lyktaw!" The dog obeyed reluctantly. The Creek on her right, creeping forward through the foliage, called to his companion.

Ena was able to make out enough of what he said to realize that he had identified her as a woman. That could mean, instead of killing her, they intended to capture her and take her back to their own camp. She could imagine the treatment she would receive.

Should she throw her knife at the brave on her left or at the one who was moving closer on her right? She knew, too, that only the knife prevented her capture. The Creek braves were keeping their distance because of it; once it left her hand, she would be helpless. Even if she dealt with one of them successfully, the other would be able to subdue her.

She also recognized the danger that she would be unable to continue to control Lyktaw, who was showing signs of restlessness. At any moment, he might hurl himself forward, thereby making himself a perfect target for an arrow.

Ena heard a faint crackling noise in the brush behind her. The first thought that crossed her mind was that a fourth enemy was approaching her from that direction. If so, all was lost.

She half turned for a moment, glancing back over her shoulder. She thought she must be dreaming when she caught a glimpse of Lyktaw, who was now wagging his tail furiously. Then she could see Rusog crawling forward through the foliage. He raised one finger to his lips in an unnecessary precautionary gesture.

In an instant, her outlook had changed from one of utter

helplessness to one in which she could hope for survival. She no longer felt independent or proud of her ability to handle any problem alone. She was relieved beyond measure that Rusog had followed her and had come to her side in a dire situation.

To divert the attention of the two Creek, she brandished the knife in broad gestures as though testing it before throwing. The warriors crouched lower, waiting until she made her move. She knew that as soon as the knife left her hand they would rush her.

Lying prone, Rusog fitted an arrow into his bow, took aim, and fired at the brave on the right. His aim was true. The arrow pierced the man's chest, and he screamed loudly with a bloodcurdling cry before he died.

The other warrior, bewildered, still had not seen Rusog. He brought up his own bow as if to fire, but it was too late. Rusog fired once more, and again his arrow found its mark. The Creek braves had been done away with; the immediate peril was past. Rusog raised himself to one knee. "Are you all right?" he called.

"Yes, I—I think so," Ena replied breathlessly. Lyktaw was wagging his tail violently, and she patted him. Lyktaw raced to Rusog.

"Let's get this job finished. What do you say, dog?" he asked, and moving forward, he expertly lifted the scalps of the three Creek. Then, wiping off his knife in the grass before returning it to his belt, he said to Ena, "Come along!"

"Where? Where are you taking me?" she asked.

"I'm returning you to your father's camp," he said

flatly, his tone one that would tolerate no argument. "You've had enough scouting for one day."

She opened her mouth to reply, but his manner deterred her. She couldn't define it, but nevertheless she knew better than to dispute him. He had saved her life, after all, and it would be wrong, she felt, to become embroiled in an argument with him.

They started toward the rear together, with Lyktaw running beside them. Suddenly Rusog halted.

"Here!" he said, handing her the three blood-smeared scalps. "I took these for you."

Ena shook her head. "No," she protested, "they're yours."

"You disposed of one of them before I arrived. As for the other two, your playacting made it possible for me to kill them. All three scalps belong to you and to no one else."

His generosity touched her deeply. "My conscience," she said, "does not permit me to accept symbols of prowess that I have not earned. Besides," she added demurely, "it is not seemly for a maiden of the Seneca to boast of her skills in battle. That is the right and prerogative only of the brave."

Rusog's lack of familiarity with the customs of the Seneca made it impossible for him to argue with her—as Ena knew it would. While he tried to fashion a suitable reply, Ena tried to end the discussion. "Not only do you deserve to keep those scalps," she said, "but you've also earned my eternal gratitude. I'll never forget that my life was in grave danger. And that only because you defied all custom and followed me am I still alive. Thank you, Rusog!''

He realized she meant every word, and he was so overcome that he reacted just as she had hoped. He fell silent, and neither of them spoke again until they reached Ghonkaba and Casno, who were walking toward them through the forest. Ghonkaba was astonished to see them together.

"I fell into an ambush of three Creek braves," Ena said, giving neither Rusog nor her father the opportunity to speak first. "I took care of one, but the other two were ready to take me prisoner. When Rusog appeared, he outsmarted them and killed them both. I owe my life to him."

Rusog's modest nod confirmed her words.

Ghonkaba and Casno first busied themselves sending two runners out. One went forward to notify the other scouts that three enemy warriors had been sighted and killed. Meanwhile, the other runner was sent to the rear to tell Colonel Sevier and Wegowa, so they could put their fighting men on an immediate alert.

Only then was it time to turn to personal concerns.

"Thank you," Ghonkaba said to Rusog, "for keeping watch over Ena and for returning her safely. I am very greatly indebted for your concern."

Realizing that Rusog was essentially a shy man, Ena favored him with a broad smile. Deeply embarrassed, Rusog shifted his weight uncomfortably. Her unexpected warmth, together with her unexpected humility, proved almost too much for him. Losing his poise completely, he backed away and soon disappeared as he departed to return to his own unit.

Ena stared at the place where he had last been visible. A half smile was on her lips, her expression unfathomable.

Ghonkaba had no interest, at least at the moment, in what his daughter might be feeling. "You will remain with me," he instructed her.

Though being demoted from her post as a scout, she made no objection. In fact, admitting the truth with reluctance, she knew that she had experienced such a narrow escape that she was genuinely glad to accept the protection her father offered.

She assumed new duties meekly, and although the responsibility was minor, she did her best to fulfill her obligations satisfactorily. It was well to know that she was safe, and for the present, at least, would suffer no harm.

As the day wore on, scouts sent word back to Ghonkaba with increasing frequency that they had sighted Creek patrols.

An unsettling new element was added when two scouts began to report sighting sentry outposts of the Tuscarora. In the North, some Tuscarora had become members of the Iroquois League, and consequently, were allies of the Seneca. But most of the Tuscarora nation had remained in the South, completely independent of the northern brethren. This nation had been the first major Indian tribe of the area to enter into an alliance with Great Britain. The Seneca of Ghonkaba's unit regarded the southern Tuscarora with contempt, even though the nation had achieved a respectable reputation as fighting men.

Late in the afternoon, Ghonkaba received a definitive message from Ranoga, the most experienced of his scouts: "I have located the main camp of the enemy!"

Notifying Ranoga to keep the foe under surveillance, Ghonkaba immediately informed Sevier and Wegowa. When they moved forward to join him, along with several of their lieutenants, he took the lead in guiding them toward Ranoga's forward position. The little party, including Casno and Ena, advanced rapidly for three miles. Approaching the crest of a high bluff, they traveled the final short distance on their hands and feet to avoid being seen by the enemy below.

Night was beginning to fall before they reached the forward edge of the bluff. As they looked down they could make out the war paint of the warriors in the valley, where cooking fires were being lighted. The scouts and officers stared down in silence as they watched the activities.

Ghonkaba busied himself in making an estimate of the enemy's strength; he counted the Creek totals three times, first noting the number of fires and then adding the tents that he could count on the plain. A stream separated the Creek from the adjoining Tuscarora. They were fewer in number than the Creek, and he had little problem in figuring out their strength.

Then, at Ghonkaba's signal, the group retraced its steps, crawling back until they had reached a safe distance before rising to their feet. They did not pause until they came to the bivouac the Seneca had established for the night.

Ghonkaba's company had refrained from lighting any fires for fear of giving away their position, so they were eating the customary Seneca prebattle meal of smoked venison and parched corn. Ghonkaba led the way to his tent, and his companions seated themselves in a circle on the ground outside.

Sevier, as the commander, was the first to speak. "What was your estimate of enemy strength, Ghonkaba?"

"I always estimate the size of an enemy generously," Ghonkaba said. "I would say that the Creek have about one thousand warriors and the Tuscarora could put perhaps half as many braves into combat."

"In brief," Sevier said, "your guess is that they can go into battle with fifteen hundred men. That's a shade higher than I figured it. But as you say, it's wiser to give them the benefit of the doubt."

Sevier looked troubled, and Ghonkaba shared his concern. Both knew that the frontier regiment and the Cherokee numbered no more than thirteen hundred men, and Sevier probably could put even fewer into battle. They were outnumbered by a margin too great to ignore.

Ena, present as an observer rather than as a participant, noted that both of Sevier's battalion commanders looked disturbed, as did several of the Cherokee war chiefs.

Only Wegowa appeared unworried. Ena could not comprehend the cause of his apparent unconcern, but he saw the developments as his chance to escape from the spell that he felt Ghonkaba had cast over him. He would be able to prove to his people that he was a warrior as courageous as Ghonkaba, a leader as inspired. He would be demonstrating his valor and cunning in battle when Ghonkaba was also participating. He felt confident that the comparison would silence the Seneca's admirers and enhance his own stature.

"I see no need for concern," Wegowa said. "My braves—acting alone—can easily defeat the so-called warriors of the Creek and the Tuscarora who have gathered here. I will gladly meet them in combat and send them fleeing from the field. But no matter how they run away, they shall not escape my vengeance. Before I am through, they will be reunited with their ancestors."

Everyone present stared at him in silence. Even his own war chiefs looked at him as though he had been robbed of his reason. Ena was shocked beyond words. To her, Wegowa's reasoning made no sense: not even Seneca veterans, the greatest warriors in all of North America, would choose to go into battle against a force several times their size.

Sevier was in an untenable position and realized it. His authority over Wegowa was limited. In theory, as commander in chief of the expedition, he had the last word, but the Cherokee were not really reporting to him. Instead, they were merely consenting to associate with him. If they happened to dislike any role assigned to them, they could— even now on the eve of battle—walk away from the alliance and go home. They would not be censured by other Indians; on the contrary, they would be much admired for it. With this in mind, Sevier chose his words diplomatically.

"I honor the readiness of the principal war chief of the Cherokee to face the enemy unassisted," he said, "but I am unable to accept his generosity. I am pleased to know that his warriors thirst for the blood of the Creek and Tuscarora. But my troops also are eager to achieve a victory. With regret, I find that it is necessary to decline his offer.''

The tension in the circle eased, but Wegowa, plainly unhappy, quickly made it evident that he did not intend to accept Sevier's decision. He cleared his throat and started to rise to his feet in order to reply.

But Ghonkaba outmaneuvered him. Jumping to his feet first, he then spoke deliberately.

''I agree completely with the wise words that Colonel Sevier has spoken,'' he said. ''The unbreakable policy of the Seneca is to avoid splitting their forces when they are planning to attack. The cardinal rule is to use every available warrior of all allies at such a time. This is particularly true when outnumbered. If any of our forces suffer a defeat at this stage of the campaign, the whole campaign is lost and so is the war. Colonel Sevier is correct. The Cherokee should not attack the Creek and Tuscarora unaided. Rather, they should share with the colonel's frontier regiment the burden and responsibility—and the glory of their forthcoming victory.''

As he sat down, he could see nods of agreement around the circle. Virtually all his listeners seemed to accept his reasoning.

Wegowa was determined to allow no dissent from his views to prevail. ''The Cherokee,'' he declared in a slap at the Seneca, ''take second place to no other nation in bravery. On behalf of my warriors, I insist that we stand alone against the Creek and Tuscarora.''

Sevier decided to handle the problem by allowing time in which Wegowa could change his mind. At the very least, the colonel thought, the Cherokee might be persuaded not to carry out his rash promise.

Sevier adjourned the meeting, and the various officers made their way back to their headquarters. Sevier stayed behind and walked with Ghonkaba several yards distant from the other Seneca.

''Here's a fine kettle of stew,'' Sevier fumed, ''with all the fish heads still in it. I'm damned if I know what has gotten into Wegowa. He's never led his men in a major battle, but he considers himself an expert. And he has the absolute command of the Cherokee. So I'll have hell's own time trying to talk some sense into him.''

Ghonkaba sighed and clamped his teeth on the stem of his unlighted pipe. ''He appears determined,'' he said, ''to lose a battle that we'd have difficulty in winning under the best of circumstances. Some may advise you to let him have his way. That would mean standing aside when he takes his Cherokee into battle and remaining inactive while he takes his licking. Only then would you strike with your own regiment.''

Sevier shook his head vehemently. ''There's no way on earth that I'm going to stand aside and watch the enemy chew up my army. I never heard of such nonsense, and I realize that you are presenting the worst solution only so that the alternatives will appear in better perspective. As for me, I am thoroughly persuaded that the only way we stand a snowman's chance in Hades of winning is to throw every man who's capable of fighting into combat from the outset.''

"If you mean," Ghonkaba said, "that we attack and attack and attack, I am in complete agreement."

"Right! We fight relentlessly. And we never let up the pressure for a single moment. I see no other way we could possibly win."

"One of the problems," Ghonkaba said, "is that we don't have time to cajole Wegowa and persuade him to cooperate. We can expect that it will be only a matter of hours before the enemy discovers us. We've got to strike rapidly, no later than dawn tomorrow morning, or we don't stand a chance."

"So the big question right now," Sevier said in a ragged voice, "is how we deal with Wegowa and bend him to a sensible approach."

"That's simple enough," said a deep, baritone voice from the underbrush behind them. "Just start your battle without the Cherokee, then invite Wegowa to join in the fun. Rest assured he will. He won't be able to resist the opportunity to share the glory and the spoils he'd otherwise miss."

Ghonkaba and Sevier were startled. The advice they heard was sound, to be sure, but its source was so unexpected that the Seneca drew his tomahawk and Sevier pulled a pistol from his belt.

The underbrush parted. Daniel Boone, clad in his usual buckskins, strolled into the open, his rifle cradled in one arm.

175

Sevier whooped in glee and pounded the newcomer on the back.

Equally delighted, Ghonkaba shook Boone's hand enthusiastically.

"You'll have to excuse me for eavesdropping," Boone said, "but it's an old habit of mine. It's one sure way of finding out what I ought to know. Anyway, don't fret yourselves. Just go into battle, and the Cherokee eventually will join you as though they'd planned on nothing else. Their pride won't let them admit they were going to go it alone."

"We'll sure try it, Dan," Sevier said. An expert on Indian ways, he nevertheless readily bowed to the wisdom of Boone.

"What are you doing here?" Ghonkaba asked.

"I'm looking for Anthony Simpson," Boone said. "He's the mastermind behind this whole British scheme. I want to get rid of him once and for all."

"Is Simpson in the camp of the enemy?" Sevier asked eagerly.

Boone seated himself cross-legged on the ground and hooked his thumbs in his belt. "From a friendly Creek warrior for whom I've done some favors, I've learned that Simpson is behind the lines of the Creek and Tuscarora at this moment. He's waiting to observe his scheme in action."

A score of questions crowded into Ghonkaba's mind, but Boone gave him no chance to ask any of them.

"Once the battle starts," he said, "the friendly warrior will hoist a Union Jack to show Simpson's whereabouts.

From there on, I'll be on my way. It'll be up to me to infiltrate the lines.''

"How can you do this alone?'' Ghonkaba asked, shaking his head.

"I said nothing about acting alone,'' Boone replied. "To accomplish my purpose, I need the close cooperation of allies on whom I can depend. I've selected your veteran Seneca scouts for that purpose.''

"You can count on us for anything you need,'' Ghonkaba answered flatly.

Sevier hoisted himself to his feet. "If I'm taking my regiment into combat in the morning, I've got a lot of planning ahead tonight. Send your deputy, Casno, to my headquarters in the next hour or so, Ghonkaba. He can hear what I have in mind, and we can coordinate our plans.''

Nothing in Boone's plan would interfere with the task required of the Seneca on behalf of the frontier regiment, so cooperation would be feasible. And nabbing Simpson would be an enormous contribution to the American cause.

One problem still faced Ghonkaba. He roused young Renno and sat down opposite him.

"You've done good work on this expedition as a scout,'' Ghonkaba said, "and you've come a long way toward fulfilling your destiny. Your great-grandfather and name-sake would be proud of you. Tomorrow, I have a special mission for you. And, believe me, the great Renno would be as grateful as I shall be when you perform well.''

"What is your command, my father?'' Renno asked.

"I don't want Ena taking part in combat,'' Ghonkaba

told him. "She takes severe risks as a scout, and today we almost lost her. Only because Rusog intervened at the last moment was she able to avoid capture by the Creek. We cannot afford such misfortune, and I want you to prevent her from having an active role in combat. Do anything necessary. I know this assignment seems unfair to you and that you will be unhappy because you are missing your chance for combat, but I swear that I will make this up to you when responsibility for your sister does not weigh so heavily. Do as I ask, Renno, and the manitous will reward you as only they can."

Renno, like any Seneca, would not think of deliberately flouting the will of a superior. The discipline that had been instilled in him was so exacting that he bowed his head and murmured, "I hear you and will do your bidding, my father." Given an unpleasant assignment, he would fulfill it to the best of his ability. He hoped that his father was right in predicting that the manitous would reward his fidelity.

Chapter VII

An hour before daybreak, as his men and the troops of the frontier regiment ate parched corn and dried venison, Ghonkaba learned that the approach to the enemy, bisected by the river he had seen, occasionally turned into a swamp. The broad section of dry ground was in the hands of the Creek, who were massed at the far end of a particularly heavy section of undergrowth. The Tuscarora held a narrow sector beyond the river and swamp.

Following Boone's advice, Colonel Sevier approached Wegowa, saying casually, "We're attacking in less than an hour's time. You and your warriors will be very welcome if you join us. In fact, I'll turn over the entire sector on the other side of the river, opposite the Tuscarora, to you. If you subdue them, you'll have the honor of defeat-

179

ing the cousins of a tribe that's within the Iroquois League.''

Wegowa promptly rose to the bait and took it. ''We accept the challenge!'' he declared loudly.

''Good!'' Sevier made no attempt to hide his relief. ''If you hadn't accepted,'' he said, ''we would have had no one to engage the Tuscarora. Now I know they'll really have their hands full!''

Ghonkaba had time only for a very brief confrontation with his daughter. ''You will abstain from combat today, Ena,'' he instructed. ''You are to remain here in our camp. You will not stray toward where the fighting is taking place. Your brother also will stay. He has been ordered to use any means whatsoever to dissuade you from taking part in the fighting. If necessary, he is prepared to tie you to a tree.''

Although bitterly disappointed, Ena knew better than to argue. ''I hear your orders and I will obey them, my father,'' she said submissively. He relented sufficiently to reach out and pat her cheek gratefully.

Then he joined his scouts, and his instructions were succinct. ''As we've done in the past so many times, we'll be acting as an advance infantry unit today. We'll be scouts only in that we'll notify Colonel Sevier when we contact the enemy. We're going into action against the Creek, who have a formidable reputation. All I say to you is: Remember you are Seneca.'' His listeners needed no other inspirational advice.

''Daniel Boone will be joining us in our advance,'' Ghonkaba continued, ''and at the appropriate time we'll be required to perform a special function for him.'' He outlined the task in detail and concluded by saying, ''He is depending on us. The man he's after is the enemy that General Washington wants eliminated.''

Finally, before going into action, Ghonkaba picked up the flag that the commander in chief had awarded to the company. The eagle embroidered on it almost gleamed in the early morning light. Ghonkaba tied the pennant onto the back of Casno, who would join him in the front rank. It was the first time that Washington's gift would be used in battle. This was an unprecedented honor, and the Seneca were more determined than ever to prevail.

In the final minutes before the Seneca were to begin their advance, Ghonkaba stood with Sevier, but they exchanged few words. They had no need for last-minute conversation. Both were veterans who knew what was expected of themselves and each other. This, Ghonkaba realized, was the great advantage of working beside men of experience. Years of hard fighting had transformed them from a raw rabble into an efficient unit.

At last, the sky turned from a velvetlike black to a sooty gray. Dawn was breaking.

Ghonkaba and Sevier shook hands, first with each other, then with Daniel Boone. The scouts struck out on the trail that would lead them on the left of the river and swamp to the position held by the Creek. So far as they knew, the enemy still had no idea that an attack was impending. They spread out through the wilderness. With Ghonkaba, Casno, and Boone in the lead, they advanced rapidly.

Again, Ghonkaba realized that Boone, as expert as any

Seneca war chief, made no sound as he trotted on light feet, his rifle ready for instant use, his Indian weapons held in reserve.

On three occasions, the Seneca encountered Creek sentries and made short work of them. They were slain before they could give an alarm. The bodies were concealed in the underbrush as the company swept forward. At such times, no Seneca would think of halting to lift an enemy scalp. Scalping was performed when a battle was already won, and warriors would never jeopardize their comrades' safety for the sake of another trophy.

Casno signaled to inform the company that less than a mile remained before the Creek lines were reached. Tension increased perceptibly. Rifles were checked for the last time.

Suddenly, from far to the right, beyond the river and swamp, they could hear wild whooping. The trio in the lead halted instantly. Casno looked dismayed, Ghonkaba cursed silently under his breath, and Boone seemed thunderstruck. The noise could mean only one thing: the Cherokee, moving without an advance guard toward the Tuscarora, presumably were more or less equal in their advance with the Seneca. What they heard was a battle cry before combat.

Ghonkaba was stunned by the stupidity of Wegowa, who was permitting his men to announce their approach, rather than attacking suddenly, silently, and unexpectedly. He was giving the Tuscarora time to prepare a defense. As a consequence, the advance would be slowed appreciably, and many Cherokee would lose their lives needlessly.

The whooping became louder, wilder, less restrained. Ghonkaba realized anew that a surprising lack of discipline by the entire Cherokee high command could result in catastrophe. Neither Wegowa nor any of his principal chiefs seemed to realize that they should have been as silent as possible, creeping up on the enemy to deliver telling blows with as much force as they could muster. The Seneca never gave their war cry unless they were on the verge of total victory. Only then did they let loose their cry, as a way of rallying their comrades on all parts of the battlefield for a final, conclusive effort.

Now, however, the Cherokee were not only doing great potential harm to themselves, but also were endangering the Seneca and the frontiersmen.

What was done could not be undone, and the first to realize it was Daniel Boone. He hunched his shoulders and advanced even more cautiously than they had been moving. Ghonkaba and Casno followed his example. One significant difference was occurring in the tempo of their advance. They moved more rapidly now, making better time in order to thwart the enemy if the Creek, having been alerted by the Cherokee, were preparing to repel invaders. The entire Seneca unit understood the need for greater speed, and all responded instantly. Behind them, the frontiersmen also moved more rapidly. Removing the safety catches from their rifles, they prepared to plunge into battle without notice.

At last they came to the main body of the Creek force, strung out at a point where the foliage had thinned considerably. The defenders were armed with the latest model of British muskets.

The Seneca dropped to the ground, and Ghonkaba immediately sent a runner to notify Sevier that they had established contact with the enemy.

Oddly, the Creek did not appear to be ready for battle. They must have heard the war cries of the Cherokee but presumably had reasoned that only the Tuscarora were under attack. The Seneca were able to fire two rounds of arrows and inflict considerable damage before the Creek even reacted.

The trio leading the advance proved their effectiveness. Ghonkaba, trained in his family's tradition, was a deadly shot with bow and arrow. He was no more accurate, however, than were Boone or Casno. All three found their targets with their first shots, and then, still lying flat, they repeated with their second arrows.

Finally, the Creek realized they were being attacked. Musket fire rippled up and down their line but was extremely ineffective. The Creek had not learned to use the weapons that Simpson had obtained for them. Their fire was far too high, their bullets passing above the Seneca, who were unscathed.

Ghonkaba, Casno, and Boone continued to set an example, firing an effective third round of arrows, each of which struck home. The other scouts quickly followed, and their fire was equally deadly.

The Seneca responded instinctively to a rhythm, a tempo of battle learned as junior warriors and practiced throughout their careers. Ghonkaba and Casno advanced together, with each maintaining the same pace that his comrade achieved.

Daniel Boone had enjoyed no such training, however, and consequently, he moved several paces ahead of his companions.

Ghonkaba was the first to recognize his extreme danger. Looking ahead, he saw an enemy warrior on one knee, his musket to his shoulder, the weapon pointed at Boone.

He had no time to lose, no opportunity to fit another arrow into his bow and fire it. Ghonkaba instantly reached into his belt, drew a knife, and flung it with full force at the kneeling enemy.

The blade found its mark, killing the foe instantly, and as he toppled over, the motion caught Boone's attention. For the first time, he became aware of his danger.

Words were impossible, but he nodded his thanks.

By this time, the front rank of Sevier's pioneers had arrived and threw themselves flat on the ground. Their long frontier rifles continued the destruction of the Creek. Their fire was so accurate that the front line of the Creek was in danger of collapsing. Rather than ordering the Creek to use bows and thus regain some semblance of control, the war chief commanding the sector preferred to draw back his braves. They did not panic, but their withdrawal was clumsy.

By now, each Seneca was on his own, firing at will and setting his own pace. The tempo of the battle increased, and the carnage among the Creek was intensified, but so far, thanks to the inept handling of the Creek by their war chief, the attackers remained unharmed.

185

Crouching low, the Seneca dashed forward and occupied the position vacated by the Creek. They were immediately followed by the frontier regiment.

Sevier inched forward until he reached Ghonkaba. "What's wrong with the Creek?" he asked. "They're not putting up the fight they're capable of waging."

Ghonkaba explained that the enemy was having difficulty in using muskets with which they were not adequately familiar.

A wry grin creased Sevier's leathery face. "We might as well take advantage of their confusion as long as it lasts," he said, and crawled away.

Moments later, his troops opened a steady, punishing rifle fire far more effective than any attack with arrows. The Seneca needed no order to switch weapons; putting aside their bows, they, too, resorted to their firearms.

The Creek again were forced to draw back, and they withdrew so swiftly and raggedly that Ghonkaba suspected they might be having trouble preventing panic from seizing their ranks.

The Creek were saved from catastrophe only when a senior war chief wearing a feather-laden bonnet appeared in their midst and rallied them. He succeeded not only in quieting them and preventing further withdrawal, but assigned new defensive positions and ordered the braves to put aside their muskets and use their bows and arrows.

Now it was the Creek who used the traditional Indian weapons while the Seneca fired their rifles.

The results were immediate. The Seneca, who had been careless, quickly realized that they must take the normal precautions of combat. They burrowed into underbrush, concealing themselves behind the large trees and clumps of bushes.

The use of familiar arms steadied the Creek. Instead of having their shots go wild, their bow-and-arrow fire enabled them to wound several militiamen. This so encouraged them that they sent another hundred warriors to augment the braves holding their front line. The easy victory seemingly within the attackers' grasp had vanished.

As the battlefront was stabilized, the combat became a grueling, cruel tug-of-war, with both sides determined to achieve a clear-cut victory. Neither was willing to retreat or give up the field. This was the type of battle in which the Seneca excelled: holding a position tenaciously, slugging hard without giving an inch, and then breaking loose and finding a weakness that had not been apparent earlier, exploiting it until they won the day.

The Creek, who had imitated Seneca tactics for years, proved to be apt pupils. They, too, clung to their positions and would not be dislodged. Their immense advantage in numbers was neutralized by the frontier militiamen. They used Indian fighting methods, and they, too, relied on defensive measures only until they could find a weak spot in their foes.

The two sides were like fencers, each probing, pushing, experimenting, prepared to throw their entire force into a sudden advance when that became expeditious. Neither could find a chink in their opponents' armor and this fueled the grim reality of the struggle.

* * *

Meanwhile, on the far side of the swamp, Wegowa's Cherokee were caught in a hornets' nest.

Having foolishly disclosed their presence, they found themselves facing a band of determined Tuscarora who were ready to oppose them. The Tuscarora were the first to open fire, employing their new British muskets. Fortunately for the Cherokee, the Tuscarora were as inept at handling these weapons as were the Creek. Their shots consistently went wild overhead, and the Cherokee, although forced onto the defensive, were able to rally. Using their bows, they steadied themselves and inflicted enough damage to drive the Tuscarora back about fifty yards.

Quicker to react than the more ponderous Creek, the Tuscarora halted their backward movement and resorted to their own bows in order to fight on more even terms.

Though the two forces were about equal in size, the Tuscarora held a decided advantage because of their greater experience. They sent bands of specially trained warriors to infiltrate both flanks of their foes while continuing to maintain pressure on their front.

Now it was the turn of the Tuscarora to unleash their war cry. Shrill, high-pitched shouts echoed from center, left, and right.

Wegowa was stunned. His entire battle plan was in tatters, and his confused commanders were convinced they were surrounded.

Instead of waiting for a command to pull back, they

began to retreat. Only the swamp prevented the entire Cherokee force from seeking safety in the heavier forests.

Inheritors of an honorable tradition of which they were proud, the Cherokee were courageous. In the end, it was this tradition that saved them. Pride restored the common sense of the senior warriors. They stopped their headlong retreat and took a stand, determined to die honorably. They opened fire anew with their bows on their eager pursuers. Soon they were joined by enough younger warriors, following their example, that they were able to halt the thrust of the Tuscarora. Their baptism of fire had hardened the Cherokee, and they held firm now, finally convinced they could achieve invincibility. Although the opportunity to launch a surprise attack was forever lost, the Cherokee were at least able to create a stalemate and fight on, holding their own against the Tuscarora. They had, however, maneuvered themselves into an exceedingly delicate position, with the swamp behind them and the Tuscarora on both flanks as well as on their front. Now Wegowa led his men in fighting bravely, if not with particular distinction. The Cherokee had stumbled, fallen, and been carried to the thin edge of utter defeat, but they regained their balance sufficiently to ensure a chance to win.

The veteran Seneca scouts and the frontiersmen smashed repeatedly at the Creek defenders, but neither side gained an advantage.

Ghonkaba realized that Boone, who had been peering intently in hope of seeing the Union Jack, finally had spotted it off to the far right. Following the frontiersman's gaze, he saw a British flag raised to the level of low treetops about one hundred yards away.

Calling to Casno that he was to be in charge of the scouts, Ghonkaba notified Boone with a quick nod that he was ready.

Together, they made their way inch by inch, foot by foot, through the foliage. They left the Seneca position behind and, crossing the no-man's-land that separated the two forces, they crept into the domain of the Creek.

They saw Simpson in a clearing located on higher ground. He was watching the progress of the battle intently. Wearing the scarlet and gold uniform of a redcoat colonel, he was unaware of the approach of Boone and Ghonkaba as he concentrated his full attention on the battle. A score of young Creek warriors, who appeared to be assigned as Simpson's bodyguard, were located from five to twenty yards from the renegade. All were busy watching the battle, so Ghonkaba and Boone had no difficulty in firing twice with their bows as they drew closer and dispatched four guards with as many arrows.

No talk was necessary; Ghonkaba knew what he should do. He was to create a deliberate diversion in order to give Boone a chance to crawl closer to Simpson.

Showing no regard for his safety, Ghonkaba jumped to his feet for a moment in order to reveal his presence before he dove forward into a deep trough.

The bodyguards' attention was riveted on him instantly, and they fired simultaneously at the spot where he was last visible.

190

This gave Boone the chance he sought, and he raced forward, still crouching low, until he was only a few feet from Simpson. Raising his rifle to his shoulder, he approached the renegade. Simpson did not even try to lift his own rifle. He realized the buckskin-clad figure closing in so grimly was determined to kill him, but he remained strangely confident of his ability to talk his way out of the perilous situation.

"I—I have been misrepresented by my enemies for years," he said, his voice gaining in both volume and confidence. "I know this is hard to believe, but you must give me a chance to prove the absolute truth of what I say. I am secretly acting for the Americans. I seek their liberty ahead of anything else. Those who claim that I'm in the pay of Great Britain are liars!"

He got no farther. He had forgotten that he was wearing a royal army uniform. Boone acted as judge and jury. He made an instant decision, squeezed the trigger, and Simpson dropped to the ground.

Now Boone had to escape from the trap he had created; he emulated Ghonkaba and dove into the tangled foliage in the trough.

The Creek guards saw that Simpson had dropped, and some rushed to his side. Others sought to capture or kill Boone and poured musket fire at the spot where he had last been seen. The scene was one of pandemonium and confusion.

In the bedlam, no one noticed Ghonkaba emerge from the underbrush in the no-man's-land more than fifty yards from where Simpson lay. As he rested on one knee,

191

brushing dirt from his rifle, Boone suddenly appeared near him. The two magicians of the wilderness, as the frontiersmen came to call them, had accomplished an extraordinary mission and had made it look easy. Now they were on their way back to the relative safety of their own lines.

Once there, Ghonkaba addressed his daring companion. "I was sorry," he said, "that you got him with one shot. I would have enjoyed putting a bullet into him, too."

"I could take no chance," Boone reminded him. "Simpson escaped the net again and again, and I wanted to make certain that I disposed of him."

"General Washington will be gratified when he learns your news," Ghonkaba said.

"I reckon he will," Boone answered, "but now we've got to start to undo some of the damage that Simpson has created."

Neither of the wilderness fighters realized that Boone's shot had not killed Anthony Simpson. The British agent had suffered a severe wound, but had survived. His Indian allies had managed to remove him from the field of battle, where he began a long, arduous convalescence.

Ghonkaba examined the positions of the two sides. "You're right, of course," he said. "It's going to be no easy matter to dislodge the Creek. They're embedded in their positions."

"No time like the present," Boone said. "We'll have to do our damnedest to get them out of there."

Ghonkaba could scarcely contain his delight. Although Boone had accomplished his mission when he shot Simpson, he also intended to see the battle through to its finish. "I gather you're staying with us, Dan?" he asked.

Boone grinned. "Nobody ever knew me to walk away from a good fight," he said, "and this is one battle that promises to be a heap better than good!"

Darkness brought a welcome respite in the battle. The two armies settled down for the night. Men on both sides ate cold meals of jerked meat and parched corn, with neither side daring to risk the lighting of campfires.

Colonel Sevier made a tour of the positions held by his regiment of frontiersmen and the Seneca scouts before he sat down with Ghonkaba and Daniel Boone to discuss the overall situation. "Things could be a damn sight worse," he said, "but I'll admit they could be better. The regiment is in good shape. Our casualties are very light. We are solidly entrenched in land that was in the hands of the enemy yesterday. With any luck, we may be able to oust the Creek from their present position, but we'll need more than luck."

"You're referring to the unfortunate situation of Wegowa and his Cherokee, no doubt," Boone said.

Sevier nodded. "This is what comes of giving the command of the Cherokee to an untried leader whose chief lieutenants also lack battle experience. Nothing is wrong with the warriors of the Cherokee. They're good solid fighting men, and under proper leadership—say that of Ghonkaba—they could be very effective. As it is, they've been almost useless and may surrender."

Ghonkaba frowned. "Is their situation that bad?"

"It's miserable," Sevier said. "They're cut off from us in the rear by that infernal swamp, and there's no way of knowing how they can find their way to get around it and establish contact with us again. They're facing alert Tuscarora on their front and both flanks. The enemy can nibble them to death."

"It seems to me," Ghonkaba replied, "that our best hope is to open a channel of communication between the Cherokee and the regiment."

"How?" Sevier demanded bitterly. "We can't risk lives by sending men out on a fool's errand to look for paths of dry land through the swamp at this time of night!"

Ghonkaba pondered the problem and concluded that he would seek to solve it in the only way that he knew. He was determined to set out on his own in the early morning's first light to find some connecting link with the Cherokee through the almost impenetrable swamp.

Later, he told his plan to Casno and Ranoga, then silenced them when they protested. "Why should I not go?" he demanded. "Do you think I've never seen a swamp and worked around its edges? If anyone in this expedition is fit to conduct such a search, I am first on the list. I assure you I shall not be taking undue risks."

In the meantime, Ena was chafing under her restrictions. As an observer of the battle, she felt utterly useless and told herself bitterly that she might as well have stayed at home with her mother.

Now she saw an opportunity to do a great service for the regiment of frontiersmen and the beleaguered Cherokee, as well as for her Seneca. Her father had forbidden her to take part in the fighting, but he had not mentioned performing other scouting functions. She felt under no restrictions now and was free to search—as only she could—for that connecting strip of land, as she had heard her father tell Casno and Ranoga.

Around her, everyone was sleeping. Ena rose silently, picked up her bow and quiver of arrows, together with her double-edged knife and tomahawk, and then took a firm grip on her rifle. Lyktaw jumped to his feet, his head cocked to one side. She motioned to him to remain silent and threaded her way out of the area.

Just as she reached the first fringe of trees she felt a firm hand on her shoulder. She looked around to see Renno gazing sternly at her.

"Where do you think you're going?" he demanded in a harsh whisper.

She explained what was in her mind. She was not even thinking of disobeying their father. On the other hand, she saw a chance to perform a deed that no one else might be capable of. Her explanation sounded reasonable to Renno. He was assuring himself that she was not disobeying. She had no equal as a tracker, and he knew that if such a land link existed, Ena stood a better chance of finding it than did anyone else.

Renno disliked acting as her jailer, and he sympathized with her so completely that he leaned over backward to see her point of view. Examining his conscience, he could find no fault with it. "All right," he said gruffly, "just make sure you don't fire any weapons."

Ena turned and started off again. Renno fell in behind her. She looked over her shoulder, paused, then asked, "What are you doing?"

"I've decided to come with you," he said, "and make sure that you obey our father's will."

Ena looked at him for a long moment, then sighed, shrugged, and started toward the river with Lyktaw beside her and her brother silently following.

Chapter VIII

The manitous, it appeared, did not approve of the mission Ena and Renno had undertaken. Though the night was still young, the sky was dark, filled with forbidding black clouds that obscured the moon and stars. Only experienced Indians familiar with scouting operations would be abroad under such conditions.

Ena directed Renno to mark the beginning of the trail with his tomahawk. Leading the way, she tried to steer a course along the edge of the swamp, but often she miscalculated and stepped into the ooze.

Lyktaw went ahead, trying to anticipate where she wanted to go, but he ran into far more trouble than was his custom. He sank into the muddy swamp, extricating himself with difficulty. Much to his annoyance and confusion,

197

Ena kept whistling to him in an undertone and calling him back to her side.

Renno followed in silence, uttering no complaint, even though his moccasins were caked with mud, making his feet cold. At Ena's direction, he marked a tree every several yards, enabling them to find their way back if necessary, or providing guidance for anyone who followed. Instinct for survival, ingrained in his family for generations, did not desert him, and from time to time he reached out and caught Ena's arm to stop her from plunging into the swamp.

Ena was dismayed to discover that all her hard-won experience in scouting and tracking were virtually useless in the swamp at night. She had no idea where she was going. At first, she could not admit the truth to herself, but little by little she came to realize that she was relying on her brother's instinct and on the natural expertise of her shepherd dog to prevent her from plunging headlong into knee-deep mud.

It was small wonder, she realized, that her fellow Seneca, even her father, were not venturing out of their camp until morning. Rarely had she known such discomfort, and at the same time, she became convinced that her exertions would be all in vain unless she concentrated her abilities to the utmost.

But actual dangers rather than mere discomforts were lurking in the mists. Suddenly she was alerted to danger when Lyktaw stiffened, his ears rising to points. He made a low growling noise that was barely audible. Something was amiss.

Ena's night vision was not the equal of that of her brother, who had inherited his forebears' ability to see as clearly in the dark as most people could see in daylight.

She could see, however, that Renno had drawn his tomahawk and was shifting its weight in his hand to make certain that he achieved an appropriate balance.

Lyktaw's growl deepened and gingerly he took several backward steps.

Then Renno let fly with his tomahawk, and a moment later he uttered a short, sharp sigh of satisfaction.

Lyktaw, still tense, became less apprehensive and advanced slowly, responding to Renno, who patted his head.

Ena peered ahead in the darkness, and objects in front of her began to take shape.

On the ground directly ahead was a rattlesnake at least four feet long and with a diameter equal to the thickness of her wrist. At first, she thought the snake was still alive, and started to shrink back, but then she realized that the tomahawk had decapitated it and that the rattler was only in the peculiar death throes of its kind. She could face almost any wild creature without flinching, but for reasons she never had been able to understand, she could not tolerate snakes. She broke into a cold sweat and rubbed her arms vigorously. "Thank you, my brother," she murmured, and then started forward again, walking with even greater care than previously.

Though she slowed her pace appreciably, she consoled herself with the thought that caution was surely the wisest course. She avoided the trap of traveling in circles.

Ena's legs ached, but she merely bent down and massaged them for several seconds before going on.

Renno appeared to know where they had been, even though he was still in the dark as to how to reach their destination.

She was determined to find their way out of the morass and she would allow nothing to stop her. Though concerned, he was incapable of halting her.

After at least two hours of walking, Renno touched his sister's arm and pointed to higher ground off to their left. Ena moved onto it, grateful for the dry soil underfoot and for the fact that even the fetid stench of the swamp faded somewhat.

She sank to the ground, as did her brother, who sat opposite her. Lyktaw moved between them and dropped off to sleep. Renno thought it safe enough to light a small fire, using some brush and twigs, to help warm them somewhat.

All at once, both brother and sister felt as though they had been struck by lightning. They heard human voices and, strangely, the sound seemed very near.

Renno, with his almost superhuman hearing, was quick to figure out the mystery. Ena, straining hard to make out what the voices were saying, required a little more time. By concentrating on the sounds, she was able to discern that several men were speaking in the tongue of the Cherokee. Then she realized that the swamp, and beyond it the river, extended for some distance yet, and that sound carried far more clearly over water than over land. Therefore, it was apparent that she and Renno were now directly across the swamp from Wegowa's camp. The wind, blowing from that direction, carried the voices of the Cherokee warriors.

Renno peered hard at the water ahead. "The swamp," he said, "doesn't seem to be too deep or too broad in this area. We've crossed much of it somehow during the night, and I'm sure it can be negotiated here. We'll have to keep watch for snakes, of course, but even that danger can be avoided. I think we're on some sort of island in the swamp—probably we are mostly through it."

"What do you have in mind?"

He smiled wryly. "I had a strange thought just now, almost a dream," he said. "I imagined that the manitous worked some of their finest magic and made it possible for us to get in touch with our father and with Colonel Sevier. Then I was able to imagine the army joining us and crossing the swamp to become united with Wegowa's Cherokee."

"What was the magic that you imagined the manitous were using?"

"Unfortunately, my mind has failed to register just what they did. What's the use?" He sounded discouraged and, drawing his tomahawk, he began to strike at a nearby pine tree in disgust. "We face a terribly serious situation, and I see no way of solving it," he said. "We can't perform the impossible." In his frustration, he struck the trunk of the pine more forcibly. Jamming his tomahawk back into his belt, he stared gloomily into space.

The tree began to "weep," and Renno unthinkingly put up a hand to halt the flow of pine tar. Suddenly he realized what he had done. When he looked at the sticky tar on his fingers, he began to laugh.

His sister was bewildered by his change in mood.

Still chuckling, he turned to her and said softly, "It may be that the manitous have shown me a way after all. We shall soon find out."

He coated an arrow with pine tar and then, handling it delicately, held it over the fire until the pitch caught and flared. Then he instantly shot the arrow high into the air. As it ascended, the arrow flamed over its entire length.

At last Ena understood what he was doing and hastily began to coat a number of arrows with pine tar.

Waiting for several anxious moments between shots, Renno lighted them in the little fire one by one and sent them up into the sky.

The flaming arrows were noted by sentries of both the Tuscarora and Creek. But, never having thought of flaming arrows as a means of communication, they failed to grasp the significance of what they saw. As far as they were concerned, the Cherokee probably were trying in some strange way to please their gods.

Renno and Ena waited anxiously for their signal to be received and understood. Because of the great care they took not to reveal their feelings, their faces showed no emotions.

In the distance, they finally heard the unmistakable screeching call of the great white owl. Renno grinned, and Ena sighed deeply. Their signal had been received and correctly interpreted, and they knew that the Seneca had found the beginning of the trail, and would now be on the way to join them, probably leading Colonel Sevier's regiment. They waited for several minutes, then Ena put an ear to the ground and listened. "The march is halting," she reported. "They are in need of some guidance."

Renno dipped an arrow in pitch and lighted it, then shot it straight up into the air. The brand flamed as it went skyward, then was extinguished as it burned to cinders and disintegrated on its descent.

The brief signal was enough to give the Seneca scouts another idea of their location. Renno and Ena had wandered off the correct course frequently, and Renno had notched trees as they stumbled along. Therefore, their comrades had to follow the same indirect and confusing route. Every few minutes, Ena listened to the approaching column halt indecisively as the scouts apparently searched for another trail marker. At each such occasion, Renno sent up another flaming arrow as a signal. They repeated this process many times before they felt certain that the scouts were safely approaching.

Brother and sister coordinated their moves smoothly, as though they had worked together for a long time. Without unnecessary conversation, each trusted implicitly in the other.

After a time that Ena estimated as about two hours—making it nearly midnight—the call of the great white owl sounded close at hand. Renno no longer needed to rely on flaming arrows and merely answered in kind, imitating the cry of the owl as a way of notifying his comrades of their location.

Eventually, making no effort at concealment, the Seneca

scouts appeared, led by Ghonkaba, who was following the directions given by his son and daughter. The first to greet him was Lyktaw, who wagged his tail vigorously and jumped up to indicate his pleasure.

The scouts were closely followed by the Tennesseans. Sevier joined Ghonkaba, and Renno and Ena led them to the edge of the islet.

"Yonder," Renno said, pointing off through the swampy marsh to the left, "lies the position of the Cherokee. Beyond, we can assume, are the Tuscarora. If our strategy is to join with the Cherokee, I believe that I could lead all of you there."

"What condition do you consider that part of the swamp to be in?" Ghonkaba asked.

"It's not bad, my father, and could be much worse. I've had to kill only one rattlesnake, and if the troops take precautions, they should suffer no casualties."

"Are you prepared to go find the Cherokee, and then lead us to them?" Colonel Sevier asked.

"Certainly," Renno answered promptly.

Ena could not help interjecting, "If you prefer, I can go for them."

"You've done quite enough already," Ghonkaba said. "You'll stay here, near me, and you won't leave my sight again."

Ena suspected that her glorious adventure had come to an end.

Carrying his tomahawk, Renno plunged into the swamp. The water was less than knee-deep, he discovered, so he was able to make better time than he had expected, but he had to walk a half mile through the ooze before he caught sight of Cherokee sentries.

The sentries, seeing his bold green and yellow war paint, withheld their fire.

Renno pulled himself onto dry land and asked to be taken without delay to Wegowa. The Cherokee chief came forward to greet him with surprise but very warmly.

"Colonel Sevier authorizes me to inform you that he is prepared to join you here and then open a counterattack," Renno told him.

"Is it possible for his men to navigate safely through the swamp?"

Renno pointed to the waterline on his legs. "The swamp rises no higher than this. It will be entirely possible for them to cross, if you are ready."

Wegowa seemed to Renno to be much chastened. His attitude had changed from one of surly recognition of the Seneca to one of a willingness to cooperate. He promptly and eagerly agreed on the desirability of having the frontiersmen and the Seneca brought forward to join his embattled men, with the idea of fighting their way out of their cul-de-sac.

Carrying their firearms and gunpowder horns at shoulder height, the Seneca scouts and the frontiersmen followed the route Renno had taken, guided by the occasional arrow he sent into the night sky. Their crossing, with Ghonkaba and Ena in the lead, was rapid.

Ghonkaba and Sevier began a hurried consultation with Wegowa almost immediately after they touched the point of land held by the Cherokee.

Despite their heroic role that made the meeting possible, Renno and Ena were required to stand aside while their elders conferred on strategy best calculated to salvage the difficult situation.

With Ghonkaba taking the lead, the officers soon agreed that they should attack the opposing Tuscarora at dawn, giving themselves some four hours to rest and make the necessary preparations.

Humbled by his unfortunate experience, Wegowa unexpectedly said to Sevier, "I relinquish the command of my Cherokee and gladly give the post to Ghonkaba if he will take it."

Ghonkaba was startled by the unexpected offer. Giving Sevier no chance to speak, he intervened swiftly. "It is right," he said, "for the braves of the Cherokee to be commanded in battle by their own principal warrior, the son of their Grand Sachem. It is not proper that a stranger should lead them."

"Ghonkaba of the Seneca is no stranger to my people," Wegowa replied. "They have followed him and his scouts through a long march that lasted many days through the wilderness. They trust Ghonkaba, and they will obey his orders in battle. I have prayed to the Breath Holder for guidance, and I know in my heart that what I am proposing is correct."

Colonel Sevier, puzzled, wisely stood aside, allowing the two Indian leaders to settle the issue.

"My pride overcame me, and I placed my nation in jeopardy. Now I am willing and eager to atone for my errors and place myself, as well as my men, under the command of Ghonkaba. Only a warrior with his knowledge and experience will lead us to victory!''

Ghonkaba was reluctant to take command of another man's army. But Wegowa was sincere. "I must prove to my brother," he said, "that I mean what I say." He called his braves to surround him and said to them, "I have offered my place as your leader to Ghonkaba of the Seneca, who has experience in battle far greater than mine. I have told him that I will follow him as will you. How many of you will obey his commands?"

Without exception, the Cherokee raised their left hands and brandished muskets or bows.

To the delight of Casno, Ranoga, and the other Seneca, Ghonkaba bowed his head and replied, "I will do my best to lead you to victory." Only he was troubled by his decision. Later in the day, his son asked, "What caused you to accept the leadership of the Cherokee, my father?"

Pleased that his son recognized the responsibilities of leadership, Ghonkaba replied, "The braves expected no less from me. They were convinced, as was Wegowa, that it was the will of the Breath Holder that I be given the command."

His son was bewildered. "But we do not believe in the Breath Holder. We do not acknowledge his powers, nor do we worship him."

Ghonkaba shook his head and smiled wearily. "Who is to say that the Breath Holder of the Cherokee is not related to the gods of the Seneca? For all we know, we worship the Breath Holder under another name. I dare not turn my back on this offer for fear that the manitous, who have favored us in all things, for so long a time, will turn their backs upon us."

Thus it happened that Ghonkaba assumed the command of the entire Cherokee force.

The question of the leadership of the Indians having been settled, Colonel Sevier called a meeting of his commanders. The army rested in preparation for fighting after its difficult march to its present forward position.

Ghonkaba called a council of war of his own, including Wegowa among those he consulted.

"I am not sufficiently familiar," he said, "with the battle techniques of the Cherokee to know whether they are capable of fighting in the Seneca manner and are willing to try. We attack! We never assume the defensive, and we attack in full strength and keep attacking until our enemies are worn down and either surrender or flee. This technique requires no greater energy or risk than does the normal give and take of battle, but it requires greater courage and unflagging willpower."

"My braves," Wegowa told him, "are not lacking in courage or in strength. If someone will show them the way, they will gladly do as they are bidden."

"My Seneca will set an example for them," Ghonkaba replied. "Let every warrior of the Cherokee do as my Seneca do, and all will be well."

And so it was arranged. Ghonkaba's lieutenants privately entertained doubts as to what their chief was proposing.

"You cannot transform Cherokee into Seneca," Casno argued. "You ask too much."

Ghonkaba shook his head emphatically. "You are wrong. I say that every warrior of every nation has the capability of acting like the Seneca in battle if he knows what must be done. By our example, we will show our new allies, and the rest will follow naturally."

When Sevier was informed of Ghonkaba's plan, he approved without reservation. "This fits in with my own scheme of things. The American frontiersman is a strange breed, you know. He functions best when on the attack, so I'm intending to turn my regiment loose. They'll go on the defensive only if it's absolutely necessary. Between them and your forces, we should be giving the Creek and the Tuscarora a lively time of it."

The rest of the night dragged for the Tennesseans, but the Indians accepted the pause phlegmatically. They slept, ate their dried venison and parched corn, and told tales of the supernatural. The Cherokee were revealed as the possessers of a lively sense of humor, and they competed in telling tales about an imaginary character named Brother Rabbit, a mischievous, four-legged creature who possessed magical qualities.

Not long before dawn, Rusog appeared in the camp of the Seneca. Instead of seeking Ena's company, as she expected, he asked instead for the privilege of conferring with Ghonkaba.

The Seneca war chief smiled broadly. "I know why you're here," he said. "You want reassurances that Ena is not going to take part in the conflict."

Rusog nodded vehemently. Ghonkaba turned to Ena and emphasized each word as he said, ''Ena has been ordered to stay in our camp and not to stray during the battle. She is to keep her dog with her as a companion and guard, and if either participates in the fight, regardless of the reason, they will be sent back as soon as the battle ends.''

''You've already made my situation quite clear to me, my father,'' Ena said indignantly.

Rusog looked hard at Ena and said to Ghonkaba, ''If she disobeys you, sir, I will, myself, speed her on her way.''

Ena glared at him. Unlike her father, Rusog had no right to interfere in her business, much less to threaten her, and she wanted to tell him what she thought of him.

But he gave her no opportunity. Barely glancing in her direction again, he raised his left arm in salute to Ghonkaba and retired.

Ena was wildly angry. She was willing to admit that women were physically smaller and weaker than men, but she would concede nothing when she was treated like a fragile being lacking any voice in her own future. The concept of obedience to the will of her father would make it obligatory that she do his bidding, but she knew of no reason to heed Rusog's orders. She hoped he would escape injury in the coming conflict so that she could show him, once and for all, what she really thought of him.

Just before dawn, the Cherokee, bolstered by the Seneca scouts and Sevier's troops, set out from the camp toward the positions occupied by the enemy.

CHEROKEE

The Cherokee, led by the small band of Seneca scouts, occupied the position to the left, and the frontier settlers held the right. Warned by Sevier and Ghonkaba to observe quiet, they made no sound as they moved out.

By the time the first light of day appeared in the sky, they were in position. Cherokee braves and frontiersmen alike crowded forward in order to bring maximum pressure on the enemy as quickly as possible. The small group of Seneca assumed responsibility for taking care of the enemy sentinels, a feat they accomplished with the efficiency of long practice. Striking swiftly and silently, they attacked the Tuscarora sentries from the rear. The sentinels made valiant attempts to defend themselves but had no chance against their veteran foes. One by one they were destroyed, and not one survived long enough to give an alarm. Breakfast fires were just being lighted in the Tuscarora camp, and their cooks were about to prepare a meal of freshly caught fish when the assault began. The Seneca, using only Indian weapons, attacked silently and surely. At least a score of Tuscarora died before one of their senior warriors managed to give a piercing war cry that caused consternation everywhere on the front.

Luck played a major role in the battle from the outset. The Tuscarora, seeing the war paint of their foes, assumed they were being attacked by Seneca and became panicky. By the time they discovered their mistake, the Cherokee had advanced sufficiently to play an active part and it was difficult for the Tuscarora to regroup.

Both sides were using only their Indian weapons, but gunfire rattled in the sector where the Tennesseans advanced.

211

Ghonkaba led the charge. With Wegowa close beside him, he advanced rapidly, fighting furiously as he and his companion unloosed arrow after arrow at their foes. Both were excellent shots, and Wegowa soon proved that he was a superb marksman and took a heavy toll on the enemy. Ghonkaba, as always, was second to none.

They did so well, in fact, that the enemy soon marked them for special treatment. The line of the Tuscarora broke as they approached it, and only when they continued to drive forward and Tuscarora warriors appeared on all sides did they realize that they had walked into a trap.

Now they were completely surrounded and would have their hands full. If they escaped with their lives, they would be fortunate.

Because of his ornate headgear, Wegowa drew the lion's share of attention, and most of the Tuscarora arrows were aimed at him.

Increasing the pace of his fighting, Ghonkaba retaliated with one rapid shot after another, losing no time fitting a fresh arrow into his bow the very second that he released one. His pace was as furious as his aim was sharp, and he opened a path in the closed ranks of the Tuscarora. He and Wegowa headed for it, and soon they were able to escape from the trap.

Instead of turning back and joining the Cherokee behind them, they continued to press forward relentlessly, shooting at every Tuscarora they encountered.

As they moved forward, Wegowa had good cause to reconsider the position that he had taken about Ghonkaba. He realized that he had been completely mistaken in his judgment. If Ghonkaba had the ulterior aim to supplant him as principal war chief, he could have stood aside just now while Wegowa was slaughtered by the Tuscarora. Instead, fighting like a madman, he had saved Wegowa's life at the risk of his own.

Ashamed for having doubted the motives of someone who called himself a friend, Wegowa vowed to go through the rites of blood-brotherhood with Ghonkaba after the battle ended. In the meantime, he had to, for his own conscience's sake, prove his intentions by fighting at Ghonkaba's side.

Never had these Tuscarora encountered such a whirlwind as that created by Ghonkaba and Wegowa fighting in tandem. Both shot their arrows with uncanny accuracy combined with bewildering speed. They took a continuing, heavy toll of the enemy, and the warriors of the Tuscarora fell back as the two men drove forward.

Wegowa was proud of his manhood, proud of the leadership he exerted as principal war chief of the Cherokee. He felt compelled to prove himself to Ghonkaba, and as the Seneca led his compatriots forward, Wegowa voluntarily took responsibility for protecting the flank of the Seneca leader.

He soon demonstrated that few warriors could be quicker or more agile with a bow and arrow. He took an arrow from its quiver on his back in a single motion and fitted it into the bow with remarkable rapidity, even as he drew the bow taut, aimed, and let fly.

Ghonkaba was virtually heedless of his own safety as he led the charge, and the expertise of Wegowa twice saved his life. One enemy was downed as he was about to unloose an arrow at the Seneca, and another met his death when he raised his arm to hurl a tomahawk at Ghonkaba.

Wegowa was so busy protecting his comrade that he paid no attention to his own safety, and he and Ghonkaba between them set an example for those who took part in the charge that stunned their foes.

Awed, frightened, and hurting at having lost so many braves, the Tuscarora fell back. Ghonkaba and Wegowa took advantage of the situation they had created and pushed all the harder.

The little company of Seneca scouts, following behind them, exploited the breach they created and widened it. Then came the main force of the Cherokee, fighting in an effort to redeem themselves and thoroughly enjoying fighting in the Seneca style, giving no quarter, accepting none, and continuing to attack incessantly.

As every enemy who had met the Seneca in combat for a hundred years had discovered to his dismay, no force could stand up to an army that drove so hard. The Cherokee, emulating the Seneca of old, were apt pupils. They maintained an unrelenting pressure on the foe.

As Ghonkaba had hoped would come about, the Tuscarora finally had taken all they could accept as a cohesive fighting force. They gave in to a sudden, unreasoning panic. Abandoning their bows, they lost their battle line, and every Tuscarora was strictly for himself.

This caused the Cherokee to alter their tactics, too, and for this they needed no instruction. The battle had degenerated to the point where it was hand-to-hand combat, so the

Cherokee resorted to their knives and tomahawks and wielded them with savage abandon and uncanny accuracy. They took advantage of the disorganized foe and turned the retreat into a headlong rout.

The Tuscarora left the right flank of the Creek dangerously exposed, and John Sevier was quick to take full advantage of the situation. Even before the Cherokee could move into the gap, he sent forward a hundred men of the half-battalion of frontier infantry he had been holding in reserve. These marksmen, eager to prove they were the equal of the comrades who had taken the brunt of battle so far, hammered at the Indians with all their might. The Creek, forced onto the defensive, lost their initiative and with it, their desire to fight. Seeing what had happened to the Tuscarora made them apprehensive, and they continued to battle halfheartedly.

Ghonkaba realized the time had come to combine his efforts with Colonel Sevier's. He had managed to keep the Cherokee under control, and he ordered them to turn now on the flank of the Creek, which they did in all their fighting fury, attacking fearlessly again and again.

The colonel's regiment continued to take a heavy toll of the Creek. Ghonkaba sensed that the battle's critical moment had arrived. Speaking in his own tongue, he said to Wegowa, "Call on the Tuscarora and the Creek in the language of the Cherokee to surrender at once."

Wegowa agreed, and raised his voice. "Surrender!" he cried. "Surrender to the Cherokee and to the regiment of the United States!"

The Tuscarora had no desire to lose their lives for a

cause in which they had lost all faith. Throwing down their weapons, they raised their hands high over their heads. They never recovered from the severe blow they suffered that day at the hands of Ghonkaba and his Cherokee and Seneca. Abandoning the home they had created in Tennessee and Alabama, they hastily retraced their steps eastward across the mountains to South Carolina, their power gone, their reputation in tatters.

Sevier, wanting to take no chance that the Cherokee would take undue advantage of helpless foes, sent troops forward to surround the Tuscarora and accept their surrender.

The move impelled the Creek, who now stood alone, to give up the struggle, too, and they began to surrender in large numbers. Although they were farther removed from the Cherokee on the field of battle, Sevier also surrounded them with frontiersmen, who accepted the surrender. The battle ended in a complete, unqualified victory for the frontier regiment and for the Cherokee. Ghonkaba made no attempt to stop the Cherokee warriors from roaming the battlefield and taking the scalps of the Tuscarora they had killed and the Creek who had been killed by the militiamen of the regiment.

The war chiefs of the Cherokee came forward to congratulate Ghonkaba on the role he had played in the victory, but to each he said the same thing: "The role that I played was not important. It is Wegowa who deserves the full credit. He is your leader, and he performed brilliantly!"

Wegowa knew this was untrue, that Ghonkaba was praising him falsely, giving him credit he did not deserve in order to build him up with his own people. Realizing it would be unseemly to deny the validity of what Ghonkaba was saying, he quietly accepted the praise.

Although the day was well advanced, hunting parties went out to search for deer and buffalo, and that night Wegowa insisted on holding the brotherhood rites that would make him and Ghonkaba close relatives for life. In the absence of Jejeno, only Casno had the rank to act as the medicine man in the ceremony. Praying impartially to the gods of the Seneca and of the Cherokee, he implored the deities to look with favor on the rites that he was conducting. Rusog and Renno stepped forward, each handing him a ceremonial stone knife whetted especially for this ceremony.

Casno jabbed Ghonkaba's forefinger with one knife and then performed the same operation on Wegowa with the other. Then the two principals each squeezed drops of blood into the other's mouth while Casno intoned a ritual as old as the land itself. Finally, Ghonkaba and Wegowa were pronounced blood brothers. Embracing, they performed a dance to win the favor of their gods. The ceremony came to an end, and Rusog commented quietly to Ena, "You can no longer ignore me, you know; you're now my sister." He chuckled at his own humor, while she glared at his retreating back.

In the morning, the Indians bade farewell to the regiment. The frontiersmen were returning to their homes in eastern Tennessee, while the Cherokee were taking a direct route to their town.

Sevier's farewell to Ghonkaba and Wegowa was affectionate. "Between us, lads, we pulled the teeth of the

Tuscarora and the Creek. We'll meet again in the next campaign.''

Ghonkaba smiled at him. "You're thinking of the Choctaw, of course?''

"You bet I am," the colonel replied. "They're acting too big for their moccasins and they need to be hauled down a few pegs. I'll call on you when the time comes. Don't let the flag that Washington gave you get dusty.''

A short time later, the Cherokee and the little band of Seneca were in the wilderness striking out for home.

Ghonkaba saw another opportunity to train the Cherokee in the ways of the Seneca. At his instigation, Wegowa appointed a number of warriors as scouts. Each of the Cherokee was assigned to accompany a veteran Seneca and to learn from him.

Ghonkaba's eyes sparkled mischievously as he asked Wegowa, "What do you think of assigning Ena as the scouting teacher of Rusog?''

The war chief was so startled that he roared with laughter. "I take it you're serious?" he countered.

Ghonkaba chuckled and then sobered. "Indeed I am serious," he said. "Rusog continues to stand in too much awe of my daughter, and she takes advantage of his good nature. They seem incapable of solving their problem by themselves. As I see it, if they're thrown exclusively into each other's company for days at a time, they'll either kill each other or reach some sort of accommodation.''

"You have ingenuity as well as courage, my brother," Wegowa said. "It will be fascinating to see whether both Rusog and Ena emerge from this ordeal with their scalps intact!"

Chapter IX

Ena glided noiselessly through the forest, studying the terrain ahead, yet never slackening her pace. Suddenly she halted, bent low to examine the ground, and then beckoned imperiously.

Rusog, who had been following at a distance of several feet, joined her and glared. "What is it now?" he demanded.

"If you will," Ena replied sweetly, "please examine the ground. Then tell me if you find anything unusual about it."

He glanced at the ground and shrugged. "I see deer tracks, if that's what you refer to," he said. "I certainly don't find them unusual in this part of the wilderness."

"Let us suppose," she said, "that you are alone as a

221

scout for the Cherokee. What do you do when you see these signs?''

''I follow them, naturally,'' he replied patiently. ''I track the deer, bring it down, and we have fresh meat for our supper. What else would I do?'' He was both belligerent and impatient.

Ena's attitude was lofty, and she made no attempt to conceal her feeling of superiority. ''You are wrong. You should digress long enough to hunt for the deer and to shoot it only if the war chief has asked you to acquire food as well as carry out your regular duties. You are not traveling alone through the wilderness. Nor are you a member of a small hunting party. As a scout, you have a responsibility to a large number of warriors, and you are acting as their eyes and ears. By going hunting, you could place the entire expedition in grave jeopardy. At no time do you forget that you are responsible for the safety of those who are following you.''

Rusog knew she was right in principle, but he could not help resenting her high-handed manner. ''I suppose,'' he said sarcastically, ''that you knew as soon as you first became a scout that you were required to pursue that duty at all times and never give in to a natural wish to hunt for game.''

Ena knew he was seething, and decided to push her lecture even further. ''As a Seneca,'' she replied, ''I've always been aware that my duty is paramount and that all other considerations must take second place.''

''As a good Cherokee,'' Rusog said angrily, ''I regard it as my first duty to provide food for myself and those who depend on me. Therefore, it would be only natural for me to take a short time from scouting in order to shoot a deer."

"That is where we differ," Ena assured him. "My primary allegiance is to the warriors who make up our force of arms. Their welfare comes ahead of anything else."

"Do you mean to tell me that fresh meat isn't in their best interests?"

She, too, became more strident. "To be sure, it is. But some of us are assigned only to procure food. As a scout, I am required to lead a force and to notify my superiors if any enemy stands between us and our goal, or if any other danger threatens. That is all I am to do."

"How do you manage to live with such perfection?" he asked snidely, his temper finally getting the better of him.

She had taken enough of his bullying. "How I live is strictly my own business."

"I'm making it my business," he said rudely, "because I'm going to be living with you, and it's to our mutual advantage for me to understand you."

"Your imagination is playing tricks on you!" Ena told him icily. "I can't conceive of a condition in which I would marry you and live with you."

"You're mistaken!" he retorted. "You have no voice in the matter. Our fathers have become blood brothers, and they will arrange our marriage. I have taken up the issue with my father, who not only gives his consent, but has told me that he will speak with your father. And he assures me that if necessary he will persuade him to grant his approval."

"No one has bothered to consult me," Ena shot back, "and since it's my future that is at stake, I warn you that my consent is necessary. And it will never be forthcoming!"

"You have performed the duties of a man," the exasperated Rusog told her, "and because you have excelled in your field, you've assumed a man's independent airs. You forget that even the sacred Corn Mother depends on her son for his help and protection. You need a lesson that will put you in your place."

"Who is going to teach me that lesson? Will it be you?"

Goaded beyond endurance, Rusog replied firmly, "Since no one else will take that responsibility, I accept it as my duty." Reaching out, he caught hold of both her wrists with one large, brawny hand and grasped them firmly.

"What do you think you're doing?" Ena demanded in outrage. "Let me go this instant!"

Having taken the lead, Rusog felt more assured and gave in to a good humor.

Laughing easily but savagely, he seated himself on a boulder, and hauling her across his lap, backside up, he proceeded to spank her soundly. "This is what you've needed for a long time," he told her, "and I've been wanting to administer just this punishment to you."

Ena struggled furiously, writhing, kicking, and trying to wrench her hands and arms free, but Rusog continued to hold her in a grip of steel. Her efforts were unavailing, so she suddenly went limp and tolerated the indignity of the spanking in unresisting silence.

Her failure to fight confused Rusog. Afraid that he might be hurting her, he released her wrists.

No sooner was Ena free than she became a demon. She lashed out with both hands, using her strong fingernails to rake his face and torso. Meanwhile, she was kicking him where he was the most vulnerable. He fell back before the fury of her onslaught. Ena persisted, determined to humiliate him as he had humiliated her.

If Rusog had used his fists, he could have ended the unequal struggle, but he didn't want to hurt her and merely tried to grasp her wrists again.

By far more agile than he, Ena managed to slip from his grasp again and again.

Eventually, he did succeed in catching her right wrist, forcing her arm behind her back. He pulled her close, and with his free hand gripping her shoulder, he bent his head and kissed her full on the lips.

She struggled for some moments, but a strange and curious effect worked its spell on her. She was not finding his kiss unpleasant. On the contrary, she was enjoying it enormously, so much so that she stopped fighting and, pressing her free hand against the back of his head, brought him closer.

Rusog was undergoing a series of increasingly complicated reactions. His desire for vengeance faded, his anger was no longer even remembered, and he was totally absorbed in their kiss.

Ena, too, forgot that she was competing with him and

that she regarded this giant as a lout. Instead, she was breathless as she clung to him.

At last, they drew apart and looked at each other soberly. Both were awakening to a consciousness of the passions they had unleashed. All they knew for certain at the moment was that their feelings had undergone a vast, significant change. No longer were they antagonistic, no longer engaged in headlong competition.

Suddenly Ena gasped. "Your face!" she cried.

Not knowing what she meant, Rusog lifted a hand to his face; his fingers came away feeling sticky. Looking down at them, he realized he was bleeding from the scratches she had inflicted.

"We need to find water!" Ena said urgently. "Quickly!" Everything else was driven from her mind, and she started off at a fast pace. Rusog followed, debating whether he should apologize for having spanked her.

In a short time, Ena again displayed her remarkable capability for finding what she needed in the forest. She came upon a small, fast-moving creek and, kneeling beside it, motioned Rusog to come next to her.

Cupping her hands, she splashed water onto his face and torso, taking bits of moss from the riverbank and gently wiping away all vestiges of blood. Then she searched for "the magical plant that the gods favored," known to some tribes as sassafras and believed to have medicinal qualities. Quickly spotting the shape of its leaves, she applied several to the cuts on his face, chest, and upper arms. After stinging for a moment, he felt much better. "This will remove the blood from your wounds," she told him, "and

226

CHEROKEE

will restore you until you are as good as new. Tonight, when we join the others, we can say that you encountered a wildcat.''

He grinned at her, then began to chuckle. "A wildcat? That would be the truth.''

Ena joined in his laugh without self-consciousness. He reached for her hand and covered it with his.

They stopped laughing and felt a new, heavy tension as they looked at each other. Then, Ena averted her head. Without another word, they both stood up and resumed their duties. For the rest of the day, they tended strictly to business, conversed as little as possible, and avoided all contact, as though afraid they had started something they might not be able to finish satisfactorily.

When they were relieved by another pair of scouts, one a Seneca and the other a Cherokee, they returned to the encampment. As they approached a cooking fire where supper was being served and were handed gourds of food, Ghonkaba and Wegowa looked at each other in puzzlement.

"Rusog looks like he fell into a bramble patch,'' Ghonkaba remarked, "and I don't recall seeing Ena as subdued as she appears tonight.''

"Look at them!'' Wegowa exclaimed. "Their shoulders touched for a moment, and neither seemed to object.''

Ghonkaba shook his head. "Don't regard it as being necessarily significant,'' he said. "I don't think they even noticed. They've moved apart again, and they're acting like complete strangers.''

*   *   *

After a leisurely march of almost two weeks, the expedition reached the main town of the Cherokee. There the warriors received the heroes' reception that they deserved.

Jejeno led a company of maidens and junior warriors in a dance of thanks to the gods, and the entire population joined in additional prayers of thanksgiving.

Because the Cherokee had not participated in any battle within recent memory, it was rightly suspected that the little band of Seneca was responsible for the victory. They were accorded a lion's share of the praise, until Ghonkaba soon called a halt. He lavished praise on Wegowa, calling him the principal architect of the victory over both the Tuscarora and the Creek.

Rather than accept praise that he felt he didn't deserve, Wegowa withdrew to the house of his father. There he was joined by Loramas, the Grand Sachem, and Jejeno. He insisted on making a full confession.

"I badly misjudged Ghonkaba of the Seneca," he said, "in believing he was trying to gain my own position. At the climax of the battle, he risked his life to save mine. He could have stood aside, let me be killed, and then hoped to move into my place. I have become his blood brother. But I feel that I have not done enough for him. Something is lacking, and I don't know what it might be."

After Wegowa went out to rejoin his warriors, the Grand Sachem spoke freely. "You and I," he said to Jejeno, "probably are of one mind in this matter."

"So it appears."

"Now, while our people are celebrating the return of the

228

expedition, is a good time to hold a secret conclave of the council and to reach certain conclusions.''

"I shall summon the elders, the medicine men, and the principal warriors without delay.''

In a short time, the council convened in the Grand Sachem's house, with only Wegowa and Ghonkaba absent. Loramas came to the point quickly. "I have learned from no less an authority than my son,'' he said, "that our debt to Ghonkaba of the Seneca is endless. He alone is responsible for our victory, and he is fashioning our fighting men into warriors who will enter battle as do the Seneca. I propose that we reward him in ways that will permanently reflect our gratitude to him.''

"Speak plainly and not in riddles, Loramas,'' one of the elders said testily. "At my age, I must hear plain talk in order to understand what is being said and why.''

"Very well,'' the Grand Sachem said. "Examine, if you will, what the small band of Seneca in our midst have accomplished. Think of the good they have done for our people and for the cause of our nation. I cannot help but wonder this: if a few Seneca have done us this much good, what could ten times their number accomplish?''

The elder raised his voice in alarm. "We would be taking a terrible risk,'' he objected. "No fighting men in all the world are the equal of the Seneca. If they have a large number of warriors here, within our walls, they would destroy us from within.''

Jejeno jumped to his feet. "That they would never do!'' he insisted. "Ghonkaba already has demonstrated that no warriors on earth are more honorable than the Seneca. His men will help us become more accomplished in the art of fighting and winning battles. We would be able to hold up our heads when we meet the Choctaw.''

"Jejeno is right," the Grand Sachem said. "We have nothing to fear from the Seneca. We have thousands of warriors we can put under arms. It would be a sign of cowardice if we turn our backs on a few hundred of them because we secretly fear them.''

The gathering echoed his feelings. The business of the conclave soon was settled in favor of the Grand Sachem's position.

That same night, in keeping with the ancient custom of the Cherokee, the entire town ate supper together. The meal was cooked on spits over large fires, and members of each clan sat together. The Seneca scouts, reunited with their families, also sat together, occupying an inconspicuous place near the rear.

At the beginning of the meal, Jejeno rose to his feet and implored the gathering to thank the Corn Mother for her bounty, and also to be grateful to the Spirit Holder for the recent victory. Then, to the embarrassment of the Seneca, he extolled their virtues in the campaign, and he paid special tribute to Ghonkaba for his contributions.

Ghonkaba wanted to protest that Wegowa, not he, was responsible. Jumping to his feet, Ghonkaba acknowledged that he owed his life to Wegowa's talent and courage, and he emphasized that Wegowa truly deserved his position as leader of the Cherokee warriors.

When he finished his remarks, his generosity was wildly applauded by both the Cherokee and his own small band of

Seneca. Then, when the assemblage grew quiet again, the Grand Sachem of the Cherokee stood and held up his hands for silence.

"I ask the people of the Cherokee nation to make a momentous decision this evening," he said, "and I will tell you that it was discussed this very day by your council and met with unanimous approval."

Ghonkaba was surprised. This was the first he had heard of the council meeting.

"Our military expedition covered itself with glory," Loramas went on. "The Tuscarora went down to defeat, and the mighty Creek were humbled. This was due in large part to the example set by the Seneca allies who live in our midst, and to the leadership of Ghonkaba, who led our own braves to victory."

Ghonkaba was dismayed. He saw Wegowa sitting beside his father, looking very much at ease and pleased.

"Our lives have changed dramatically for the better since the Seneca came to live in our midst," Loramas said. "Therefore, I propose that we make their welcome permanent by extending to them full privileges as Cherokee. From this moment forward, no difference will exist between them and us. Just as Wegowa, my son, has become the blood brother of Ghonkaba, whom I also recognize now as my son, all the Seneca among us will be full-fledged Cherokee. What do you say?"

His listeners sprang to their feet, roaring their approval. Loramas raised his hands for silence. "I also propose," he said, "that we increase the number of Seneca to whom we offer citizenship, homes, and the full rights of the Cherokee nation. I do not know how many would accept our offer. We have unlimited land, limitless hunting grounds, while they are sorely limited, and I understand that many of them are chafing under restrictions placed on them by the United States government, which has not forgotten that they are allies of Great Britain. I propose that we place no limit on the number of Seneca we will accept. Let all who come here be made welcome. They are members of the Indian nation that is more successful than any other. We have much to learn from them. Our gates should be open wide to all of their people who would join us and become a part of us. They can strengthen the Cherokee and make more firm our hold on the land and the hunting grounds that we call our own. Let all the braves and women of our nation have a voice in this matter. And, since future generations will be deeply influenced by what is decided tonight, let the young also have a free voice. Let us now determine whether we should so extend an invitation to the people of the Seneca nation.''

The vote in favor of admitting more Seneca to the land of the Cherokee was overwhelming. The few who objected were talked out of their stand by Loramas and Wegowa, and the vote was made unanimous.

Ghonkaba was overwhelmed, and the look that he received from Toshabe spoke volumes. The decision made by Loramas meant that the customs and beliefs of the Seneca would be kept alive in the lands west of the Appalachian Mountains because enough of their people would be on hand to maintain them in ways that their little band of pioneers could not do. The gods of the Seneca would still be worshiped, and the manitous would continue to intervene with the gods on the behalf of mere mortals. Even the language of the Seneca would continue to live.

Casno uttered a prayer of thanks to the gods for making this vastly important decision feasible. Ghonkaba, Toshabe, and all the Seneca joined in the prayer with all their hearts.

Ghonkaba and Toshabe remained awake until the small hours of the morning, talking over the unexpected development that was certain to change their lives and those of their children for the better.

"We have been assuming," Ghonkaba said, "that the Seneca will respond eagerly to the invitation, but we are forgetting how proud and independent our people are. They may reject the invitation, even though their lives in New York will be regulated by the state government."

"Life has become so pleasant for us, and the future seems to hold such promise for the children," Toshabe remarked, "that I can't help hoping—purely selfishly—that a large number will join us here. Then we'll have good reason to hope that our grandchildren will continue to worship the ancient gods of our people and will obey the customs and the laws of the Seneca."

"I'm trying to look beyond my selfish reasons," Ghonkaba replied, "and I hope, as you do, that we'll be joined by a number of our brothers and sisters. As sad as it is to concede, I must admit that the days of the Seneca greatness in the North are numbered. The Iroquois League has been assigned now to history. Their brilliant exploits will become a thing of the past alone. They'll live lives of isolation in their own land without participating in the active life of their neighbors. Neither will they participate in any of the wars that America will fight, so there will be no opportunities to win fresh glory. Only if they send an appreciable number of families to join the Cherokee will there be a chance to keep alive the glorious name and heritage that the Seneca have won through the ages. As I grow older, I gain a greater appreciation of what my distinguished ancestors, Ghonka and Renno, accomplished for our people. I can only hope their exploits live on in the memories of the Seneca.''

"I share that hope with you," Toshabe replied. "How do you propose to deal with the generous offer that Loramas of the Cherokee has made?''

"It would be best if I could travel to the town we left and explain, myself, what the Seneca will gain if they choose to move here. But, alas, I feel that the circumstances here obligate me to remain, regardless of my preferences. Ena would undoubtedly do well and act competently if she were to go in my place, but it would not be seemly to send a woman on such an errand. That means the natural choice is our son, Renno.''

"Do you think he is old enough to bear such a responsibility?''

Ghonkaba's reply was firm. "He truly earned his feather as a senior warrior on this expedition," he said. "As to his other talents, we shall find out when we either greet some new arrivals from the land of the Seneca, or he returns alone and empty-handed. He bears the most illustrious name in the annals of our people, and he is old enough to learn to live up to that name. He will gain far more than we will if Seneca come to join us here. And Renno must learn that we are required by the gods to earn whatever benefits we receive.''

Toshabe knew he was right. A great burden would be placed on their son, but nevertheless Renno had an opportunity if he could summon the skills to take advantage of the situation.

Ena and Renno enjoyed the privilege of sleeping late, one of the benefits of having participated in a successful military venture. El-i-chi joined his parents for breakfast; after gulping his food, he went off to fish and find some vegetable roots.

"I wish that Renno would get up," Ghonkaba said. "He knows nothing as yet about the journey in store for him."

"Let him sleep," Toshabe replied. "It's already too late for him to go out on the trail today. It will do no harm for him to rest."

Ghonkaba grinned a trifle sheepishly. "That's true," he said. "I'm just eager to see him prepare for what will be ahead."

They were interrupted by the sound of banging at the entrance, and Ghonkaba hastened to answer the summons.

Rusog stood on the threshold. Very clearly, he considered this to be a special occasion. His head was newly shaved on both sides of his scalp lock, and he wore new trousers of buckskin, as well as a Cherokee senior warrior's robe, a buffalo skin garment decorated with dyed porcupine quills laid out in a mathematical design.

Ghonkaba welcomed him, then led him into the house, where Toshabe greeted him cordially and offered him breakfast.

"No, thank you," the young giant replied. "I have no appetite these days. May I have a word with you, sir?" he asked, addressing Ghonkaba.

"Certainly," was the prompt reply.

"Shall I leave the room?" Toshabe inquired.

Rusog shook his head vigorously. "No," he said. "This concerns you as much as it does War Chief Ghonkaba. Sir," he continued, his voice quavering in spite of the bold front he tried to present. "Sir, I seek your permission to ask Ena's hand in marriage."

The first thought that came into Ghonkaba's mind was that his scheme had been successful when he had assigned Ena and Rusog to work together as scouts. "If you have reason to believe she will respond favorably, by all means, ask her. If you think there's a good chance she'll reject you, however, I urge you to keep silent for the time being."

"My husband knows our daughter, as do I," Toshabe said, "and the point he is trying to make is that rather than have her reply negatively, it would be far better to wait. She can be incredibly stubborn, and once she rejects you, it would take a superhuman effort to persuade her to change her mind."

"I have reason to think," Rusog said, "or at least to hope, that Ena will accept my proposal."

"Under those circumstances," Ghonkaba said, "I can only offer you the best of good fortune."

"You'll have to exercise more patience," Toshabe said with a smile. "Ena is still asleep."

"At this time of morning?" Rusog asked incredulously, and before his hosts could stop him, he cupped his hands over his mouth and bellowed, "Ena! Wake up! I need to see you!"

Toshabe looked at her husband in despair. Such bull-like tactics were certain to antagonize Ena, who then would reject a proposal regardless of whether she approved of Rusog.

To their astonishment, Ena's voice, floating from the rear of the house, was calm and moderate. In fact, she sounded sweet. "I've just been awake for a few minutes, Rusog," she called. "Have patience and wait for me, please."

The young man nodded and grinned, in no way surprised by her temperate response.

Toshabe insisted on giving Rusog breakfast and piled the food high on his plate. In spite of his protestations that he lacked an appetite, he ate ravenously. When Ena appeared at last in the doorway, he clambered hastily to his feet.

Toshabe and Ghonkaba regarded their daughter in stunned silence. Instead of the buckskin shirt and trousers that had been her uniform on the expedition, she was wearing a gown of flowered white silk that had been Martha Washington's parting gift to her. She had also enhanced her natural beauty with cosmetics: Rims of kohl around her eyes emphasized the most vital of her features, and her mouth was scarlet. She had acquired perfume, too, while living in civilized communities, and now a mysterious, musklike scent filled the room. A faint, enigmatic smile touched the corners of her mouth. Going straight to Rusog, she reached out and touched him on the bare arm, a gesture that women ordinarily reserved for the men they had married.

"It's so nice to see you again," she said softly. "Thank you for coming here."

Ghonkaba was stunned. Ena's conduct did not mystify her mother, however. Toshabe knew from the dress, makeup, and attitude that Ena had already made up her mind. "Come along, Ghonkaba," she said. "We're wanted elsewhere." Taking her husband's arm, she guided him firmly from the chamber.

He looked at her in bewilderment, only dimly recognizing facts from the look on her face.

Rusog could not wait to bring up the subject that weighed heavily on his mind. As soon as he and Ena were alone, he said, "I slept very poorly last night. My mind was filled with the invitation that my grandfather extended to the people of the Seneca nation to move to this land."

"It was a generous offer," Ena said as she brewed herself a gourd of herb tea, "but it was nothing that my father and the warriors of his company have not earned."

The last thing Rusog wanted to discuss was the validity of the invitation. "I suppose," he said, "that among those who will accept the invitation will be many who are friends of Ena."

"Yes," she replied with a smile. "I'm sure I'll have many friends in the group that will join us here."

"Included will be many who are warriors." He sounded belligerent.

Ena had no idea what he was talking about. "Yes, I'm reasonably sure that a number of warriors will be in the party," she murmured.

"These are braves who are admirers of Ena." Rusog was working himself into a fury. "They wish to marry Ena. Being Seneca, they think highly of themselves and recognize no members of other nations as competitors for her hand!"

At last she understood and tried unsuccessfully to hide her smile.

That was the last straw, and he lost his temper. "I will not tolerate competition for the hand of Ena from warriors of the Seneca or from men of any other nation!" he roared.

He misinterpreted her silence, thinking that she was disagreeing with him. Catching hold of her shoulders, he began to shake her. "I will accept no warrior of any land as a rival for the hand of Ena!" he shouted. "You are my woman, and you will be as long as we both live!"

She tried to speak, but he was shaking her too hard. She dug her fingernails into his arm as a way of persuading him to desist. Rusog's arms began to sting, so he stopped shaking her long enough to brush away her hands. Now she addressed him quietly. "In only one way," she said, "can you make certain that no Seneca warriors will compete with you for my hand."

"What way is that?" he bellowed.

"Marry me!" she replied promptly. "Then no warrior of any nation will dare to pay court to me."

He remembered belatedly that he had intended to propose to her. "You will become my wife, then?" he demanded.

In complete control of the situation and of Rusog, Ena became demure. "I've had no choice," she replied, "since you revealed your true nature to me the day we first were assigned duty together." Giving him no opportunity to reply, and wanting to end the suspense, she placed her hands on his shoulders and raised her face to his.

Rusog had intended to make several comments, but when he became aware of her liquid eyes peering into his, of her scarlet mouth beckoning invitingly, he forgot everything else and took her into his arms.

Her response made him forget potential rivals in the company of Seneca who might be coming to the land of the Cherokee.

To observe necessary amenities, the young couple went to Ghonkaba and Toshabe. "I proposed marriage to Ena," Rusog boomed, "and she's done me the honor of accepting me."

They looked at their daughter for confirmation.

"Rusog honored me by asking me to become his bride," Ena said meekly, "and I was pleased to accept."

Ghonkaba was startled. Ena the firebrand had vanished, and in her place was a girl so passive, so mild, that he scarcely recognized her. He turned to Toshabe, hoping to be given an explanation, but saw that his wife was accepting the miraculous change as normal and natural.

Ghonkaba grasped the young warrior's left wrist in a sign of friendship and acceptance and then turned to Ena, who came into his arms for his kiss. In her eyes, he saw no meekness, no passivity. They were bold and forthright as usual, and a glint of mischief appeared in them. That gleam gave him a clue: Rusog would learn in due course that he had not taken an average squaw.

She was still his daughter, and the blood of the great Renno continued to flow in her veins. Now that he thought of it, Rusog might never realize how he was being handled and directed by a wife who had few equals.

The wedding of Ena and Rusog was an event of consequence in the Indian world. Representatives of more than a score of nations, from the Algonquian of Maine to the Seminole of Florida, were in attendance. Also on hand were emissaries from the distant tribes of the Rocky Mountains and of the Great Plains that approached them. Even the Creek, recent enemies of the Cherokee in war, sent the daughter and son-in-law of their sachem to represent them.

Only one prominent tribe ignored the wedding. Significantly, the powerful Choctaw, the near neighbors due south of the Cherokee, paid no attention to the occasion.

This snub was responsible for a conference the day before the wedding between Ghonkaba, the father of the bride, and Wegowa, the father of the groom.

Ghonkaba, who was delighted because the nations of the Iroquois League had sent a full-scale delegation to the ceremonies, took a grim view of the Choctaw slight. "I can see this only as a deliberate insult," he said. "The Choctaw know that the homeland of the Seneca is too far away to enable my people to meet the challenge and face them in a war. But that is not true of the Cherokee, their neighbors. Once the wedding has taken place, you and I will have to sit down with Loramas and decide what to do."

"I know of only one response that an honorable nation can make," Wegowa replied. "We must declare war against the Choctaw. To do anything else would be to lose face with every tribe that has sent delegates to attend the wedding."

"You're right," Ghonkaba agreed, "but all the same, we must examine every facet of the issues at stake in order to make certain of where we stand before we become involved in a war against a nation as large and powerful as the Choctaw."

They made a serious effort to put the problem out of their minds in order to concentrate on the wedding festivities.

On the night before the ceremonies, a great banquet was held in an open field. There, volunteer cooks roasted whole quarters of three buffalo on spits, along with a dozen deer and any number of wild turkeys, ducks, and other game. Dozens of fish were broiled or fried, and an almost bewildering array of vegetables was prepared.

The banquet was opened with a long prayer to the gods,

alternately recited by Jejeno and Casno. Lesser medicine men engaged in a ritual dance. Then, before food was served, Ghonkaba and Wegowa were required to make speeches. They spoke at length, wishing happiness and long lives to the bride and groom.

No one wanted the meal to grow cold, so the ceremonies were suspended while everyone ate the delicacies and took turns wishing well to the bridal couple.

The bride and groom had sat apart during this earlier portion of the banquet, but now, Ghonkaba, Renno, and El-i-chi conducted Ena across an empty, open space that separated her family from the groom's. She was taken to a seat adjacent to Rusog's.

It was an acknowledged part of the ceremony, in the land of the Seneca as well as in the land of the Cherokee, for the bride to put bits of various foods into the groom's mouth. This was done, but at Ena's instigation, something new was added to the ceremony: the groom also fed the bride. The younger people present, particularly the women, regarded this as being of great significance and approved heartily. By taking a firm stand for her sex, Ena had already assured herself of even greater popularity with the women of the Cherokee.

The massed drums of the host nation provided music for the dancing that followed. More than forty Cherokee drums spoke in unison, reverberating through the wilderness for miles in every direction.

Then Casno and Jejeno engaged in a special dance to the goddesses of marriage and of fertility. In the case of the

Cherokee, the dance honored the principal goddess, the Corn Mother. The medicine men were succeeded by the bridal couple, who were required to invent a dance of their own. It was customary for the bridegroom to take the lead in this dance. Rusog lived up to expectations, leading Ena through a series of foot-stamping gyrations that brought the audience to its feet.

Once again, Ena inserted her own ideas into the ceremony. She and Rusog proceeded to do a dance that she had devised, a graceful, dervishlike series of movements that left both of them panting for breath.

They were joined in the open space by their parents, then their friends, then the members of the respective clans, and finally, by the entire assemblage. Here the festivities reached a grand climax.

Hundreds of braves, from white-haired elders to the youngest junior warriors, each with an appropriate partner, thundered up and down the field in time to the pulsating beat of the drums. The dancers twirled and stamped, gyrating madly. Now and again, an individual or a couple would unleash a loud war cry as a way of expressing the exuberance that the occasion inspired.

The dancers were led by Rusog and Ena. Each appeared determined to wear out the other. As Toshabe commented to her husband with a laugh, "I've never seen such determination in two people. They're not even married yet, but they're going to exhaust each other—if it's the last thing they ever do."

Ghonkaba knew that when their daughter and her husband-to-be started making love in earnest, their competitive athletic spirit would ebb, but he held his peace.

Tired couples fell to the ground and, laughing and panting, crawled out of the path of those who had greater endurance. The dancing went on and on, with a score of young couples determined to win the prize traditionally offered by the bride and groom to those who were still on their feet at the end.

Once again, Ena and Rusog broke with tradition. They had made up their minds to outlast all the other dancers. This they did, recklessly expending energy as they stamped and whirled. Perspiration gleamed on their faces and bodies, but both were in superb physical condition, and they found it easy to maintain their frenetic pace. Two by two, other dancers dropped out of the competition, but the bride and groom did not falter.

"My grandson," Loramas announced proudly, "has met his match at last!"

When the last of the dancers dropped out of the contest, it was the moment Ena had been waiting for. Smiling broadly, she deliberately increased the tempo of her dancing. The drummers did their best to keep up with her, but she left even them behind.

Rusog stubbornly refused to be defeated by his bride. Calling on his hidden reserves of strength, the giant danced more vigorously than he had previously. Thumping and stamping, he outdanced Ena. In order to make certain that everyone present realized that he was the victor—and wanting in particular to make sure that Ena was aware of it—he scooped her off the ground and, carrying her in his arms to her seat, bent his head and kissed her.

She curled her arms around his neck and returned his kiss with passion as well as with good humor.

The crowd applauded vigorously. It soon became apparent, however, that the bride and groom were not acting for the benefit of spectators. They were lost in their own world, and after they fell into their seats, holding hands, laughing and leaning against each other, they had eyes for no one else.

"They deserve each other," Ghonkaba said to Toshabe.

After the prenuptial ceremony finally came to an end, the bride was conducted back to the Seneca compound by an honor guard consisting of members of the former company of scouts. There she entered a small tent made of animal skins that Casno had erected. She was under orders to remain until her mother came for her in the morning in order to dress her for the wedding. This was to be her opportunity to commune for the last time as a single woman with the spirits of her ancestors and of others.

It grew quiet in the compound, but through the open window of their bedchamber in their nearby house, Toshabe and Ghonkaba could hear the soft voice of their daughter in the tent.

"She must be dreaming," Toshabe whispered. "Perhaps she is seeing Renno and Betsy in her dream and is communing with them."

Actually, although Ena indeed was dreaming, she was not enjoying a visit with her ancestors. Instead, she was stunned to discover that she was confronted by Clem Dawkins, her first love, who wore a bandage low on the forehead over his left eye, where he had been mortally wounded. He looked at her, his face resembling an expressionless Indian mask. She shivered as he said, "It has come to my attention that you are going to marry."

Afraid that he sounded accusing, she lost her voice and could only nod, rather than reply in words. "Have you forgotten me already?" Clem asked.

Somehow Ena found her voice and gained the courage to speak up. "No, Clem," she said, "I have not forgotten you. I shall never forget you. But I am young and alive. And I cannot spend my entire youth grieving for a lost love that can never be fulfilled. You will always hold a special place in my heart, Clem, and I will love you as long as I live and perhaps forever after that when I go to the land of my ancestors. But I must fulfill my destiny as a woman and as a Seneca. It is my duty to act as a bridge between the Seneca and the Cherokee, to bring children into the world who will honor both the people from whom I have come and the people I have joined. It is important that the traditions and ways of the Seneca live on in this new land. I am responsible for the carrying of that tradition, so I must beg you not to be annoyed or angry. I have not forgotten you. I do you no dishonor by giving myself to Rusog as his wife."

To her pleased surprise, Clem nodded and then smiled boyishly. "Well said, Ena," he told her. "You have expressed noble sentiments, and I'm proud to have loved you."

She was confused but nevertheless felt infinitely relieved.

"I do not ask you to be true to my memory," he said. "That would be demanding far too much, more than I have any right to ask, more than you have the right to give. If I have learned one thing since I crossed the great river into the land where your Seneca ancestors dwell, it is that life is meant to be lived for the living. Those whom we have left on the far bank of the great river that separates us from the living may remember us with affection and try to do justice to our memories in the way that they live from day to day. But they must overcome their grief and go on and find the happiness that is the right of every person to pursue."

Tears came to her eyes and she bowed her head.

"I give you my blessing, Ena." His voice became soft and she felt that he was caressing her, although there was no physical contact between her and his spirit. "May you have many years of joy and contentment with Rusog. May your children and their children after them look up to you and revere you and love you as I once loved you. May your days forever be filled with happiness."

The tears ran freely now. Her cheeks were wet, but she made no attempt to dry them.

Slowly, the benign figure of Clem faded, first becoming transparent, and then vanishing from the glade in which he appeared to her.

Ena realized she had made a smooth transition and was no longer asleep, but wide awake. She was lying on a bed of small boughs in the tent that had been erected for her last night as a single woman.

Strangely comforted and quietly exhilarated, she reached up in wonder and touched her cheeks, where tears still glistened. She was convinced that her dream had been very real and not a figment of her imagination. Her tears had bridged the vast distance between sleep and wakefulness, and between dream and reality.

Clem had really appeared before her and had given her his blessing. Of that she was certain.

It was right and good—good for her, good for the Seneca—that she was marrying Rusog. Her last doubt had been stilled. Now she could enter the marriage with a heart filled with love and compassion. No woman could ask for more.

Casno and Jejeno, wearing their ceremonial head masks and embroidered leather capes, officiated at the wedding. The rites were interminable, lasting for hours because of the relationship of the bride and groom to the rulers of Seneca and Cherokee.

For several hours, Ena and Rusog prostrated themselves on the ground before the two medicine men who performed dances, chanted incantations, and offered prayers to their respective gods for the health, welfare, and fertility of the young couple.

In spite of the solemnity of the occasion, the bridal couple occasionally could barely prevent themselves from laughing aloud. All of the older married couples present sympathized with their giggles, having undergone similar experiences.

Finally, they swore in the names of their gods that they would be faithful to each other for as long as they lived on earth. Ena promised to obey her husband at all times. She appeared to have no trouble with this oath, and those who knew her among the onlookers wondered if she secretly had reservations. They could hardly imagine Ena being obedient to any man.

What no one realized was that she found it easy to promise to obey Rusog because she could not imagine her husband ordering her against her will. She would make her wishes known, her stand would be clear, and that would end the matter—at least in her opinion.

The bride and groom each drank a drop of the other's blood and were pronounced man and wife.

Rusog presented Ena with a very small, thin slice of raw buffalo meat, which she quickly seared in the flames of the high fire. He then cut the meat into two equal pieces with his knife. When they had eaten it, the ceremony came to an end.

The couple intended to make their home in a new house, which they had built with the help of friends. Rusog swept Ena off her feet and, carrying her in his arms, started off toward their dwelling. She resented the indignity of being carried and demanded that he put her down. He laughingly refused. The last that anyone saw of them that day, Rusog was chuckling and shaking his head as Ena pounded her fists against his chest. The Seneca and Cherokee women were quick to speculate at length as to whether the marriage was off to a bad start.

The following day, around noon, most of the Seneca were gathered in a field inside the town wall, where a number of Cherokee were teaching the intricacies of a game played with a stone ball.

Two teams, one of Cherokee and the other of Seneca, ranged up and down the field, pursuing the ball, which they were striking with curved sticks.

The activities came to an abrupt halt when Ena and Rusog appeared, holding hands as they joined the throng at one side of the field.

"Please don't stop on our account," Ena urged pleasantly, and the game was resumed.

According to the rules of the game, only the opposing goaltenders were allowed to use their hands. The Cherokee scooped up the ball as it was thrown toward his goal and threw it with all his might back out into the field.

Rusog was distressed. "That's no way to throw the ball," he called. "How do you expect the Seneca to learn to play properly if you don't show them by example the right way to do things!"

"Will you object," he asked Ena meekly, "if I show them the proper way to throw the ball?"

"Why would I object?" Ena said sweetly. "I'm sure you're an expert at this game. Both sides can learn from you."

His chest seemed to expand as he reached down and scooped up the ball with both hands. "Always use two hands," he said to the Seneca players. "When the ball is moving rapidly, you'll need both hands to stop it. And two hands are absolutely necessary if you're going to get any direction and thrust when you throw it.'' He hurled the ball with both hands and it went far down the field.

Ena applauded. "That was a marvelous throw,'' she said in admiration.

"It was nothing special,'' her husband replied modestly.

"Well, I think it was,'' she insisted. "And if you want to play for a time, please go ahead, Rusog.''

He was torn. "What would you do?''

She looked at him brightly. "Oh, I'll watch you play. That will be quite enough for me!''

"All right, I will play,'' he said, "provided that the Seneca team will accept me as their goalkeeper.''

The Seneca were delighted, and that settled the matter.

Rusog played for the better part of an hour, his presence providing the Seneca with the strength that equalized the odds. Ena was content to remain on the sidelines until he departed from the lineup; she cheered and applauded every move he made, and he basked in her admiration.

When the game ended, Ghonkaba, who had been present as a spectator, left for home with Renno and El-i-chi at his side.

"I had no idea,'' El-i-chi said, "that Ena knew anything about that game.''

His father looked at him and laughed wryly. "I very much doubt that she does.''

"From the way she was screaming and carrying on with every move that Rusog made,'' El-i-chi said, "you'd think she was an expert.''

"She was applauding strictly for Rusog's benefit," Ghonkaba said. "I didn't think she had that much guile in her, but she's an expert, like any other woman."

"I don't understand."

Again his father laughed. "By the time that you're old enough, wise enough, and experienced enough to understand, El-i-chi, it will be too late for you. Just as it's now too late for Rusog."

Chapter X

Renno and Ghonkaba sat cross-legged before Loramas. For the occasion, the Grand Sachem wore his feathered headdress and beaded buffalo robe. "Say to the Seneca," he intoned, "that our land shall be their land. Our homes shall be their homes. The plenty that we enjoy, they shall share."

"I hear you, O Loramas," Renno said, "and I shall do as you have bidden me."

"Say also to the Seneca," Loramas went on, "that in return, by their example, by the way they live and bring up their young to follow in their footsteps—they shall give the Cherokee the benefit of being feared and respected by all Indians, as are the Seneca."

"And I," said Ghonkaba diplomatically, "am equally

certain that the Seneca will learn much from their Cherokee brothers. We are forever grateful for your openhearted gestures of true friendship and hospitality. We need your continued example in many respects."

When Ghonkaba and Renno returned home, they found Toshabe waiting to bid farewell to her son. Now it was Ghonkaba's turn to give messages to Renno.

"Give to Ja-gonh, my father, and to Ah-wen-ga, my mother, the love and respect that is due them from their son. Tell them that Toshabe and I have found happiness here, and it is our wish that they join us in this lush and bountiful land. But we know that the duty that Ja-gonh faces as Great Sachem of the Iroquois will keep him in the land of the Seneca for the rest of his days. Tell them I think of them often, and I do my best to follow the precepts that I learned from them."

Renno promised to deliver the message.

"When Ah-wen-ga asks for additional information about the marriage of Ena, say to her that Ena grows more like her grandmother in spirit each day. That will tell Ah-wen-ga all she needs to know."

Renno did not fully understand the message but dutifully promised to convey it to his grandmother.

It had been agreed that Ena and her new husband properly should pay a call of respect on her grandparents in the land of the Seneca. The young couple would take several days or a fortnight to settle themselves in their new home, and then they would set out on their long, sentimental journey. Meanwhile, Renno would be off with all due speed, traveling rapidly and alone, to carry the message of

Loramas and the Cherokee. Ghonkaba decreed that any delay might unfortunately suggest to the Grand Sachem and his people that their heartfelt, unprecedented invitation was regarded lightly by the Seneca.

When the time came for the young warrior to depart, he submitted to the ritual of allowing his father to apply his green and yellow Seneca war paint. Then he took up his emergency food rations and his weapons. Soon he was on his way. His mother's final words rang in his ears: "We shall pray to the manitous that your journey is safe and successful."

Bidding farewell to his parents and an envious El-i-chi, Renno started out on his long journey. He was in no great hurry but, nevertheless, traveled at the usual Seneca trot, the most rapid of paces, because he knew of no other way to travel. Game was plentiful, and the wilderness was filled with edible berries, plant roots, and other vegetation, so he had ample food.

Moving in a northeastern direction, he headed toward Kentucky before crossing the Appalachian Mountains. Not until he headed into the rugged Appalachians did he observe rudimentary precautions, having left the land of the Cherokee. Ahead, he faced hostile tribes, from the Miami of Ohio to the Erie of Pennsylvania, traditional enemies of the Seneca.

He brought down a deer and also enjoyed good fortune fishing. He made a small fire at night and rekindled it in time to prepare his breakfast each morning before he resumed his journey. Occasionally, he found evidence of hunting parties, ranging in size from one or two warriors to a dozen or more braves, but he took care to avoid them. In that way, he made certain that he did not become involved in any unpleasant incidents.

He was unprepared for the sight that he saw shortly after noon one day. Adjacent to a bush filled with ripe berries was a large man-made hole in the ground covered with leaves and branches to camouflage it. Peering into the hole, he saw a huge brown bear, a shaggy creature that weighed hundreds of pounds. Trapped at the bottom, the animal had no way of escaping.

Renno was horrified. He had no idea how long the beast had been imprisoned, and aside from the shocking cruelty to the animal, as a member of the Bear Clan he particularly resented the treatment. In addition, he had been raised with the family legend that his namesake, having made friends with a bear in his youth, had called the animal Ja-gonh, a name subsequently borne by young Renno's grandfather.

Renno immediately determined to do something to assist the trapped creature.

The bear looked up at him, clawing ineffectually at the side of the pit. Drawing his knife, Renno first hacked off several long branches of the berry bushes. These he threw into the pit, reasoning that the bear would be kept busy eating the berries for some time. Meanwhile, he could try to figure out some way to help.

In spite of his size, the bear delicately plucked the berries one by one from the branches and ate them. Renno stood at the lip of the hole, lost in thought as he looked around the forest. Suddenly, an idea occurred to him.

Removing his tomahawk from his belt, he began to hack at the base of a nearby birch tree. The tree, six or seven years old, already was tall enough that one end could rest on the base of the hole while the other end touched the top edge.

A plentiful stand of birch trees was nearby. He attacked them vigorously, cutting down a half dozen, and then dropping them into the pit, top first. He laid them out adjacent to each other, and although they were fairly narrow and slender, they were nevertheless resilient and appeared strong enough for what he had in mind.

The bear watched in apparent fascination as the trees descended into the pit.

To make the trees more secure, Renno cut a length of vine and bound them together, thus making a narrow platform.

Now he wondered how to convey to the bear the idea that it could use the trees as an escape tool. Perhaps he could show the bear by example.

Ignoring his own safety, he lowered himself partway into the pit, using the trees as a springboard. Although he was within the bear's reach when he ended his descent, the bear made no attempt to attack him.

Then, slowly, he inched his way upward to ground level again.

Almost miraculously, the bear remained absolutely motionless, watching intently. Looking back at the beast across one shoulder, Renno could have sworn that he saw intelligence in the animal's eyes.

Hauling himself to his feet, Renno turned back toward

the creature. ''Come on, mister bear,'' he muttered. ''Do as I've done, and you'll be all right.''

After a long wait, while the bear sniffed at the raftlike arrangement of the birch trees, it reached out experimentally with one huge paw and swiped at the tree trunks. Its claws made ripping sounds as they tore through the soft, pliant bark.

Then, while Renno held his breath, the bear dropped to all fours and laboriously began to climb toward the ground level. The birch trees sagged beneath the animal's great weight, but they did not break, and little by little, the bear managed to move out of the pit.

At last, to Renno's joy and relief, the bear reached the ground and half hauled, half rolled itself off the logs that had been the bridge between it and captivity. Then the animal pulled itself to its feet.

Renno, who was six feet tall, suddenly realized that the bear would be taller by at least a full head. He was standing so close that the animal could have reached out and, with a single swipe of a powerful paw, knocked the mere human to the ground and inflicted severe—perhaps permanent—injury. If the bear decided to cuff him, Renno could do nothing other than put up a feeble resistance. He could not use either a bow or his rifle at such close quarters. By the time that he could draw his tomahawk and wield it, the bear could kill him.

But the beast made no move to attack. Instead, it appeared to understand and be grateful.

It stood so close to Renno that he caught a whiff of its hot, fetid breath.

The Seneca knew his life depended on the bear's whim. The animal could enfold him in its arms and crush him to death. One swipe of a paw could knock him unconscious to the ground. The long, powerful teeth that showed in the bear's open mouth could close on his flesh and tear off an arm or a leg with great ease.

Yet nothing happened. The bear remained utterly motionless.

Renno made no move either. He and the bear looked at each other, and at that moment, something so extraordinary happened that Renno knew he would remember that second for the rest of his life.

He and the bear seemed to achieve an understanding. A great sense of peace enveloped Renno, and he felt no fear in the presence of this wild, savage creature. Renno *knew* that the bear would not harm him, then or ever. Somehow he understood that he had been destined to find and to save the beast from captivity and to establish a relationship that would last for years.

He felt the presence of the manitous, and the air was heavy with their invisible attention.

In those few seconds, the bear, too, seemed to be transformed, to climb out of itself and to become one with the man. In a way that Renno could never understand, much less explain, his soul seemed to merge with the soul of the bear, and they became one for the brief second. Or was it for all eternity? Neither then nor later could he answer that question to his satisfaction.

All at once, the bear drew back and moved toward the

edge of the clearing, still looking directly at the man. Then it turned swiftly and disappeared into the wilderness.

Renno continued to stand for a very long time, looking at the spot where he had last seen the bear. In one sense, he was inclined to believe that he had imagined the incident, but the hole in the ground was still there, and so were the birch trees that he had cut. Imagination certainly could not have been responsible for what he had seen and experienced. This extraordinary episode, he realized, matched the experience that the original Renno had undergone so many years earlier. Therefore, he concluded, the manitous were looking out for him, were watching over him, and were preventing him from suffering harm. Like his ancestor and namesake, he appeared to be blessed.

This knowledge encouraged him, making him realize that he had been singled out for special treatment. At the same time, he could not help but become badly frightened: might he prove unworthy, unable to live up to the expectations of the manitous? His disgrace would be far worse than that of an ordinary mortal.

He uttered a heartfelt prayer to the manitous, asking them to give him the strength and the courage to live up to whatever assignment they would have for him in the future.

For the first time, he was able to make sense of a family saying attributed to the first Renno: "He who has won the favor of the manitous must work harder and more conscientiously than ordinary men in order to fulfill the mission given him in this life. And he must earn his way toward the happiness that all men seek."

The sense of responsibility weighed him down, but

Renno did not feel depressed, nor was he worried about the future. The bear, he was convinced, was an intermediary sent by the gods through the kindness of the manitous, and he felt blessed and honored. He was not yet invincible, to be sure, but invincibility was within his grasp. In ways that he could not foretell, he would be able to serve his people as they had not been served since the first Renno had walked through the wilderness. Yet that certain knowledge did not frighten him, nor cause him to doubt. In that magic moment when his soul had merged with that of the bear, he had been endowed with the animal's superhuman strength. That strength would stand him in good stead for the rest of his days.

Refreshed and ebullient as he resumed his journey, Renno belatedly realized that his encounter with the bear—which he refused to regard as an accident—had obligated him to his fellow human beings through service to the Seneca, to whom he was related by blood and by belief, and service to the Cherokee, who had made him one of them.

Renno wondered when, if ever, his path would cross that of the giant bear again. But something deep within him told him they would meet only if he persevered in his pursuit of the right and in his attempts to help his people.

He knew now that a turning point had been reached in his existence. He was a senior warrior of the Seneca, committed to a life with the larger and potentially more potent Cherokee nation, but he would live up to his own potential only in the services that he performed.

If that was the will of the gods, so be it.

*   *   *

The night was unbearably hot and humid. Swarms of mosquitoes made life additionally uncomfortable, and Ah-wen-ga slept fitfully. At breakfast she was in an unhappy mood, but her reasons were far more basic than the lack of sleep to which she attributed them. She peered at the loaf of corn bread that was baking, then irritatedly threw down one of the stones that constituted a lid for her stove. "Breakfast will be ready at any minute," she announced testily.

Ja-gonh had the good sense to humor her. "Take your time," he urged. "We have nothing special to do today, so we can eat whenever it's convenient."

"We rarely have anything special to do any day," she grumbled. "Every day is like the one that has just passed. That's the effect of the new regulations made by the state of New York."

Her husband sighed and shook his head. "We have as much or as little to do," he replied, "as our people have had for generations. The authorities are doing us a favor, you know. By making it more difficult for us to wage war, they're helping us to preserve life. We'll raise a generation that doesn't know the meaning of war."

She looked as annoyed as she felt. "When that day comes," she said, "our Seneca traditions will die. When I was a child, we reveled in the tales of the wonders performed in battle by Ghonka. We cheered the great victories won by our fathers. What exploits can the young celebrate these days? Shall they cheer when someone shoots a deer in the forest or catches a fish as long as a man's arm? Will such deeds become the measure of a warrior's worth?"

She was exaggerating, of course, but Ja-gonh knew that the point of view that she was expressing had validity.

"The new United States," he said, "has created an entire continent in transition. The freedom achieved by the American people changes everything. Just as the former colonists must find new ways to exist, so must we Indian nations who share their lands find new ways to live."

"We are being untrue to our Seneca heritage," Ah-wen-ga insisted. "Think of what Renno would say if he were alive today. What would Sun-ai-yee do? Would they accept the passive role assigned to us by the Americans or would they continue to practice their warlike ways?"

"I can't answer your questions," Ja-gonh replied. "I'm not sure anyone alive can answer them. We are required to move slowly and cautiously, one step at a time. We can only pray that we're moving in the right direction. The Seneca can and will play certain roles in the future of the United States. Of that much I'm certain. What those roles will be, I don't know, any more than I know the extent to which our future is tied to that of Ghonkaba."

Ah-wen-ga removed the corn bread from the oven and her mood softened. "Forgive me, Ja-gonh," she said. "I don't mean to be overly critical. But I know something is going to happen, and I cannot for the life of me determine what it is to be. I try to exercise patience, but it seems as though I have been patient forever. Now that quality no longer exists within me."

"Our people look to me for guidance," he said, "but our present existence is so new and so different from anything we have ever experienced that I am uncertain where to lead them. As I pray to the gods for help, I live in the certain knowledge that they will not desert us."

The foliage of spring contributed to Renno's ease of travel. Not only was game plentiful, but a hunter found it far easier to conceal himself in the heavy underbrush. After his extraordinary encounter with the bear, he managed to avoid contact with Indians until he reached the land of the Erie in Pennsylvania. Ever conscious that he was alone, he took special precautions. He lighted no cooking fires, he took pains to cover footprints, and he slept only in hollows and other relatively safe spots. Because the season was approaching when warriors wandered farthest from home and invaded the hunting grounds of their neighbors, every nation now maintained a more vigilant system of sentries. It was virtually impossible for Renno to escape surveillance.

One morning, as he was making his way through the thick forest, he realized he was being followed. He held his ear to the ground and listened. He was not in the least surprised to hear more than one pair of footsteps. He increased his pace, and when he arrived at a hilltop covered only with evergreens, he paused long enough to look back and survey the terrain he had just covered.

His vigilance was rewarded when he saw two warriors wearing the war paint of the Erie. He had no idea whether they knew he was a Seneca, but he felt that they could be expected to pursue him until they caught up with him. He had to either escape or confront them.

Escape was preferable, but he realized that his pursuers, experienced trackers, were having no difficulty in keeping on his trail.

He tried every stratagem he had been taught, every trick he knew in an attempt to throw them off his trail, but they remained quite close to him regardless, and it proved impossible to shake them.

He had to face the fact that he would have to confront them and, if possible, do away with them in order to save his own skin. With this in mind, he increased his pace to a rapid Seneca trot, knowing he could make far better time than could his pursuers, who had to search the ground for his tracks. This would be true unless they came close enough to actually see him.

When Renno came to an open space to his liking, he paused and then rapidly but deliberately went around the clearing, first to the left and then to the right, circling, doubling back, and leaving a multitude of footprints in the tall grass. When the result satisfied him, he climbed fifteen feet into the branches of a large oak tree, where he was invisible from the ground below. This suited his purpose, and here he awaited the approach of his enemies.

After a time, his patience was rewarded. Two tall, husky braves with the feathers of senior warriors in their scalp locks came into the clearing. Examining the tracks that Renno had left, they were completely confused by his tactics. They followed the crisscrossing markings that he had left on the ground, and their bewilderment only increased. Eventually, they stopped to try to decide how to proceed.

This gave their quarry time to consider his next move. His hold on the branch on which he was perched was too precarious to permit use of either his rifle or of his bow, so he reluctantly put these weapons out of his mind.

He debated whether to throw his tomahawk at one of the braves, and although he felt certain he would strike his target, he abandoned the idea because, without his tomahawk, he would be left only with his knife while facing the second of the Erie.

His mind functioned coolly, swiftly, and analytically, and he concluded that the best action would be to attack the pair directly, one at a time. Having made up his mind, he immediately put his plan into action.

Drawing his knife, he leaped down at one of the Erie, waiting until he was in midair before giving the fearsome war cry of the Seneca. He crashed into the shoulders of the brave, bearing him to the ground, and as they went down together, Renno's knife found its target in the man's heart.

Now the odds were equal for a direct confrontation with the surviving Erie. Leaving his knife protruding from the body of the slain brave, Renno drew his tomahawk and faced the other warrior.

The Erie was easily as tall as Renno and was far huskier, outweighing him by at least thirty pounds. He had a longer reach. As he crouched, holding his tomahawk in front of him, his footwork suggested that he was a veteran with long experience in this type of combat.

Renno emptied his mind of extraneous thoughts and devoted his concentration to this primitive duel. It was either kill or be killed. One mistake would be fatal.

They circled the clearing, each waiting for the other to make a false move. The Erie lost patience first, flicking his tomahawk in a feint. Refusing to be taken in by this strategy, Renno held his ground and slowly continued to move in a lateral direction. Afraid of being outmaneuvered, the Erie was forced to do the same, and they circled on and on tirelessly.

The Erie tried a number of ruses, all so elementary that Renno saw through them at once. Glancing over Renno's shoulder, the Erie called out to an imaginary confederate, but the Seneca's gaze remained unwaveringly on his foe. The Erie also pretended to stumble but gave himself away by taking a firmer grip on the tomahawk. He had intended to thrust forward if Renno tried to take advantage of his apparent clumsiness.

Engaged in the first duel of his life, Renno discovered that he was endowed with a useful patience. He was prepared to wait as long as necessary for the break that would enable him to step in and achieve victory. He stopped himself from growing tense, and his gaze remained catlike.

The silence in the clearing was profound. Neither the Seneca nor the Erie uttered a sound. They had pitted their strength and cunning against each other, and one surely would die.

The Erie clenched his teeth, and Renno guessed that he

was about to strike. The surmise proved correct when the brave suddenly lashed out with his tomahawk.

Anticipating the blow, Renno bent his body away from it, and the hatchetlike weapon grazed his arm but left him unscathed.

Renno saw his chance to retaliate and swept his own tomahawk in a sharp downward motion.

But the Erie was too quick for him, and shifting his own weapon to the target area, he managed to deflect the blow.

Both men leaped backward and gave themselves the opportunity to recuperate and once again assume their watchful waiting.

The thought occurred to Renno that he was playing his foe's game. The Erie was also waiting for a break of some kind. More experienced, he probably would be better able to take advantage of any such development.

A bolder strategy and a calculated risk were called for. By now, Renno had the opportunity to gauge the other's strength and ability, and although he did not know the Erie's weaknesses, he was able to weigh his own strengths against those of his foe. He remembered a lesson from his father in the art of fighting with a tomahawk. "Think of your weapon as an extension of your arm and hand," Ghonkaba had told him, "and use it as you would employ your own arm. If you think of it as an alien weapon to be handled separately, you will be depriving yourself of a natural advantage."

That advice, applied literally, enabled the young Seneca instantly to develop a whole new tactical plan. He put it into use without pondering it too long.

He struck swiftly, aiming a blow with the blunt, hammerlike edge of the tomahawk at the head of the Erie.

The man brought his own weapon up to ward off the blow, but Renno changed direction. Instead of aiming at his foe's head, he brought the sharp edge of the weapon in a slashing, sweeping strike to the Erie's shoulder.

His aim was slightly high, and the sharp edge of the tomahawk cut deeply into the base of the Erie's neck.

Stunned by the excruciatingly painful blow, the brave stood rooted to the spot, paralyzed for the moment, unable to move.

It was easy now for Renno to terminate the combat at his leisure. He felt a twinge of compassion, a real sense of pity for the warrior who had lost. There, but for the grace of the gods, he himself now stood. Had his foe been more agile, mentally and physically, it would be Renno whose life was now ending in the wilderness of the Pennsylvania hills.

A few sharp blows with the tomahawk brought the combat to a decisive close. Renno wiped his tomahawk on the grass, then did the same with his knife. He looked at the still bodies of his enemies, their sightless eyes staring up at the summer sun, and he uttered a brief prayer to the manitous, thanking them because it was two Erie and not one young Seneca who had died.

Then, true to his heritage, he removed the scalps of the two warriors and placed them on his belt. Retrieving his rifle, his bow, and his arrows from the crotch where he had placed them in the tree, he resumed his northward journey.

CHEROKEE

It did not occur to him that he had done anything particularly noteworthy by killing two foes. The thought that some might regard him as a hero was furthest from his mind. He had faced an emergency and had emerged unscathed, while the scalps of his enemies dangled from his belt. This was the true Seneca tradition, the tradition of Renno, the invincible.

Krystan, a Seneca of middle years, looked her age and disposition. When young, she had been known for her beauty, but now her face was haggard and her eyes reflected her embittered nature. Her skin and blue-black hair had lost their luster. Her troubles were easy to understand: she had been married to the wrong man for many years.

Crolbu was a senior warrior of the Seneca, a well-built, handsome man whose looks concealed a lack of both talent and ambition. Instead of advancing to the rank of war chief at an early age and then going on from there to become one of the rulers of his nation, he had been satisfied with the rank of senior warrior and had never tried for any higher position.

The power and prestige that his wife had sought through him had been sadly lacking throughout his life, leaving her bitter and angry. Nevertheless, Krystan had not abandoned her dream.

Now her hopes were centered on her only child, Dalnia, who at seventeen summers was endowed with her mother's natural beauty. Additionally, she had developed the crafty nature that made Krystan so different from her peers.

By the standards of the Iroquois—and those of all other Indian nations—Dalnia was exquisite. She had high, firm breasts, an incredibly tiny waist, and legs so long and slender that in her childhood she had been nicknamed "the deer." She had such a saucy way of twitching her buttocks that every brave, from a junior warrior to an elder, watched her walk.

Her eyes were huge, liquid, and full of promise. Her lips were large, soft, and inviting, and her chiseled features were those of a perfect Indian maiden. Dalnia had always preferred the company of males, and since she was small she had been a flirt, instinctively knowing what other females had to learn slowly and laboriously.

All of her mother's hopes for the future rested on Dalnia. For years she had been taught that never would she marry an ordinary brave like her father. She would save herself for someone very special, someone who would give her the high stature she deserved and could attain only through making the proper marriage. Until that day arrived, Dalnia was free to live as she pleased and gain the experience necessary to the achievement of her goals. The only restrictions on her behavior were that she not become pregnant, nor become involved in a scandal that would make her less attractive as a wife for the right man.

Krystan shared the wild excitement when Renno, the grandson of the Great Sachem of the Iroquois, Ja-gonh, appeared unexpectedly as an emissary from his father, Ghonkaba, who had successfully settled in the distant land of the Cherokee.

That noon, after her family had eaten its customary light

meal, Krystan deliberately waited until Crolbu went off to join his cronies. He spent his afternoons sitting on the ground smoking and exchanging stories.

She looked at her daughter across the table, then demanded sharply, "Have you seen him?"

Dalnia was busy admiring her image in a little hand mirror of burnished steel. "Seen whom?" she demanded negligently.

"Renno!"

Dalnia laughed. "The great Renno has been dead for many years, and I don't think that his spirit has come back from the land of our ancestors."

Krystan was not amused. "I refer to his grandson!"

"Oh, you mean *that* Renno. No, how could I have seen him? He went off with his parents some time ago to join some tribe in the South."

Krystan spoke slowly and distinctly. "Young Renno, the great-grandson of the great Renno, returned here this very morning. He went straight to the home of Ja-gonh, escorted there by two sentries. I saw him with my own eyes. He's become a grown man. He's gained a great deal of stature and is no longer a scrawny boy. He wears the feathers of a senior warrior in his scalp lock, and he has scalps hanging from his belt."

"I remember him well from the days before his parents left here." Dalnia remained indifferent. "What a serious-minded boy he was! There was no fun in him! He was so filled with his destiny as a descendant of Ja-gonh and of the great Renno that he couldn't think of anything else."

"He appears to be fulfilling that destiny, although I

274

don't know any details. See him and judge for yourself. And when you see him, make sure that he remembers you, as you remember him. Make certain you make a good impression on him!''

Dalnia shrugged prettily; she was incapable of doing anything unattractive or less than graceful. ''Why should I bother to impress him, Mother?''

''Because it's very possible that he is the warrior for whom you have been waiting. Come to think of it, wear your new dress—the doeskin with the short skirt.''

''You can't be serious, Mother! Renno is probably the dullest person I've ever met!''

''You haven't seen him in years,'' Krystan said. ''You've changed and grown up. He's become adult, too.''

''I'm sure he can talk by the hour about duty and honor and similar subjects to put me to sleep. He's dull, I tell you.''

''His grandfather is the most powerful Seneca alive today, and his family is the most famous in our history. Think of it! His great-uncle is our sachem at this very moment, and the boy's father undoubtedly holds a position of importance and trust wherever he may be. I'll soon have the full story on Renno's background, never fear. Do as I tell you, and make every effort to call yourself to his attention. Do I make myself clear?''

Something in her tone made Dalnia realize that her mother was very serious. Perhaps her own easy way of living was coming to an end. If so, she had been waiting for a long time for the ''right'' man to come along and enter her life. She had always known that she would not necessarily like him, but that was unimportant. It was odd to think of Renno as that man, but the ways of the gods were strange.

"I hear you, my mother, and I shall obey," Dalnia said submissively.

No one could prepare a marinated venison steak equal to the one Ah-wen-ga cooked for her grandson. Renno, who had talked solidly for hours, sat down at the dinner table and discovered his favorite meal. He took one look at the steak, and melting, looked at his grandmother with a soulful smile.

Ah-wen-ga was reminded of her own youth, when she had been kidnapped and taken to France in a plot against the life of the king. Ja-gonh had followed to rescue her, and they had married immediately thereafter. Now Renno reminded her so much of her husband in those days that she was filled with bittersweet memories. No warrior was ever as alert and courageous, as dashing and romantic as Ja-gonh. A half-century later, here was Ja-gonh of old grown young again. The resemblance was astonishing, and she found it difficult to concentrate on what her grandson was saying.

"My mother and father wished with all their hearts that you, my grandparents, could have come to the land of the Cherokee to attend the wedding of Ena. They realized it was not possible. But they wanted me to be sure to express their great desire that you be present."

"Tell them in return," Ja-gonh said with a heavy sigh,

"that we appreciate their thoughts. Ena and her husband are with us in our minds and our spirits, and we shall pray to the manitous for their welfare."

Renno hesitated for a long moment, then made up his mind and plunged ahead. "I have something further to relate regarding the marriage of Ena."

Ah-wen-ga waved impatiently. "Can't this talk wait? Your venison steak will grow cold, Renno."

He grinned again at his grandmother. "Never fear. This is a meal for the gods! I will pay it the attention it deserves."

He sounded so much like his great-grandfather that Ja-gonh was startled.

"After Ena and Rusog have had an opportunity to establish themselves in their new home, they also will come to pay you a visit," Renno went on. "They will be escorted by the delegation whom you sent as your representatives to the wedding, as well as by various members of the company of scouts, who will come to visit relatives."

Ah-wen-ga and Goo-ga-ro-no, his great-aunt, reacted identically, exclaiming joyfully and clapping.

Ja-gonh showed no emotion, as that would have been improper for the Great Sachem of the Iroquois to display. But his eyes nevertheless lighted with pleasure.

"These scouts will have one additional function," Renno continued. "I will explain when I have eaten my venison steak." He ate steadily, without hurrying, and when he finished the meat on his plate, he happily accepted another portion from his grandmother.

Only when he was done eating did he tell them about

the invitation extended by Loramas of the Cherokee to the people of the Seneca to join his nation and make their homes with them, living among them as Seneca, rather than as Cherokee. When he was finished, Ja-gonh and No-da-vo looked long and hard at each other and then bowed their heads.

"The gods are great and all-knowing," Ja-gonh said. "They have heard our prayers. They have been aware of our needs and they have found a way to solve our nation's greatest problem."

"Many Seneca," No-da-vo said to Renno by way of explanation, "especially the younger generation, feel that their opportunities for living lives of adventure in the great traditions of our people are very limited. They believe that the Seneca will become staid and listless with no wars to fight and no great adventures beckoning. We have been very much worried about the future of our younger people. The solution worked out by Ghonkaba and the Grand Sachem of the Cherokee fits the need perfectly."

"We have been worried, too," Ja-gonh went on, "but now I am grateful to the gods, as well as to my son and to Loramas of the Cherokee."

Renno could not help marveling at how the manitous were meeting the needs of the Seneca nation.

"Will you present this plan, Renno, to our people?" Ja-gonh inquired.

"If that is your wish, my grandfather."

The meeting was scheduled for seven days later, which allowed those who were in other parts of the Seneca realm to return home. Renno occupied himself throughout that week by renewing old acquaintances, going hunting and fishing with friends from his childhood days, and regaling his grandparents with tales of family exploits in the land of the Cherokee.

One morning he went to a little clearing in the forest, not far distant, a place known only to his family. Since the time of Ghonka the warriors had prayed there to the manitous for help and guidance. He engaged in the ancient rituals and, feeling much better, stood up, intending to return to town.

He was astonished to find his path blocked by the most beautiful young woman he had ever seen. Her blue-black hair, which was not braided, shimmered as it fell loosely to her shoulder blades. Berry juice, red and shining, accented the sensuality of her full mouth. She had used a scorched stick to accent around her enormous, limpid eyes. Unlike most Seneca women, who were modest in their attire, her skirt fell open inches above her knees to reveal her long, firm thighs. The neckline of her jacket was low cut and it was easy to see the delectable swelling of her breasts.

He took in her appearance in a glance and then looked away in confusion.

"I hope I haven't disturbed you, Renno," she said politely.

"Not at all," he replied, certain that he must be dreaming.

"I had no wish to disturb you," she said, "but I saw you leaving the town this morning, and on impulse, I followed you. You looked as though you were offering prayers to the manitous in the clearing, so I stayed back.

But I decided I'd make myself known to you now that you are done with your prayers.''

Still overcome by her radiant beauty, he wondered how he could have allowed her to follow him through the wilderness without becoming aware of her presence. Perhaps she was a product of the manitous, a creature invented by them as a messenger.

She smiled at him, her red lips glistening invitingly. ''You don't know me,'' she said, and the observation was a statement rather than a question.

''Should I?'' he countered.

''I am Dalnia,'' she said. ''We played together as children. I was friendly with your sister. And I recall one occasion when you dropped a spider down my back.''

Renno felt distinctly uncomfortable. ''I can remember being punished for putting a spider down *someone's* back,'' he said, ''but I can't remember that I played such a trick on you. Are you quite sure it was you who was the victim?''

''I'm positive!'' Relishing his lack of ease, she laughed aloud.

''You have changed a great deal since you were small,'' he said gallantly, trying to recoup.

She appreciated his effort and thought more highly of him. Her laughter died at her throat as she examined him with care and then said candidly, ''You, too, have changed for the better. You were a horrid little boy. But now, frankly, you look like one who associates with the manitous as their equal.''

Renno was embarrassed by the extravagance of her

praise. This was no ordinary person who was talking to him, but a most attractive creature. He gestured vaguely, as though brushing aside her remarks.

Dalnia was enjoying herself. She had merely been obeying her mother's command when she had followed him into the forest, but she found pleasure in this experience for its own sake. It was true that he had grown into an exceptionally handsome man. His heritage was partly Indian, partly white, and in him was the best of both races. No other warrior of his generation in the community could match him for good looks. A campaign to become his bride promised to be far more pleasurable and exciting than she had anticipated. As for a life as his wife, she began to think that perhaps it might not be as dull as she had assumed.

His embarrassment began to subside.

Dalnia knew that she had to make one bold movement, one strike toward achieving her end. "I followed you this morning," she said, lowering her voice as though making a confession, "because I was eager to renew the friendship we once enjoyed." She well knew she was talking pure nonsense. If he analyzed her remarks, he would realize that they had never been close and that their "friendship" was strictly a figment of her imagination. She was counting on her beauty to deprive him of realistic thought.

Her gamble succeeded. "I'd like that very much," Renno said. Fascinated by her mouth, he was wondering if she would object strenuously to being kissed once their association became a little stronger.

"I'm glad," she replied, sounding a trifle breathless. "I

was so busy following you that I'm not sure I can find my way back to the town without help.''

Renno's chest seemed to expand. He was so distracted by her praise of him that he failed to observe how transparently false her statement was. "You have no need to worry," he said. "I'll guide you safely back. You never need to worry when you're with me in the wilderness. I'll always see to it that you're safe."

"Thank you," she replied softly. "That's good to know." She favored him with a radiant smile that left him weak.

Soon they started toward the town. Renno indicated with a wave the direction they were to travel, and Dalnia took the lead on the narrow portion of the trail that required them to go in single file. Renno, following her at the easy pace she set, was conscious only of the waggling of her hips from side to side. Never before had a woman's posterior held such fascination for him, and he could stare at nothing else. He was regretful when the trail widened sufficiently for them to walk side by side. All he knew was that he wanted this woman badly.

His experience with women had been limited, and never had he felt this way. He was conscious only of Dalnia. Everything but his overwhelming desire was obliterated from his mind.

She brushed against him from time to time, now with an arm, now a leg. He had no idea that these contacts, which served to increase his desire, were anything but accidental. She calculated brilliantly, using these seemingly casual physical contacts to keep his interest at fever pitch.

Never before had she made such concerted efforts to

gain the interest of a man. Consequently, never had anyone responded to her so wholeheartedly.

They had covered no more than half the distance to the town when Dalnia knew she would be able to report to her mother that her campaign was a rousing success. She could manipulate Renno as she pleased, and he would propose marriage whenever she wished it.

Still scheming, wanting to make certain that he would fall hopelessly in love with her, she pretended to twist an ankle and literally threw herself at him, pressing close to him as she clung to him.

"Oh, I'm so ashamed of myself!" she cried, her hands on his bare chest. "I'm as clumsy as a city dweller who has never spent a day of her life in the wilderness. Whatever will you think of me?"

At the moment, enjoying her warm closeness, Renno found it difficult to think coherently.

"It doesn't matter in the least," he assured her. "Anyone can trip over a hidden tree root."

Pretending that the "accident" caused her to limp, Dalnia said she needed assistance, and she was not satisfied until Renno put one arm around her waist and supported her weight as she leaned against him. Their progress was slow thereafter, but he did not mind in the least. He could not recall when he had enjoyed himself so much.

Not until they approached the open fields near the town did Dalnia recover sufficiently to walk unaided. By that time, Renno had become putty in her hands, and was eager to do her bidding. She invited him to dine at her home, and when he accepted, she secretly pleased her mother and astonished her father by insisting on preparing the meal herself.

By the time that Renno returned to the dwelling of his grandparents after dinner, he was badly smitten.

The three senior emissaries of the Choctaw were deeply impressed by Anthony Simpson as they stared at him around the fire at his encampment. When they had last seen him in battle, he had been more dead than alive after being shot by Daniel Boone. Now, after a difficult convalescence, he had recovered his health. The only vestiges of his close call were the facts that he was considerably thinner than he had been, his voice was more gravelly, and he walked with a decided limp.

But his cunning generosity, as always, was boundless. He had made them gifts of fine woolen blankets and bolts of tightly spun cotton cloth for their families, as well as new muskets and pistols for themselves and, as special gifts, bottles of Scottish whisky.

Their farewell breakfast eaten, the Choctaw listened attentively as Simpson addressed them. "When you return now to your own land, let it be known to all your people that I offer rich rewards to any who successfully attack warriors of the Seneca and Cherokee nations. If they are attacked and defeated in a full-scale battle, the rewards will be great. If the assaults are smaller and merely harass the Seneca, the rewards will be less. But I assure you that all will receive rewards."

"Before we left our towns to meet you," one of the

leaders interjected, "the invitation to attend the wedding of Rusog, grandson of the Grand Sachem of the Cherokee, to the daughter of the leader of the Seneca, was rejected. Is there any reward for this?"

"Of course!" Simpson said heartily. "I will give you a new musket and knife to take to him who refused the offer to attend the festivities." He made no secret of his all-consuming hatred for the Seneca, since it was they who had ruined his carefully crafted plan to enlist the Cherokee on the side of the British.

Simpson seldom erred, but he had made a major mistake when he had underrated the Cherokee, and he was paying for his mistake both personally and professionally. While recuperating from his injury, he had taken a solemn vow to pursue his enmity to the Seneca to the ends of the earth if necessary. He had no intention of resting until he had repaid them in full for the grievous blows that he had suffered.

The Choctaw made up one of the instruments he was employing in his war against the Seneca. Certainly he had no intention of calling off his campaign until he achieved total victory and crushed the nation whose representatives had dared to raise their hands against him.

Chapter XI

The council chamber of the Seneca was crowded, filled with members who had come to hear Renno speak. In the front rows sat the elders of the clan, grizzled, retired warriors who were honored by the entire nation. Directly behind them sat their wives, the heart and soul of the Seneca, the women on whom the nation depended for its stability. Then came the senior warriors and their wives—the men who went off to fight whenever battle was necessary, and the women who carried on the sacred traditions of the clan and the nation. Next came junior warriors and the younger women. Solemn and quiet on this occasion, they were monitored by their instructors. In the rear were the young children of the clan, and even they sat quietly, watched as they were by their guardian-instructors, who held long whips of reeds used to quell any misbehavior or disturbance.

Ah-wen-ga and her sister-in-law, Goo-ga-ro-no, sat with the elderly women; neither held a special place because of the prominence of Ja-gonh and No-da-vo.

These leaders now walked to the ceremonial fire burning in the center of the circular building beneath a hole in the roof.

They were followed by Renno, who held his head high. He realized that this was his initiation as a leader of his people, and conscious only of the responsibility that he bore, he was already preparing his speech in his mind.

Using his words sparingly, Ja-gonh introduced his grandson without fanfare.

Renno began by reminding his listeners of the small band of Seneca who had left in 1775 to cast their lot with the American patriots. He outlined how they had played major roles in battle after battle, going from the despair of the early days of the Revolution to the triumphs that the Continental Army of General Washington had won.

He related how the scouts had been relieved from duty and presented with an eagle flag that carried the insignia of the commander in chief. Then he told how the party had migrated to the land of the Cherokee, west of the Appalachian Mountains. There they had participated in a military campaign against the Tuscarora and the Creek, and fought so efficiently, covering themselves with glory, that the Grand Sachem of the Cherokee now was offering to open the doors of his nation to any members of the Seneca who wished to migrate to his land.

Stressing that these immigrants would be free to retain their identity as Seneca, Renno also made it clear that they would enjoy the full privileges and rights of the Cherokee. Their only obligation would be to accept their share of responsibility for day-to-day living.

His eyes glowing and his voice impassioned, Renno went on to describe daily life in the land of the Cherokee, including its benevolent climate. He told about the large permanent dwellings, the wonderful hunting and fishing, and the infinite variety of vegetables and fruits. He dwelt on the amicability of the Cherokee and their reliance on the Seneca, from whom they hoped to learn much about the arts of war and of government. "We are not strangers there," he concluded. "We are truly at home."

As his audience began to inundate him with questions, he noticed Dalnia sitting in the company of the other unmarried women of the clan. Seeing her with her contemporaries made him realize more than ever how strikingly beautiful she was. In order to concentrate on the questions that were being asked, he tried to shut her out of his mind.

Dalnia, however, took no chance that he might overlook her. Rising frequently to her feet, she asked many questions about the dress and social life of the Cherokee, and the differences between them and the Seneca.

Renno answered each of her questions fully, and she seemed satisfied. It appeared, in fact, that he paid more attention to her questions than to the queries of others.

After everyone else had exhausted the inquiries, Dalnia had one final question: "Who will lead the party?"

Her question left Renno confused. "It is customary,"

he said, "for the Seneca to acknowledge the warrior who holds the highest rank as their leader. As to who will guide the party, I will act as scout and guide because I have made the journey between the lands of the Seneca and Cherokee and am familiar with the way.".

As Dalnia resumed her seat, she indicated her delight in pantomime, clasping her hands together ecstatically as she smiled. It was apparent to every young woman present that she was making a play for Renno. Many older women saw it, too, but Ah-wen-ga was whispering to Goo-ga-ro-no at that moment, and both missed the byplay.

Renno's persuasive efforts, combined with the situation in which the Seneca found themselves, produced spectacular results. Nearly five hundred voted to move. Of this number, one hundred and fifty were warriors, which meant that they would need no large escort on the trail. One hundred and fifty Seneca fighting men could take care of themselves and their dependents under the worst of circumstances. Those who were departing would need time to wind up their affairs; private property had to be assigned to someone who was remaining, and many goods had to be transferred. Ja-gonh estimated that the process would require several weeks.

Renno was content to remain until the large party was ready to go. He was enjoying himself greatly at the home of his grandparents, savoring particularly his favorite foods, which his grandmother took pleasure in preparing.

A few days after the vote, Renno went fishing with a number of other young warriors. When they strolled back carrying their catch, Dalnia was lingering outside the town gate. She had eyes only for Renno, smiling at him invitingly. His companions continued to walk into the town without pausing. Renno, however, halted to speak with her.

"Your grandmother told me where you had gone," she said, "and I've been waiting for you. I have some wonderful news."

He waited expectantly.

"My parents," she said, "have been discussing the possibility of making the move, and now they've decided to go. We'll be included in the party, whenever you leave."

"You'll enjoy living there," he said. "The weather is much warmer than here."

Dalnia had no interest in the southern climate. "Tell me about the maidens of the Cherokee," she asked.

"What is it you want to know about them?"

Dalnia managed to look very young and helpless. "Are they better looking than those of the Seneca?"

Renno pondered the question. He had never thought to compare the maidens of the two nations. "I suppose," he said, sounding apologetic, "that they're more or less alike."

He had not told her what she wished to hear, so she tried again. "Are they prettier than I am?"

"No maidens anywhere are more attractive than you are!" Renno replied quickly.

Her eyes became soft and her voice was like a caress. "You aren't just saying what you want me to hear, I hope. Do you really mean that?"

"Indeed I do. No maiden there is your equal, just as there is none here. But you don't need me to tell you that

291

you're beautiful. Your mirror must tell you, and so do your many admirers.''

Dalnia shook her head. "I know of no admirers," she said flatly.

Renno looked at her in astonishment. "How could that be?''

For his sake, she pretended to be very naive. "My mother tells me that I am too handsome for my own good. I can't see that, of course, but she insists that my looks frighten away suitors who feel the competition is too great for them. The truth is that I know of no suitors.'' What she failed to mention was that she had discouraged every senior warrior who was seriously interested in her because of her cold-blooded decision that none was good enough. She would be satisfied only with a leader of the people. He was greatly pleased to hear of the absence of rivals for her hand—precisely as she wanted him to believe.

He looked at his day's catch, two strings of fish. The four fish on one would be sufficient for supper for him and his grandparents. The other string's six fish included several that were quite large. On impulse, he handed her the longer string.

She feigned surprise. "For me?''

Overcome with embarrassment, Renno could not speak and merely nodded. Only later would he think of the many graceful compliments he could have paid her. Handicapped by shyness in the presence of this beauty, he felt unable to speak. He bolted, hating himself as he moved rapidly through the town toward the dwelling of his grandparents.

Dalnia looked after him, a half smile on her lips as she

twirled the vine on which the fish he had given her were strung. He was responding exactly as she had hoped, and the road ahead was clear. She would wait until they left and were on the trail before she intensified her campaign. But she felt confident of one thing: he would propose marriage to her and she would become his bride shortly after they reached their destination.

Ah-wen-ga kept her mounting concern to herself, but she finally became so upset that she decided it would be best to confide in her husband. "I'm worried about Renno," she told him.

"You're upsetting yourself needlessly," Ja-gonh replied. "He has the family eye with both rifle and bow. I don't think you need be concerned about him in the least."

"You don't understand," she replied impatiently. "I'm not referring to his talents as a warrior. I'm concerned about his future as a man."

Seating himself opposite her at the fire, Ja-gonh looked at her questioningly.

"It's Dalnia," she said. "He's developing a strong interest in her—far stronger than I like."

Ja-gonh was lost in thought for a moment. "Crolbu, her father, has a good record as a warrior," he said. "I don't remember him in battle, but that doesn't mean much. I can't remember every one of the hundreds of warriors who have served with me. As for Krystan, to the best of my memory, she's never been known to be guilty of what could be considered misconduct."

Ah-wen-ga could see that the conversation was going to be even more difficult than she had anticipated. "It's Dalnia herself," she said. "She's conniving and two-faced, in my view."

"She's the maiden you pointed out a few days ago in the cornfield?"

"That's the one."

He smiled faintly. "She's exceptionally good-looking," he said. "In fact, I can't recall any Seneca woman that pretty since you were that age."

Ah-wen-ga shook her head. "There's no comparison!"

"No, I suppose there isn't," her husband said hastily, trying to avoid an argument.

"When I was old enough to become aware of males," Ah-wen-ga said, "I fell in love with you. And from that day to this, I've never looked at another man."

"I'm grateful to the gods for your constancy, although I can't say I admire your taste," he replied with a smile.

She did not smile in return. "Dalnia," she said severely, "is a natural-born flirt. She has a reputation for flirting with every handsome warrior she meets and for chasing after men."

Ja-gonh chuckled. "I'm surprised she hasn't caught up with any of them. She seems rather graceful on her feet."

"According to the gossip," she told him, making a judgment on Dalnia, "she has indeed caught up with a number of warriors. In fact, it's said that she has no right to be in the Bear Clan's house of maidens."

"She's never been caught and punished," Ja-gonh said

with some heat, "so anything you've heard does belong only in the realm of gossip."

Ah-wen-ga was not afraid to stand up to the Great Sachem. "I've watched her for many months," she said, "smiling her most beguiling smile and waggling her rear end at various warriors. I can't believe that she's honorable and sincere, and I'm convinced she's looking for a husband who will give her increased standing."

"I've never been able to blame anyone for trying to improve his place in the world," Ja-gonh said. "Your only valid criticism of her is that she makes a stunning appearance. And, as you know from your own experience, beauty is no reason to treat a person like a criminal."

Ah-wen-ga sighed in exasperation.

"You say that Renno is appreciative of Dalnia's appearance?" he asked.

Ah-wen-ga snorted. "He's dazzled by her!"

"Well," he said thoughtfully, stuffing his pipe. "He's old enough to fight when the situation calls for it, so I daresay he's old enough to take a bride if that's his desire. If his parents want my advice, I'll gladly urge that they give their consent to Renno's marriage, and I urge you to do the same."

"Unfortunately," Ah-wen-ga said, "Ghonkaba and Toshabe probably won't learn about their son's romance until it's too late. I don't mind telling you that I intend to try to prevent him from marrying her. I'm sure it would be a catastrophe!"

* * *

The honeymoon that Ena and Rusog arranged was out of the ordinary, but they were no ordinary couple. They asked for Seneca who were in the land of the Cherokee to volunteer to accompany them on their trip in order to provide ample protection for members of the Bear Clan who intended to come south.

Eight warriors responded, so that left places for eight Cherokee under the terms of the training scheme Ghonkaba had devised. Sixteen experienced warriors, all veterans of the recent campaign, would be sufficient to protect the bride from any bands they might encounter on their journey. Ghonkaba was satisfied and approved the plan.

What made the party unique was the fact that the groom was to be its commander, and at the bride's insistence, she was the chief scout.

They traveled north through eastern Tennessee and then Kentucky, Virginia, and Pennsylvania, avoiding combat, and their journey was without serious incident.

When they came to the land of the Seneca, Ena relaxed completely, as did the Seneca scouts. That night they built a large fire to cook their supper and eased their security precautions.

"You see no risk that we'll be attacked by a Seneca war party?" Rusog asked his bride. "I wouldn't relax until we've met a sentry and identified ourselves."

Ena smiled. "You have much yet to learn about my people, Rusog," she replied. "It's true that we have not encountered a sentinel of the Seneca, but I assure you that we no sooner crossed the border into their land but they sent a full report on us ahead to the sachem, who is my great-uncle. Each of us was described. I was identified, as were our eight companions who are also Seneca in good standing. Tomorrow, when we arrive at the town of my grandfather, you'll find everyone on hand to welcome us.''

''How is it possible for the sentries to have seen us without being seen?''

''They are Seneca!'' Ena replied, and her words had to suffice. She saw no need to explain that the sentinels sent runners ahead who would reach the town silently, in relays.

The journey came to an end the following morning. As Ena had predicted, a large crowd was on hand to welcome the travelers.

Renno was on hand, too, to see his sister, as were a number of Ena's childhood friends. The other Seneca in the arriving group also were welcomed by relatives and friends, and the scene was a happy one. Rusog, who had expected to find the Seneca a ferocious and exacting people, was surprised by their warmth and kindness.

Then it was Rusog's turn. As Ena's husband, he was overwhelmed with cordiality. No-da-vo made him an honorary Seneca, and he was invited to don their war paint as well as put on the three hawk feathers that would mark him as a senior warrior of the nation. Ena proudly introduced him to those who thronged around. He saw so many new faces that he made no attempt to remember them.

Only one of those whom Rusog met that day stood out in his mind: Dalnia was an exquisitely beautiful woman whose limpid eyes and full, moist lips he could not forget. Later in the day, when he had an opportunity to sort out his impressions, he wondered about her. He loved his bride and had no intention of being unfaithful to her, but at the same time, he was curious about the maiden who, it seemed to him, had invited him to participate in a dalliance. No one mentioned her name, however; so he knew he would need to bide his time before he learned anything about her.

What Rusog had no way of knowing was that Dalnia was deliberately flirting with him in accordance with a preconceived plan. As she told her mother, she had no intention of relying exclusively on her relationship with Renno to assure her future.

The appearance of Rusog gave her a chance to expand her prospects. From the moment she set eyes on the barrel-chested giant, she decided he was her kind of man. She easily brushed aside the fact that he had very recently married Ena. Dalnia simply did not consider Ena as serious competition. Once she made it clear to Rusog that he interested her, he would forget his bride, Dalnia felt certain. Then, with the grandson of the Grand Sachem of the Cherokee as her protector, she would have a bright future in the land of her choice.

To be sure, she had no intention of abandoning her efforts to persuade Renno to propose marriage. That was the preferable course of action, but it would do no harm to add another arrow to her arsenal.

Her future in the land of the Seneca seemed dismal, but in the land of the Cherokee her potential was without limit. She was determined to seize her chance and make the most of it.

CHEROKEE

*   *   *

Rusog and Ena listened attentively as Renno described
his meeting with members of the Seneca. What impressed
them was the large number of Seneca willing to emigrate.

"We knew," Ja-gonh told them, "that many of our
people, particularly the young, would be eager to leave
because the future here promises to be bleak, but I was
surprised by the number who responded to Renno's plea.
The manitous have given him my father's gift of tongue,
and he was eloquent in his descriptions."

Rusog was irritated by the praise given his young brother-
in-law. Here Renno could do no wrong, and Ena, too, was
regarded as a model of perfection. In fact, Rusog resented
the praise of his wife more than he objected to that spoken
about Renno. It bothered him that Ena remained constantly
in the limelight. He did not know why she had regarded it
as necessary to act as a scout on the journey north, while
his record as a warrior took second place to her exploits as
a scout.

Ja-gonh, who had no idea of what was seething below
the surface in Rusog, remained lavish in his praise of the
grandchildren of whom he was so proud.

When the talk turned to family matters, Rusog was glad
to escape for a time. Excusing himself, he went out into
the open and wandered aimlessly through the town.

It was sheer luck—or perhaps the will of the gods—that
unexpectedly brought him face to face with Dalnia.

"Well, hello," she drawled, halting and smiling broadly.

299

She had not planned on this encounter, but she was instantly determined to make the most of it.

Ordinarily, Rusog would have nodded a greeting and continued on his way. But in his present frame of mind, he paused. A sense of rebellion against Ena was welling up within him and ruling his actions.

"If you're going someplace in particular," Dalnia said, "don't let me detain you."

"No, no," Rusog protested. "It's perfectly all right. I was just getting some fresh air."

"Have you seen our lake yet?" she asked, her face innocent. "If not, I'll gladly take you there."

"I—I hate to impose on you," Rusog told her.

She reached out in a seemingly impulsive gesture and touched his arm. "Oh, it's no imposition at all, I assure you," she replied, and still holding his arm, she started toward the town gate. Rusog self-consciously fell in beside her.

As they made their way toward the gate, and beyond it, to the open fields that led to deep woods, Rusog suffered sudden pangs of conscience. Everyone in the town knew him by sight, and if he should be seen strolling with this attractive woman, what possible excuse could he give Ena? If he told her the literal truth, she would find it difficult to believe he had been so naive.

He increased his pace unconsciously, which forced Dalnia to walk more rapidly. After he reached the shelter of the wilderness, however, he slowed to a crawl and felt a great sense of relief.

She had no idea what was troubling him, but she shared

his relief. Smiling up seductively, she led him through the forest to the near shore of the large lake a short distance from the town.

"This lake," she said, "is very important to the people who live here. We catch many of our fish in it, and we obtain water for drinking and cooking from the two rivers that feed into it." She sat down on the mossy bank and dipped her hand into the water. "At this season of the year," she said, "the water is most refreshing. I think that of all the things I shall miss, this lake will be high on my list."

"You shouldn't miss it," he said. "We also have lakes, as well as rivers."

Her face lit up. "Ah! You swim, then?"

"Of course," he replied.

Dalnia jumped to her feet and, turning her back to him, began to disrobe swiftly. "Let's go for a swim right now," she called out enthusiastically. "The day is so hot, the water will be just right."

Rusog stood still, unable to move as he watched her disrobe. Apparently, the Seneca saw nothing wrong with individuals of different sexes swimming together, but the practice was strictly taboo among the Cherokee. He was rooted to the spot.

Stepping out of her dress, Dalnia immediately plunged into the lake. She swam underwater for about ten yards before coming to the surface. She turned and called over her shoulder, "This is wonderful! Join me, won't you?" Not waiting for an answer, she swam farther out.

Rusog hesitated for a long moment, then, discarding

modesty and caution, as well as his clothes, he jumped into the lake and began to swim with long, powerful strokes, soon overtaking Dalnia.

"Isn't this wonderful!" she cried.

"Yes," he replied, "it's grand."

Suddenly her arms were flung around his neck, and he was forced to tread water for both of them. Her body, warm and slippery, pressed close to him, and he knew that he must exercise the most rigid self-control. He began to swim to some distant point up the lake.

Dalnia still clung to him, laughing as he dragged her along.

Rusog was becoming frantic. Her superbly proportioned body was rubbing up against his. Her lips were only inches from his face, and he was sorely tempted—as never before—to move into shallower water and to take her without hesitation or apology. She had already made her availability evident, and he no longer cared what her reasons might be. No man but a fool rejected a gift such as the one Dalnia offered him.

Dalnia fought him playfully, her breath warm in his ear, her body still rubbing against his.

All at once, Rusog was drained of all desire for her. He felt only a stinging sense of contempt, not only toward her, but toward himself.

He wrenched her arms away from his neck and freed himself. "Enough!" he roared. "Damn you, woman, keep your distance!" His violence sent a shiver of apprehension through Dalnia.

"What's wrong?" she whispered, treading water. "What have I done?"

"It's not what you've done, it's what you were about to do," he told her bluntly. "You know better than to tamper with the emotions of a man who has just been married."

"I'm sorry," she murmured, "but I have feelings, too, and I was carried away by them."

He made no reply but swam toward the shore where he had left his clothes. Pulling himself up onto the land, he rolled in the tall grass to dry himself.

Within moments, Dalnia joined him, but Rusog jumped to his feet, dressed swiftly, and folding his arms, turned his back on her.

Dalnia took her time drying and dressing. Her hair remained wet, and using her long, tapering fingers as a comb, she ran them through her hair.

"I'm sorry you took offense, and I beg your pardon for it," she said, her voice cold. "What you don't seem to realize is that I was carried away by the desire of the moment. I don't know if anyone has ever told you this, but you're hardly an unattractive man." Her voice broke, and she succeeded in looking and sounding pathetic.

He weighed her words and had to admit that the point she made was valid. He had come within a hair's breadth of giving in to his emotions; how much easier it had been for a young woman lacking the self-discipline of a senior warrior to be overwhelmed by her feelings. At least she recognized him as an attractive male, someone with stature in his own right who was not merely Ena's husband. His anger melted and he smiled.

"I must admit, you were completely right about one thing," he said. "The weather today is just right for swimming."

She looked up at him, her eyes shining. "I'm forgiven, then?" She had known that she could persuade him not to carry a grudge, but she was making certain that there would be no repercussions.

"Nothing untoward happened," Rusog said. "If anyone asks, we went for a swim and enjoyed it a great deal. But unless asked, I don't intend to volunteer the information."

"Thank you," she said simply. "Thank you very much." She reached out, and the fingers of her left hand closed around his wrist.

He returned the gesture, encircling her narrow wrist.

This was the best of all solutions, Dalnia thought. By promising her not to mention the incident, Rusog would share the guilty secret and therefore would remain in her debt, pliable and relatively easy to manipulate.

She moved from the shade into the hot sun so her hair would dry before they returned to town. "It is good that we have this understanding," Dalnia said softly. "We will be related to each other for many years to come."

He was startled and made no attempt to conceal his surprise.

"You are married to Ena," she said. "Renno doesn't yet know it, but he will become my husband."

The news left him in a terrible dilemma. He couldn't speak to Renno, warning him away from Dalnia, without admitting his own intimate experience with her.

"Renno has spoken of you, and I know he thinks highly

of you," she said. "If he comes to you for advice, I hope you will urge him to marry me."

"To be sure," Rusog muttered.

"That is good," she said sweetly. "It would grieve me if I were forced to give Ena my version of what happened this afternoon." Her crass effrontery was breathtaking. She had made it plain that she was blackmailing him. Her attempt to seduce him had failed, but if she went to Ena, she would state that he had seduced her against her will. He would be able to stay out of trouble with his bride only if he supported Dalnia's efforts to become Renno's wife. The boldness of her scheme was as stunning as was her malice.

She was smiling, and he became upset when he read the cool calculation in her eyes. Never had he misjudged anyone as badly as he had failed to understand the character of Dalnia. Every move was planned with her ultimate goal in mind, and she did nothing on impulse. If he had succumbed to her charms and had engaged in an affair, he would be her slave. She still intended to use him as an instrument to attain her ends, but she failed to recognize a stubborn streak in the depths of Rusog's character. He had been foolish, recklessly giving in to feelings of anger and frustration in his relations with his wife. He had almost ruined his marriage, and he was determined to right whatever wrong he had created. He realized that Dalnia was shrewd and that he was no match for her cleverness. He would have to appear ready to cooperate while he figured out how to oppose her without harming his relationship with Ena.

Reaching out, he patted Dalnia's hand. "You can count on me," he told her, hoping he sounded as though he meant it.

Ja-gonh and Ah-wen-ga gave a small feast in honor of their granddaughter and her husband. Invited guests included the hierarchy of the Seneca nation, among them the principal medicine men, the war chiefs, the heads of clans, and their wives. For three days, Ah-wen-ga, aided by Goo-ga-ro-no and Ena, had been cooking and baking. The open-pit fire outside the house of the Great Sachem was lighted day and night. Ah-wen-ga believed that simple meals were the best, and her menu included fish chowder, roasted venison, and beans and squash enclosed in a pastry crust of corn bread.

Renno invited Dalnia, who naturally was delighted to accept. Ena and Rusog reacted with shocked incredulity when he appeared with her. Both politely concealed their private feelings.

Dubious as she was about Dalnia's morality and her standing in the Bear Clan and the community at large, Ah-wen-ga had too much else on her mind and was distracted from thinking about her.

Dalnia had learned an important lesson at the lake with Rusog. She devoted herself almost exclusively to Renno, talking with him in a low, confidential voice, smiling at him, and touching him from time to time as though by accident. Before supper, when she and Renno went to the Great Sachem to pay their respects, Dalnia made a supreme effort to impress Ja-gonh with her demure, ladylike behavior. She knew from his reaction that she made a good impression, and she was content.

Her instinct told her that Ena had not changed her opinion and still disliked her as had been the case when they were children. Rusog shared his wife's opinion, thanks to Dalnia's blunder. She treated them both pleasantly, hoping that her influence over Renno would be greater than they might exercise.

The banquet was a success. Rusog and Ena exerted all of their charm on the company. The influential guests were unanimous in their admiration for Ena and their approval of her choice of a husband.

When the social evening came to an end, Renno walked Dalnia home to the Bear Clan lodge for unmarried women. Lively and animated all evening, Dalnia fell silent now, her expression pensive.

Renno became concerned. "What's wrong?" he asked.

"Nothing," Dalnia replied hastily, and then sighed, the tremulous quality of that sigh indicating that indeed something was very much amiss.

Renno continued to stare. Her reply did not satisfy him.

"If you must know," she said, sounding a trifle petulant, "I've been thinking. For the first time in my life, I begin to see how certain things are arranged. Your father, who already held one of the highest of places in the Seneca hierarchy, was a hero in the recent military campaign and won himself a position among the Cherokee. It was only natural, then, that Ena and Rusog should marry. Each had the high social standing that the other demanded. It made me realize how hopeless is my own position."

He looked at her blankly. "I don't understand."

"My father," she said, "is an ordinary warrior. Now look at you. Your father already stands high in the council of the Cherokee. Your grandfather holds the most exalted position open to any Seneca. What's more, you are directly descended from your namesake, renowned in song and in story and to be remembered as long as Seneca live on the earth."

Dalnia looked very chagrined. Playacting superbly, she spoke with what seemed to be great difficulty. "I've been wrong, and I freely admit it. I'm a romantic, and I've foolishly indulged in daydreams of a life that is impossible for me to attain. Please, Renno, forget that I've said anything." She fell silent again, averting her face.

He began to suspect what was troubling her, and he became insistent. "Tell me!"

Her talent was all but unlimited. Her distress seemed genuine, and her apparent embarrassment was mortifying. "I've stupidly allowed myself to imagine the life I'd lead married to you," she said, her voice barely audible as she looked miserably down at the ground. "I realize now that I was indulging in a ridiculous dream that can never come true." Her voice faltered, and she appeared incapable of continuing.

"I demand to know," he said, his voice grating, "why such a simple dream is impossible to fulfill!"

The talk was coming to its climax now, and Dalnia halted in the shadows behind the longhouse of the Bear

Clan's maidens. The moonlight did not reach this corner, and they were obscured by darkness.

"You are the eldest son of the first family of the Seneca, while I am nobody," she said piteously. "Your family would never permit a marriage between us."

He stiffened and became belligerent. "My family does not tell me whom I will or will not marry," he said flatly. "I am a senior warrior and my own master. I do what I think is right at all times!"

Dalnia astonished him by throwing herself at him, pressing close to him, and curling her arms around his neck. "Oh, Renno!" she exclaimed. "You do care! My dreams are real after all!"

Not knowing what to say, he put his arms around her. He hadn't consciously allowed himself to imagine making love to her. Delighted by this opportunity, he put everything else from his mind for the moment.

"You'll defy your family—for me?" she asked breathlessly.

The question was unfair, he decided, and he felt the need to put the record straight. "I'm not so sure it will be necessary to defy my family," he protested. "My grandfather hasn't said one word against you, and I have no idea how my father will react."

Again she sighed and lifted her face to his. Able to resist temptation no longer, he kissed her, gently at first. Dalnia's lips parted. His kiss became more passionate, more demanding.

Dalnia responded in kind, making it plain that she was prepared to give him whatever he wanted.

Renno felt an overpowering urge to sink to the ground with her, but he managed to remember, barely in time, that they were in the most heavily traveled part of the Seneca town, and that twenty girls were on the other side of the wall.

Dalnia was losing no time now. Leaning back in his arms and regarding him with a smile, she asked archly, "Do we marry now, or do we wait until we reach the land of the Cherokee?"

He was taken aback by the question. According to the rules by which he had been raised, he must go to her father and ask permission to court her, but apparently Dalnia's family dispensed with formalities. He was uncomfortable, even though he failed to realize how he was being manipulated, and he said, "I—I think we should wait. My parents would feel cheated if they didn't attend my wedding."

"Then we'll wait," she told him, curbing her sense of disappointment with the expectation that he would find it increasingly difficult to disentangle himself from her.

"But I'm so happy, darling," she went on. "I want the whole world to know we're going to be married!"

The speed with which she was making arrangements left him bewildered. He could not really repeat their conversation of the past half hour, but so far as he could recall, he had not actually proposed marriage to her. On the other hand, he was hardly objecting. It seemed incredible to him that so beautiful a woman would consent to become his bride, and he felt fortunate that she had accepted him without his having to propose.

Sleep evaded Renno for hours that night. Whenever he closed his eyes, visions of Dalnia's lovely face appeared before him, and he became wide awake. He was lucky beyond compare, he told himself, and was being rewarded far beyond his worth.

In spite of his lack of sleep, he was up early and had breakfast with his grandparents. Ja-gonh seemed preoccupied with messages just received from two of his partners in the Iroquois League, the Mohawk and the Onondaga, so Renno saved his personal news until later, when his grandfather would pay proper attention.

Ah-wen-ga suggested that he hunt for a deer, and he departed at once. His luck proved exceptional, and he returned before noon, carrying a buck that weighed at least one hundred and fifty pounds. While his grandmother butchered the carcass and prepared some venison, Renno went in search of Dalnia's father.

At the council lodge, a score of elders and braves were sitting in the sunlight, leaning against the wall as they smoked their pipes. One of them pointed out Crolbu.

The young warrior hesitated for a moment, then squared his shoulders and approached the brave, who was staring into space as he sucked on his pipe.

"Excuse me for interrupting, sir," Renno said, "but I am Renno, son of Ghonkaba—"

"I know very well who you are," Crolbu interrupted impatiently. "What do you want?"

"May I speak for a moment in private, sir, on a confidential matter?" Renno asked, noting that the braves who had been napping near Crolbu were looking at him curiously.

Hoisting himself to his feet, Crolbu wandered off a short distance with Renno.

The young man swallowed hard and said, "Sir, I seek your permission to pay court to Dalnia."

"My permission, did you say? Ha!" Crolbu gestured wearily. "Dalnia hasn't paid any attention to what I've wanted or haven't wanted for years. For all practical purposes, she's forgotten she even has a father!

"If you want to marry her or just plain bed her or whatever your goal may be," Crolbu continued bitterly, "help yourself, young man. Don't come to me now, and don't complain to me later. My daughter does what she damn well pleases. She excludes me from her life, so I know where I'm not wanted."

Shaking his head, he returned to his place at the wall, and sitting down again in the sunlight, he clamped his pipe between his teeth and raised his face to the sun.

Disconcerted by the rude reception, Renno retreated. Normal rules of social intercourse evidently did not apply to Crolbu's family. If what he had said was correct, Dalnia was an adult who made her own decisions and did not need her father's approval before a suitor could pay court to her.

Telling himself that Crolbu's indifference simplified matters, Renno went back to the house of his grandparents. He arrived just as Ah-wen-ga and Ja-gonh, along with Ena and Rusog, were sitting down to a meal.

Ja-gonh chuckled. "If what I hear about you is true, Renno, you'll need all the practice you can get hunting and fishing."

"What do you hear, sir?"

His grandfather looked at him, smiling broadly. "I heard three times this morning," the Great Sachem said amiably, "on each occasion, supposedly on the best of authority, that you and Dalnia are going to be married."

Ena and Rusog stopped eating, then looked at each other in consternation. Aware of their reaction, Ah-wen-ga was at least equally upset.

But Renno was unaware of the furor he had created. "I won't deny that the story has validity," he said. "All that surprises me is that it's all over town already."

"Each of my informants," Ja-gonh said, "told me that he had gathered the information from no one other than Dalnia."

"Is this true, Renno?" Ena demanded. "Are you truly expecting to marry her?"

Her brother smiled at her. "I won't deny the accounts that my grandfather heard."

Ena looked first at her grandmother, then at her grandfather. "I have been hearing very distressing tales of how Dalnia has carried on with many warriors. I doubt that her morals are equal to our standards."

"How can you question her morals?" Renno demanded, challenging her. "What do you know of them?"

Ena smiled fleetingly. "Haven't you noticed," she asked, "that her walk is exactly like the walk of the women in the cities who are called doxies by the troops of the Continental Army?"

"I'm ready to substantiate every word that my wife has

spoken about her character," Rusog said flatly. "Dalnia is a young harlot!"

Ena looked at him in surprise, a question in her eyes.

He returned her gaze without flinching, his own eyes telling her that he would explain when they were alone. It was more important that he support her in a family crisis than protect himself by remaining silent.

Ah-wen-ga shook her head. "My own impression has been strengthened by what several women have said in recent days, as recently as last night." She turned abruptly to her grandson. "Are you sure in your own mind, Renno, that you want to marry her despite what you are hearing?"

"I am very sure, my grandmother," Renno replied, interrupting her. The family's opposition to Dalnia resolved his doubts and strengthened his intention. He was no longer a boy, as his senior warrior's feathers and the scalps that he carried on his belt testified. He would insist on being treated like a man who could make his own decisions. He set his jaw stubbornly.

Ena remained so indignant that she failed to see she was rubbing him the wrong way. "We are a very old and illustrious family," she said. "Our warriors are men of great valor and have taken more scalps than have any other braves. Our women, being of great virtue, unfailingly worship the gods and bring up their children to believe and do right. Above all, we are people of great common sense who understand the values of sound human relationships. We have lived for the principles that must take first place. Would the great Ghonka have welcomed Dalnia into the family? I think not. Would the great Renno have recognized her as your wife? Assuredly not. Now that your own grandparents have learned the truth about her, I defy you to ask them what they think! Do they look forward to welcoming her as a granddaughter? Look at them and tell me that they are eagerly awaiting such a day!''

Drilled in manners as a boy, Renno could not bring himself to be responsible for creating an unpleasant scene. Asking to be excused, he leaped to his feet and left.

Even after he was gone, Ena continued to sputter.

Ja-gonh raised an admonishing hand, smiling because his granddaughter reminded him of his wife when she was young. "Enough, Ena!" he said. "I do not for one moment doubt that your claims about Dalnia's character are true—"

"They are true!" Rusog interjected quietly.

"—but you'll accomplish nothing by beating at Renno," Ja-gonh went on. "He is of an age when every young warrior rebels. When his judgment is questioned, he is determined to vindicate it by pushing his decisions to their limit. If her moral standards leave something to be desired, that will make itself known to Renno in time. If you are wise, you will stop pounding at him and let him find the truth in his own way and allow him to deal with it himself.''

"Renno already carries a heavy burden," Ah-wen-ga added. "He has generations of achievements and heroism to try to equal. I have little doubt that he will succeed. I've seen his growth with great joy and pleasure, and I'm sure he'll be a worthy successor to the men who have made our family great. But he is stubborn, as any man worthy of being called a warrior is stubborn. Do not beat at him for his faults. Let him discover them for himself, and he will correct them.''

"I hear your words," Ena said, bowing slightly to each of them. "I agree with them and I will follow your suggestions."

That ended the subject—temporarily.

Ena helped her grandmother remove the empty gourds and dishes from the circle around the fire pit, and she washed them all. Then, accompanied by Rusog, she retired to the nearby tent that had been made available to them.

Rusog told the whole story of what had happened when he and Dalnia had gone to the lake.

"You're a senior warrior, a future leader of your nation," she said, shaking her head, "but I'm afraid you're hopelessly juvenile."

"I deserve whatever you choose to think and say about me," he replied. "I couldn't believe that any woman would be that forward. I still find it difficult to think that the whole scene actually took place."

"Any woman would have known that Dalnia was demanding that advances be made," Ena said, "and when you failed to make them, she decided to become the aggressor. I marvel at the stupidity of men."

"I may be stupid, but I don't make the same mistake twice. She's kept her distance from me from that moment to this. Although she's distinctly uncomfortable around me, I'm sure she will have no idea that I've told you about the incident. She believes, I'm sure, that I lack the courage to be frank with you."

"I advise her to keep her distance from me, but I'm sure she will, anyway," Ena replied, her eyes narrowing. "I would urge you tell Renno what you've just told me, but I'm afraid that in his present state of mind, he wouldn't believe you."

Rusog nodded gloomily. "You're right, I'm sure. He's incapable of seeing any fault in Dalnia. He'd be convinced that I was making up a tale simply to accommodate you because, for some vague reason, you don't like her."

"The question now," Ena said, "is whether we do try to make use of the incident."

"You forgive my indiscretion?" he interjected.

"Of course." She smiled and patted his hand. "You did well, seeing that Dalnia's attack took you by surprise." She frowned in concentration and became lost in thought.

Her husband began to fidget. "We owe it to Renno to be completely candid and to tell him the whole truth."

"I have decided not," she replied. "At this point, he'd merely resent what he'd regard as our interference. I believe we'll be wiser if we keep the information to ourselves and let it simply put us on our guard."

Rusog wanted to protest, but Ena silenced him with a gesture. "No," she said, "the more I think about it, the more convinced I become that my way is right. Dalnia's pride caused her to make a mistake. If she had succeeded in enticing you into an affair, she would have convinced herself that that made her superior to me as a woman. Unless I'm badly mistaken, she's one of those women whose vanity demands constant reassurance. She has Renno now, but that won't satisfy her permanently. She'll grow restless again within a short time and will be reaching out for fresh conquests.''

Rusog wondered at his wife's ability to understand another woman so well.

''We'll say nothing more to Renno about our opinion of the woman,'' she said. ''We'll appear to accept his betrothal and coming marriage as settled facts, and we won't show our disapproval any further. But we'll keep our eyes open, and one of these days, she's going to make another mistake. She'll have to prove to herself that some other man finds her irresistible. We'll be lying in wait and we'll catch her as she tries to land her fish. That should end Renno's obsession with her. I'd rather not play games when Renno's whole future is at stake, but I can think of no better way to handle all this.''

Chapter XII

As their departure drew near, the Seneca emigrants hastened their preparations. Some insisted on taking seeds for corn, squash, and beans, while others more sensibly preferred to wait and take their chances on obtaining locally grown seeds in return for goods or services that they would barter. All were told again and again by Renno to carry only such essentials of clothing, blankets, and the like that they needed, and to bring enough food for several days on the trail. A very few, Dalnia among them, tried packing more clothing than was regarded as a fair allotment, but they were stopped by the alert monitors appointed by the clan to supervise packing arrangements.

The senior warriors were summoned to a meeting, and there it was quickly agreed that the members of Ghonkaba's

319

company of scouts would act in that capacity on this journey. Renno, who was to serve the party as a scout, felt it his duty to declare, "My sister, who served as a scout in the Continental Army of General Washington, has volunteered her services for this journey."

Rusog was annoyed by his wife's offer, but he said nothing to block it, and the warriors accepted her offer.

According to the strict rules of seniority, the overall command of the expedition fell to Mogudo, a senior warrior appointed a war chief several years earlier by Ja-gonh. He had never served in that capacity, however, as the Seneca had not taken an active part in the war. Regardless of how talented he might be, he was totally lacking in experience as a war chief.

This brought Renno to his feet again. "Since we are going to be passing through the lands of several nations hostile to us, and since we are a large and very conspicuous party, it seems to me that we need a high command that is experienced and wise in the ways of war. I urge that we elect a deputy commander to assist Mogudo in leading us, and I recommend Rusog of the Cherokee. He fought with distinction against the Creek and the Tuscarora, and I will feel much more secure knowing that he is in the high command."

Rusog was deeply grateful to Renno; never did he learn that Ena had suggested his nomination to Renno. She realized that he would be far more inclined to accept her as a scout if he held a high rank, and tensions between them were much improved. Rusog took his part in all command meetings and consultations from that time forward.

CHEROKEE

The scheduled day for departure dawned bright and clear, and people began to gather in the fields beyond the gate of the town shortly after daybreak. Ja-gonh and Ah-wen-ga were on hand to wish all those departing a safe journey. The Great Sachem made a brief address, as did No-da-vo.

Then, bidding farewell to Renno and Ena before they took their places with the advance guard, Ja-gonh told them, "Say to your parents that if Ah-wen-ga and I were twenty-five years younger, and if I were not weighed down here by responsibility, we would be present in this company. If circumstances continue to prevent your father from visiting us, we shall lose patience and shall come to see him and Toshabe and our grandchildren."

The scouts moved out silently, and Mogudo—with Rusog beside him—set the main column in motion. The warriors led the column, followed by the women and younger children. Those who were going were in a festive mood and waved cheerily. Those who were staying behind shared their mood and smiled courageously.

Dalnia had assumed that, as Renno's future wife, she would receive a place of distinction in the line of march. Her mother had encouraged such thinking, and she was bitterly disappointed because no one paid the slightest attention to her. Her father was far ahead with the other warriors. Her mother was bringing up the rear among a large number of women. Dalnia trudged along with a pair of heavy travois poles digging into one shoulder. Inhaling the dust of those ahead of her, she thought bitterly that she could see nothing glamorous about this journey, and a sense of high adventure was sadly lacking.

Perhaps she was making the greatest mistake of her life. On the other hand, a bleak future awaited her if she had remained. She was relying on Renno to salvage her life for her and to brighten the future. In one way or another, she intended to see to it that he lived up to that expectation.

Using only their bows, the scouts shot ample quantities of game. The season was just right for hunting, and game was everywhere in the wilderness. By arrangement with Mogudo, a scout did not halt after he brought down a deer or other animal, but instead planted a conspicuous stake to mark the spot, and when the main column came along, it was the women's duty to butcher the animal.

Ena did no hunting but performed her scouting duties with her customary efficiency. Each day, she was relieved shortly before sundown, and retiring to the rear, she went directly to the bivouac of the headquarters detachment. There, Rusog awaited her, and she realized that in addition to his pleasure when he saw her, he nevertheless still felt an undercurrent of resentment because she was a scout. That, she thought, was just too bad—for Rusog.

In time, she reflected, he would accept her for what she was. Until then, she would continue to live her life as she thought best, and he would have to accept it.

Renno was spared the distress of a painful and even ugly scene with Dalnia only because of his future mother-in-law's intervention. One day after a particularly arduous march, Krystan moved forward a short distance and found Dalnia sitting near the bank of a small river, her bare feet wrapped in wet moss. She made the mistake of asking, "How are you?"

Dalnia was out of sorts. "I'm hot and tired, and my feet ache as though they're going to drop off!"

"The weather was perfect today," Krystan said, "and I heard that Mogudo wanted to take advantage of it by covering even more territory than usual."

"I'm utterly exhausted," her daughter declared. "When Renno appears—he goes off duty and should be showing up here at any moment—I intend to tell him how I feel and let him know how unhappy I am."

Krystan stared at her. "Have you gone mad? No one cares about your feelings and won't until after you've become Renno's wife. Even then, you'll be expected to submit to the will of the majority. Ena is the daughter of Ghonkaba and the wife of a very important Cherokee, but she nevertheless covers twice as much ground on her scouting tours as you do in a day's march. Mogudo's wife is married to the head of this expedition, but she doesn't complain, no matter how she feels, and she's more than twice your age. If you make a scene and complain to Renno, you'll be cutting your own throat. I warn you, Dalnia, that's one thing that he won't tolerate. He was brought up to expect hardships in travel. To him, this is normal and natural."

"I think it's disgusting," Dalnia replied, sulking.

Krystan caught her daughter's shoulders. "Throw away that moss! Comb your hair! Put some stain on your lips. When Renno appears, you'll be bright and cheerful. Not one word of complaint will he hear from you. Do I make myself understood?''

''I hear you,'' Dalnia whined, ''but I don't see why I—''

Her mother silenced her by shaking her vigorously. ''If you want the benefits that you will enjoy as the wife of Renno, you'll do precisely as I tell you. If you want him to turn away from you, to cut you off, complain to him the moment you see him. But don't come crying to me later. You have a clear choice ahead of you, and the rest is up to you.''

Dropping her hands to her sides, Krystan stalked off. Dalnia was lost in deep thought.

When Renno joined her, her hair fell to her shoulders in an attractive wave, her lips glistened with fresh stain, and her eyes looked enormous. She greeted him with a tender smile and she wore no moss poultices on her feet.

She prepared a simple supper, concealing her dislike of food preparation, and was solicitous. She quickly prepared a bed of boughs for him and insisted on covering him with her own blanket. Renno soon dozed off.

Later that night, he awakened to find Dalnia cuddling close to him beneath the blanket. No one else seemed to be nearby.

Her head rested against his shoulder, their legs were intertwined, and her breasts, firm but yielding, were pressing into his chest. Half asleep, he reached for her and pulled her still closer.

She, too, appeared to be sleeping but managed to raise her head to his. Their lips met, and the earth seemed to rock and shake beneath them. Never had Renno felt such intense desire. He did not stop to ask how it happened that his breechcloth had been removed and that Dalnia's skirt was absent. It was remarkably easy to become intimate with her, and he was unable to resist the temptation for more than a few moments.

Their lovemaking became fervent, and her passion matched his. She guided his hands, and then her own hands became equally busy. Renno no longer was thinking, no longer was capable of logical thought. He knew only that they were finding a natural outlet for their lovemaking.

Ultimately, peace descended once more on the little glade. Renno drifted off to sleep and Dalnia ran a hand through her long hair, smiled secretly, and placed her head once more against his chest.

The first streaks of dawn awakened Renno, and his first thought was that he had dreamed that he and Dalnia had made love. But immediately he knew better. She was still in his arms, their legs were still entwined. The lip stain on her mouth was awry, her eye make-up smudged. It was too late now for regrets, so he tried—but without success—to put the night's incident out of his mind.

Silently, gently disentangling himself, he swam in the river, then dressed in his breechcloth and slipped on his moccasins for the coming day's march.

He looked down at the sleeping Dalnia before he moved off to relieve the scout who had been on sentry duty in his place all night. The thought occurred to him that he had never seen anyone as beautiful. The thought also crossed his mind that he was now obligated to her.

*   *   *

Ena, inevitably accompanied by Lyktaw, made up an unusual scouting team together with her brother. Their methods were unusual because each so thoroughly understood the techniques employed by the other. The results they achieved were superior to those of any other scouts. As they approached the land of the Cherokee, nearing the end of the long march, they continued their usual pattern of operation.

They roamed through the same sector of the forest, sometimes separating by as much as one hundred yards or more, at other times searching the ground side by side. They did not follow any definite plan of operation but let the terrain and what they found there guide them.

At noon on one particularly sunny and warm day, Renno was advancing alone through the deep forest, his progress steady and swift, when suddenly he halted and stared hard at the ground. He dropped to one knee, and he examined the terrain with great care.

The sound of an owl calling to its mate echoed through the trees. The cry was answered instantly, and Renno waited until his sister joined him. He pointed to the ground.

Ena, too, silently examined the earth. Then, looking up at Renno, she nodded affirmatively and by common consent took the lead. No one was her equal at following a trail.

With her brother studying the terrain to her left and Lyktaw following her, she made no sound as she advanced. A number of other human beings were in the area, and so far as she could tell, they were male. She raised a hand as a signal, frowned at the dog, and put a finger to her lips to warn him to remain silent, and then, slowing her pace, she crept forward.

Renno did the same, with Lyktaw sniffing the ground.

Ahead, through the foliage, Renno caught a glimpse of the near shore of a large lake. The sight that he saw there made his blood run cold.

Many husky warriors were taking their ease. All wore the stark, black and white war paint of the Choctaw, the most warlike and dreaded tribe in the south. Some were swimming in the lake, others were resting on the bank, and a number were cooking food over small fires.

For what seemed like a very long time, Renno and Ena made no move. They were busy counting heads in order to determine the number of their foes. When they had estimated to the best of their ability, they backed away in absolute silence.

They retreated discreetly but with increasing speed for almost a half hour, and then, at last figuring they were far enough from the Choctaw to move freely, they broke into a run toward the advancing Seneca. They came to Mogudo and Rusog, who halted the column while they listened to the report of brother and sister. Then the acting war chiefs of the expedition were summoned. Renno repeated the story, with Ena adding a word here and there.

Mogudo finally broke the silence that followed. "It seems to me," he said, "that we handle this in the traditional Seneca manner. We attack the Choctaw without warning, and we press our assault until we put them to flight.''

Renno saw a number of faults with such a plan but was reluctant to be the first to speak against it. Rusog also was less than satisfied. "If we were on a strictly military expedition," he said, "I'd take the risk and proceed, but we have more than two hundred women and children in our party. We'd be operating on too narrow a margin to ensure their safety.''

"Do you have an alternate plan to suggest?" Mogudo demanded, challenging him.

"I believe I do," Rusog replied calmly. "If the estimates that Ena and Renno obtained are fairly accurate, the Choctaw outnumber us by approximately fifty warriors. That number isn't necessarily significant, but I beg to remind you that these are Choctaw, not Creek or Tuscarora or some minor tribe. They're ferocious fighters who never panic, and they are known for quickly recovering the initiative when they are put on the defensive. We'll have a far better chance if we can draw them into an ambush that they don't expect and then launch an all-out attack.''

"I agree," Renno said loudly and firmly. "I think Rusog's plan has by far the greater chance of success.''

The others were deeply impressed. None of them had been leaders in actual combat, and Rusog was the deputy leader of the expedition. Furthermore, his plan was endorsed by the warrior who had the most renowned name in the history of Seneca warfare.

"Why is your plan preferable?" Mogudo asked Rusog.

"I am not necessarily objecting, I am simply asking for my own information."

"As I see the situation," Rusog replied, "we'll be forcing the Choctaw to change their stance. They'll think they are attacking. But suddenly they'll find themselves on the defensive, and once you lose the initiative in battle, it's doubly hard to regain it. If we had the greater number of braves, I'd be in favor of your plan. But I think we need a cushion to safeguard ourselves. The ambush is the best method to supply us with that cushion."

The other leaders agreed unanimously with Rusog's plan. Ena noted that her husband spoke like one who had complete confidence in his planning. This was not the Rusog who had sulked because he was known as the husband of a renowned scout. He was an authority now, one who had the foresight to play a major role in planning a battle. He had developed a remarkable degree of self-assurance. She was delighted and hoped that the battle would work out as he had predicted. If that should happen, she felt sure, any marital problem could be minimized.

The Seneca baited their trap with care as well as with cunning. Renno, accompanied by two other scouts, went back to the Choctaw encampment beside the lake. When they neared it, they deliberately left footprints disclosing that they had spied on the expedition. Then they left a trail that would be easy to follow back toward where the Seneca warriors were waiting.

Women and children had been sent far to the rear and

ordered to stay until the battle ended. Rusog insisted that Ena accompany the other women. "You have already made a valuable contribution to our cause," he said, "and we have nothing more for you to do. The Choctaw would love to take you prisoner. You're no ordinary woman, remember. You're my wife and the daughter-in-law of Wegowa, so it would be an accomplishment for them to capture you and hold you as a slave. Lyktaw will look after you and protect you until I come. I shall come myself, and until I appear, you are not to leave."

Ena knew he was worried that she would take further risks with her life, and she replied meekly, "I'll do your bidding, Rusog. It shall be exactly as you say." He was satisfied when he saw her going off with the other women toward the rear, with Lyktaw frolicking at her heels.

Renno and thirty-five other Seneca, all sharpshooters with long rifles, sat in the open, their firearms concealed in the tall grass beside them. They appeared unprotected, but each placed himself in such a way that a boulder or a large tree trunk stood between him and the point from which a Choctaw attack would come.

The rest of the force, more than one hundred strong, concealed themselves in the foliage of the adjacent forest. Mogudo and Rusog were stationed at a point nearest to those exposed in the clearing. The hidden warriors would hold their fire until they received specific instructions from Rusog to join in the battle. The scheme, as it had developed, required great self-control by every warrior; the few Cherokee who were present knew that no tribe other than the Seneca could carry off the venture successfully.

The next few hours proved to be a time of tense waiting. If the Choctaw followed the clues so liberally left behind by Renno and his comrades, Rusog's whole plan could be put into operation, and the efforts expended would be justified. If the Choctaw failed to respond in any great numbers, however, the scheme would fail, and the enemy would be warned that an alien force was nearby, waiting for battle.

Two hours before sunset, the air above Renno's head suddenly was filled with flying arrows. Throwing himself headlong into the tall grass, he paid no attention to his danger and rejoiced because the scheme had been effective. The Choctaw had taken the bait, and were attacking in force.

Furthermore, they seemed confident of success, having waited until so late in the day before launching their drive. Ordinarily, a nation would be much more cautious and would initiate military proceedings only early in the day when they would have ample time to maneuver.

Renno and his comrades, heeding the specific instructions from Rusog, fired a single volley into the air high over the heads of the attacking Choctaw. This, too, was meant as a further enticement to those making the assault. The Choctaw were delighted to discover that their foes appeared to be poor shots. Nevertheless, because enough of their foes were armed with modern muskets, the Choctaw braves were prepared to take no chances. Their entire force, two hundred strong, took part in the assault.

Rusog's gamble had paid off. Now it was up to the individual warriors to prove their mettle.

When the Choctaw force was committed to battle, the Seneca's aim miraculously improved. Renno set the standard by putting a bullet into the forehead of a Choctaw warrior who made the mistake of leaving himself exposed for a fraction of a second too long.

Little by little, as ordered by Rusog, the other Seneca and the few Cherokee in the party joined in from the relative safety of the woods in which they were concealed. By their expert marksmanship, three dozen Seneca were holding off an enemy force several times their own size.

As the din of battle soared, at last it dawned on the Choctaw that they had walked unwarily into an ambush. It was too late now to withdraw in good order, and their warriors heeded the calls of their war chiefs, who pleaded with them to hold firm. This they did, even though they suffered heavy losses as a result of their courage.

Mogudo tried to demonstrate that he alone was in command of the Seneca and Cherokee forces. He made the mistake of appearing in the open as he tried to rally his warriors into initiating an attack. He bravely exposed himself for a long time, and it was inevitable that he was shot down. He crumpled with five arrows protruding from his head and body. He was dead before he struck the ground.

Now Rusog was truly in command, and he did not hesitate to let his warriors know it. Giving them no time to think about the loss of Mogudo, he ordered them to attack in full force.

This was what the Seneca did best, and their bloodcurdling war cry erupted and echoed through the forest. Far to the rear, the women heard the cry and rejoiced, knowing

that their men had taken the initiative. Wild animals heard
the savage call and took to their heels. The Choctaw heard
it and knew they faced the fight of their lives.

Keeping themselves in concealment, the Seneca advanced
swiftly but never exposed themselves, keeping their forma-
tions intact. They were led by Renno and the other scouts
who had acted as decoys. The agile young warriors were
daredevils who recklessly took great chances as they appeared in the open again, and then again, while they bore
down on their startled foes.

The wave of Seneca warriors advanced, with Rusog
appearing in the lead, waving his tomahawk as he urged
his men forward. They responded to him, as they always
did to acts of daring and courage, and followed him as he
made his way toward the Choctaw.

Renno and Rusog found themselves advancing shoulder
to shoulder. They fired their rifles, reloaded, and fired
again, never halting, always pushing forward. Both were
alert, alive, and enjoying themselves. This was battle as it
was meant to be, and they were doing what they knew and
understood best. They were succeeding, and therefore had
overcome their fears, if not their sense of caution. They
were not fighting now for the sake of enhancing their
names for posterity, but for the sheer joy of fighting and
overcoming a foe. Victory for its own sake was a sweet
reward.

Suddenly a new force loomed up in the wilderness,
directly ahead of Renno and Rusog. About a dozen Choctaw
warriors, all armed with British muskets, were surrounding

a white man in buckskins. They seemed to be guarding him.

Renno's blood ran cold when he recognized Anthony Simpson.

He could have sworn that Simpson had died in battle at the hands of Daniel Boone months earlier, but the British agent was here, in the flesh, very much alive, seeking vengeance against those who thought they had destroyed him. In fact, they were close enough so that Renno saw the hard gleam of malice in Simpson's eyes as the man recognized the young Seneca's distinctive green and yellow war paint.

Renno knew instantly what had to be done. Fate, in the form of the manitous, had decreed that he, the direct inheritor of the mantle of Ghonka and the first Renno, should meet Anthony Simpson at this climactic moment. Simpson fired.

For whatever cause, he missed, and his bullet sang through the air, passing harmlessly to Renno's left.

In this confrontation, Renno was conscious only of the existence of two people—Simpson and himself. In his mind, Rusog faded into the background, as did the Choctaw braves, who were surrounding the British agent.

If Simpson survived, the battle would be lost to the Cherokee and the Seneca, even if the Choctaw were dispersed. Simpson, the incarnation of evil, was the key.

In this moment of supreme crisis, Renno prayed to the manitous to give him their assistance. He asked them for vision sharp enough to sight his target, for skills sufficient to bring down the mortal enemy of his people with a single

shot. Then, barely taking the time to look down the barrel
of his gun, he squeezed the trigger.

The scene appeared to be etched in a timeless eternity.
For what looked and felt like a long moment, no one
moved. Then Anthony Simpson flung his hands high over
his head and collapsed in a heap on the ground. The
Choctaw who comprised his bodyguard had falsely been
led to believe that he was endowed with godlike qualities,
but now, seeing that he was dead, they fled, each disappearing into the wilderness.

Renno had won the important personal duel with his
nation's enemy, but this was no time to rejoice, no time to
celebrate his victory. The combat itself was soaring to a
climax of its own.

Never had any military force succeeded in halting a
forward thrust of the Seneca, and the Choctaw were no
exception. They fell back before the blazing fire of their
foes. The dauntless leadership of Rusog and Renno, who
knew no fear as they were exposed to enemy fire, set an
example for all the Seneca.

The most that could be said for the Choctaw was that
they retired in good order. They left their dead behind, but
they did not panic and did not lose their formation. By the
time they disengaged and retreated from the field of battle,
it was evident that they would be adequately discouraged
from any thought of harassing the travelers further.

Only when the victory was won did the Seneca disperse
and take the scalps of their slain foes.

Rusog accepted the congratulations and thanks of his
subordinates, and then Renno, grinning, smeared green

and yellow Seneca war paint on him to replace his own. The other Seneca cheered mightily, and Rusog was hoisted onto the shoulders of several brawny warriors as they began a victory parade.

Someone remembered to notify the women of the victory, and they hurried forward now, coming to the field of battle. Ena, in the front rank, halted abruptly when she saw her husband on the shoulders of several brawny braves. She noted the Seneca war paint on his face and saw his expression of weary pleasure as he accepted the accolades. She was glad for him and pleased for herself. No longer would he be a satellite to a blazing star. He had proved himself in the most difficult of arenas, the theater of war and, henceforth, could hold up his head with any man.

Rusog's smile broadened when he saw Ena and told her that from then on he would no longer regard her as competition, and she would be free to enact the role of a scout whenever necessity demanded it.

Renno, meanwhile, was tired and wanted only to throw himself down on the ground and rest. But he had no such opportunity. He saw Dalnia pushing through the throng of women, and her expression was proprietary as she made her way toward him. He knew now that, regardless of whether it was right that he marry her, he no longer had a choice. Escape was impossible. By taking her to bed, he had strengthened her claim on him, and he realized she had every right to insist that he marry her. He had an uneasy feeling that she did not measure up to the standards of other women of the family, but he could do nothing about it now.

Dalnia came to him, threw her arms around him for the entire company to see, and then kissed him long and hard. She was letting everyone know that she had won this warrior.

Renno caught a glimpse of the disapproving look in the eyes of his sister and Rusog. He could not pay any attention to them. Caught in Dalnia's trap, he could only ask himself why he should try to escape from such a glorious future as the beautiful seductress promised. He reached for her and pulled her into a closer embrace, relishing the scandalized gaze of the women and the admiring stares of his fellow warriors. Whatever the days ahead might bring in the way of occasional regret, he was determined to make the most of an exciting life—in his own home as well as on the battlefield.

The festivities were at an end. Ghonkaba and Casno greeted the newly arrived Seneca, and Loramas was on hand, too, to express the pleasure that the Cherokee felt in the joining of forces with the newcomers. Homes were assigned, as were plots of ground for individual gardens. Ghonkaba listened as Renno and Ena told him in detail about the health and outlook of his parents and of his other relatives who had stayed behind in the land of the Seneca.

Then, with Rusog's help, Renno told his father about the unexpected battle with the Choctaw and the sudden, shocking reappearance of Anthony Simpson. Modestly, he let his brother-in-law relate a blow-by-blow account of Simpson's death.

"Thanks to you—and you alone, my son—the scourge of Simpson has been lifted from us. By performing this deed, you have demonstrated that you are worthy of assuming the mantle of the great Ghonka."

The praise was too much for Renno, and he stared down at the ground.

"We shall have other missions for you to perform in the future," Ghonkaba continued. "Now, however, I shall take pleasure and pride in a ceremony I must perform. Never in the history of our people has a warrior of your age been awarded the rank of a war chief. You have earned that rank, however, by disposing of Simpson, the greatest threat to the Seneca and to the United States. I shall award you this rank, not because you are my son, but in spite of it.

"Let all our people be gathered together for this event, so that all who are Seneca may rejoice!"

CHOCTAW

Donald Clayton Porter

The hardy band of Seneca who has settled in the South under Ghonkaba's leadership now faces one more threat to its security—the mighty Choctaw. The danger from these warrior Indians is sharpened by their alliance with the wily half-breed, Rattlesnake, son of Anthony Simpson and a sworn enemy of Ghonkaba's son, Renno.

Renno, newly made a war chief for his valor, heads a mission to confer on strategy with George Washington, who advises a preemptive strike against the Choctaw. But when this attack is carried out, the toll is very heavy—because of someone's treachery.

When Renno realizes that the source of the trouble lies close to him, he acts decisively to end the threat for all time—then must seek forgiveness from the manitous.

Meanwhile, a lovely young white colonist, whom Renno has saved from Choctaw captivity, has set her cap for her Seneca rescuer . . . and in a climactic battle, a token of her love is all that stands between Renno and certain death.

FROM THE PRODUCER OF WAGONS WEST
AND THE KENT FAMILY CHRONICLES—
A SWEEPING SAGA OF WAR AND HEROISM
AT THE BIRTH OF A NATION.

THE WHITE INDIAN SERIES

Filled with the glory and adventure of the colonization of America, here is the thrilling saga of the new frontier's boldest hero and his family. Renno, born to white parents but raised by Seneca Indians, becomes a leader in both worlds. THE WHITE INDIAN SERIES chronicles the adventures of Renno, his son Ja-gonh, and his grandson Ghonkaba, from the colonies to Canada, from the South to the turbulent West. Through their struggles to tame a savage continent and their encounters with the powerful men and passionate women in the early battles for America, we witness the events that shaped our future and forged our great heritage.

☐	24650	White Indian #1	$3.95
☐	22715	The Renegade #2	$3.50
☐	24751	War Chief #3	$3.95
☐	24476	The Sachem #4	$3.95
☐	22718	Renno #5	$3.50
☐	20559	Tomahawk #6	$3.50
☐	23022	War Cry #7	$3.50
☐	23576	Ambush #8	$3.50
☐	24492	Cherokee #9	$3.95

Prices and availability subject to change without notice.

Bantam Books, Inc., Dept. LE3, 414 East Golf Road, Des Plaines, Ill. 60016

Please send me the books I have checked above. I am enclosing $_____ (please add $1.25 to cover postage and handling). Send check or money order—no cash or C.O.D.'s please.

Mr/Mrs/Miss _____

Address _____

City _____ State/Zip _____

LE3—11/84

Please allow four to six weeks for delivery. This offer expires 5/85.

★ WAGONS WEST ★

A series of unforgettable books that trace the lives of a dauntless band of pioneering men, women, and children as they brave the hazards of an untamed land in their trek across America. This legendary caravan of people forge a new link in the wilderness. They are Americans from the North and the South, alongside immigrants, Blacks, and Indians, who wage fierce daily battles for survival on this uncompromising journey—each to their private destinies as they fulfill their greatest dreams.

☐	24408	**INDEPENDENCE!**	$3.95
☐	24651	**NEBRASKA!**	$3.95
☐	24229	**WYOMING!**	$3.95
☐	24088	**OREGON!**	$3.95
☐	24848	**TEXAS!**	$3.95
☐	24655	**CALIFORNIA!**	$3.95
☐	24694	**COLORADO!**	$3.95
☐	20174	**NEVADA!**	$3.50
☐	20919	**WASHINGTON!**	$3.50
☐	22925	**MONTANA!**	$3.95
☐	23572	**DAKOTA!**	$3.95
☐	23921	**UTAH!**	$3.95
☐	24256	**IDAHO!**	$3.95

Prices and availability subject to change without notice.

Buy them at your local bookstore or use this handy coupon: